GOOD and GONE

ALSO BY MEGAN FRAZER BLAKEMORE

For Teens
Very in Pieces
Secrets of Truth & Beauty

For Younger Readers
The Firefly Code
The Friendship Riddle
The Spy Catchers of Maple Hill
The Water Castle

GOOD and GONE

MEGAN FRAZER BLAKEMORE

HARPER TEEN
An Imprint of HarperCollins Publishers

HarperTeen is an imprint of HarperCollins Publishers.

Good and Gone

ISBN 978-0-06-234842-5

Typography by Kate J. Engbring
17 18 19 20 21   XXXXXX   10 9 8 7 6 5 4 3 2 1

First Edition

[dedication tk]

GOOD and GONE

ONE

Once upon a time.

NOW

$\mathcal{C}$harlie is in his pajamas on the couch watching one of those inane sitcoms where the wife thinks her husband is stupid and he thinks she is neurotic. The actual plot of this episode seems to be that the husband forgot their anniversary because, you know, men don't really care about such things. Then when he tries to make it up to her and asks her what she wants, she's all, "You pick it out, honey, I know it will be perfect." Which of course is a trap because, you know, women are manipulative like that.

Do adults really think like that? And if they do, why do they get married?

Charlie laughs—loudly, guffawingly—at a joke, which, as if I need more of a clue that *things are not okay*, tells me so in bold letters. I look at him, at his messy hair, at the bit of spit or something dried at the corner of his mouth, and wonder as I have so many times in the past few weeks what the hell is wrong with my brother.

I sit down on the couch by Charlie's feet. They're hairy. My brother has hairy feet and a black bruise on his left big toe. My parents haven't said anything to me about his still being here even though it's the beginning of February. It's like they think I'm too stupid to notice. Like maybe I'm assuming that Essex College offers study abroad programs to Paris, Kyoto, and our family's living room.

I'm not that stupid.

I pick up the blanket and cover his hairy, bruised feet.

Charlie wound up on the couch because he fell madly in love with Penelope (definitely not Penny) when he was a junior and she was a sophomore and I was in eighth grade. They dated all of his junior and senior years. It was a salivating kind of love. If I didn't live with him, I never would have seen him alone. I certainly never saw her without him, not even when I was in high school with them. There could be a whole classroom full of chairs, and they'd be squashed into the same one. There is nothing grosser than coming around the corner and seeing your older brother entwined with a lanky, greasy girl, lips mashed together.

Here are the things Charlie stopped doing:

1. Making awesome playlists for anyone but her
2. Running cross country
3. Playing D&D with his friends (okay, maybe this was an improvement)
4. Treating me like a human being

He disappeared into her. She told him to wear more black, and he did. She told him to cut his long hair, and he did. She told him to grow a goatee, and he tried, but his facial hair would not comply. It was total Penelopification.

It sucked.

My parents were concerned, but thought if they said anything it would only make it worse. "There's no more powerful aphrodisiac than parental disapproval," said my father, who taught in the sociology department of Essex College.

But then Charlie did something unforgivable. Charlie had always wanted to design video games. Always. So when it came to college, we all knew where he was going to go: Carnegie Mellon, home of the best video game design department in the country. He got in early. My parents sent the deposit. Then, without telling anyone, he called Carnegie Mellon, told them thanks but no thanks, and instead enrolled at Essex College, right here in good old God-awful Essex, New Hampshire. My parents were livid. Charlie said that it was awfully funny that they didn't think it was a good-enough school for him considering both Mom and Dad worked there and all. Mom said of course it was a *good* school, it just wasn't the *right* school.

So then Penelope decides to go to Whitman College in Walla Walla, Washington. And then Charlie decides to morph with our living room couch into a single being. He's like one of those eels that plants itself into the ocean floor and waits for food to float by.

It's true, of course, that going to school in the same town

where we lived, he could have decided to move out of the dorms and back home (why, why, oh God why would anyone do that?), but he hasn't been to class. He just sits on the couch and watches reruns of sitcoms.

He couldn't have dropped out. He is too into school for that. Nor would he have been kicked out. Too smart. None of it makes sense, but it's like since no one's talking about it, and we talk about everything in our family, well, I know I shouldn't ask.

"This show sucks," I say.

"It's not so bad. That one guy, he's kind of funny."

Before, my brother never would have admitted to watching a sitcom—to even knowing what a sitcom was—and now here he is defending it to me. And watching it intently. Purposefully.

He is avoiding me. Or wanting to avoid me.

"Fine." I sigh.

But then the TV crackles and the special news broadcast tones come on and a voice announces, "We interrupt this broadcast with a special report."

Cut to the news desk where the guy who normally does the sports is sitting at the desk. He is smiling, but then he seems to realize that he looks like a jackass, so he puts on his serious face. "Breaking news out of Pennsylvania this hour. Musician Adrian Wildes is missing. The star wandered away from his tour bus yesterday afternoon and has not been seen since."

"Good riddance," I say.

"Could you stop being a bitch for, like, three minutes? I

want to hear this." He is sitting up, which is a change for him. He swings his feet around and places them on the floor and leans into the television.

"Fine. Screw you very much. I'm going for a walk."

Outside I press my earbuds in so the music fills my ears. Alanis Morissette. "Hello, 1995," Charlie said to me when he looked at my playlist. "What's with all the angry dyke music?" He doesn't believe I have anything to be angry about. Only Penelope-broken Charlie has any reason to be upset, that's what he thinks. He doesn't know everything that went down with me, though, so screw him all over again.

"Maybe I'm an angry dyke," I replied. I should have known then that something was up. Charlie was not the kind of guy who referred to women as anything other than "women."

I storm down the street, my boots clomping through what's left of the snow. The music pushes me forward. I have the bass turned up too much, boom boom boom right in my ear.

In the summer, the trees are so full of leaves and the branches so long they create a canopy over the road. We moved to this street when I was nine, and I thought it was like something out of a fairy tale. I don't exactly believe in fairy tales anymore.

Still, it's kind of a pretty street. The older houses are small and the newer houses are too big, like anywhere else I guess. There are a ton of kids who tear around like some sort of a biker gang, wobbly on their two-wheelers, but Charlie and I are the only teenagers. Well, and Germy Zack Donovan. We used to ride the bus together. While we waited we played twenty questions and druthers and fuck, marry, kill, only he called it bone, marry, kill, because he said I was too young for the F-word. We had completely opposite taste in guys in terms of who was a keeper and who was a throwaway. Like he'd want to marry one and I'd want to bone him. Generally we'd agree on who to kill. But then he got his car. The awful two-door subcompact that I become all too familiar with over the course of this story. He got that car and he didn't even once offer me a ride. I thought at first it was because he had gotten himself a boyfriend, and driving to school was special time together, and I thought that was cool because even though our school is pretty accepting, there are assholes everywhere, and it still might be hard to be the only boy-boy couple. But then I thI'd see him cruising into the parking lot all alone while I stood in the side courtyard with Hannah and Gwen.

We're having an early thaw and everything is melting, but I know we're going to get hit with some sort of storm before spring finally gets to Essex. I'm wearing a sweat shirt, one I haven't worn since the fall, and it still kind of smells like October, which feels both ages ago and all at the same time on top of me.

But I'm thinking that maybe things are okay. Maybe this thaw is like a metaphor. Or a simile. I can never quite keep them straight. Anyway, I can almost believe that things are going to be okay. The snow will melt, the leaves will come back, Charlie will go back to school, and me, well, maybe I'll start putting myself back together, too. Maybe I can try to undo what happened.

And then the song switches and it's Adrian Wildes singing into my ear and I know that nothing is going to be okay.

"Nothing, nothing, and nothing again," croons Adrian Wildes.

Crap.

I thought I had erased every little piece of Seth Winthrop from my life, but here it is: our song. Not that the song that defined our relationship, but it was the one that made us look at each other and say, "Oh hey."

Another bit of the past to dredge up: It happened over the summer at Gwen's house. She has a pool and there was always the most random assortment of people there. Seth was one of them. Earlier in the day I'd watched him scoop a mouse out of the pool with his hand. He'd placed it gently on the pool deck, and there it sat still and soaked. Seth just stared at it and I swear it was like he willed that thing back to life. It was dead and lifeless and then it stirred and then it stood up and shook the water off itself before scurrying out into the woods. He looked up and saw me watching and gave me a little smile. I just blushed and turned away. But later. Later, we were sitting next to each other, only in different conversations—him with his friends, and me with Gwen and Hannah—when the Adrian Wildes song came on. He leaned back and I leaned forward and at the same time we both said, "Man, this song sucks." It was like we had practiced it, but it was totally spontaneous. We all laughed, even his stupid friends Alex and Torrance, the latter of whom is deep into some sort of goth-emo phase, and maybe that should have been the end of it, but we both stayed at Gwen's house past sundown, and one thing led to another. "I can drive you home," he said. Casually. Because to him driving was nothing new, not something you had to beg your parents to let you do once a weekend. And so he drove me home, and in my driveway, he kissed me sweet and long, right on my lips. He didn't even try to slip me the tongue or anything, and I remember being disappointed, because it was my first real kiss, but it wasn't a really real kiss. That would come later. All of it. I went to the pool free and single, and came out hooked up with Seth Winthrop, a coupling that wasn't completely radical, but strange enough to send ripples of excitement through the school. That's what happens when you live in a town where nothing happens.

I push the button to skip the song, but it comes right back around and repeats.

Nothing, nothing, and nothing again.

Really, who thinks starting a relationship with words like that is a good idea?

I push the Stop button but it won't stop.

You slip beneath the surface and I pull you up again.

"It's cheating," Seth said. "You can't make the rhyme with the same word." Ah, bitter irony. Our first conversation and he talked about cheating.

I clomp all the way around the block trying to get Seth Winthrop and Adrian Wildes out of my head. Even three go-rounds of Ani DiFranco's "Untouchable Face" can't seem to do the trick.

When I get back home, Zack Donovan's rolling two-door wreck is in the driveway and he and Charlie are deep in conversation. I hear the name "Adrian Wildes" and I think maybe they are playing bone, marry, kill without me. I know what I would say for Adrian Wildes: kill, kill, kill. Or maybe bone. It would depend on who else was in the game.

All of this races through my head in about three seconds. Long enough for them to notice my arrival and then exchange one quick look. Charlie looks back at me. "Adrian Wildes is gone," he says.

"Yeah, hello, I was there with you when the news came on. And anyway, who cares?" I ask.

"Adrian Wildes?" Zack suggests. "I mean, probably." When he smiles, his chipmunk cheeks have one dimple, not two. I usually hate one-dimplers. It's like they are trying to be adorable, but half-assing it as if they really don't care if you think they are cute or not. But with Zack it's more like the one dimple just jumped on his face and surprised him. Like he's not quite sure how it got there so he's going to make the best of it.

"We need to find him," Charlie says.

"Find him?" I ask.

"He's out there somewhere hurting, and we need to find him."

I do not need any more proof that my brother has had a complete personality upheaval, but here it is. It's like the un-Penelopization has left him completely devoid of any of the characteristics of pre or post Hell Girl Charlie. In his place is this changeling.

"I'm sure there are people looking for him," Zack suggests.

"Like a hundred thousand fangirls," I said.

"That seems like an exaggeration," Zack replies.

"Okay, ninety-seven thousand sixty-three fangirls."

"Closer to ninety-seven thousand and sixty-four."

"I wish you still rode the bus."

"They won't find him," Charlie interrupts. "So I'm going. I'm going to find Adrian Wildes. You can go with me or not."

I realize that he is serious. His eyes have this strange mix of sadness and desperation. I also realize that this is the first time he has expressed any interest in getting off the couch in weeks. "Okay. I'll go," I say.

"I guess I'll drive then," Zack says.

Charlie says, "Sure, okay, I guess."

"Of course he's going with us," I tell him. "We are completely carless whereas Zack has that car-like object." I turn to Zack. "You should've held out for payment."

"I'm a white knight, Lexi, I thought you knew that."

"Wait, don't tell me you have a big gay crush on him, because, ew."

"Him, Adrian Wildes, or him, your brother?" Zack asks.

"Ew and double ew."

"No crushes. I mean, no offense, man. No, it's just that my parents are getting a divorce only they don't know it yet. The farther away I can get from them, the better. A little road trip seems perfect right about now."

"That's a decent reason, I guess."

Charlie reaches for the passenger-side door. "Wait, wait, wait," I say. "We can't just hop in the car and go. Where are we even going?"

"He was last seen in Pennsylvania," Charlie says.

"Which is, what? How far?"

Charlie shrugs and so Zack says, "A good eight to ten hours."

"So we'd better get going."

"No, we'd better get *stuff*," I say. "We should call Mom and Dad and ask first."

Charlie raises his eyebrows at me.

"Okay, fine. Leave them a note. I am going to get some supplies." I kick off my sneakers when we get inside, but Charlie leaves his on and makes little wet footprints across the floor. Mom and Dad would cut my feet off at the ankles if I did that, but they'd probably be so damn happy that Charlie was on his feet that they'd just crawl behind him with a towel if they were here.

Zack stands right inside the doorway looking a little useless and confused, which is, frankly, the way he frequently looks, so maybe he has useless resting face. I bet I could come up with about a million types of stupid resting faces that guys have, and all anyone would say is that I put the bitch in resting bitch face. Anyway, I say, "Make yourself useful and get some snacks from the kitchen."

I run up the stairs at the exact moment the cat comes tearing down between my legs. I swear it is her plan to get me to tumble to my death on these stairs. She's never been happier since Charlie took up residence on the couch. The two of them snuggle together like best bosom buddies. All the while she's getting meaner and meaner to me. The other morning she hid beneath the couch and lunged out at my ankles as I walked by, drawing blood.

In my room, I grab a change of underwear, a purple long-sleeved T-shirt, and a sweat shirt. Clean socks, too. Life is always better if you have clean socks. And that's not a metaphor or anything. Clean socks is good living.

Then I take my old piggy bank down from the shelf. The pig has blue eyes and long lashes and a little tail that curls like a corkscrew. I pop open the bottom and pull out the bills: seven twenty dollar bills, four tens, a five, and three ones. I keep most of my money in the bank account I've had since I was seven, but I like to have a little emergency cash on hand. I roll it up and jam it into the pocket of my jeans.

When I put my piggy bank back up on the shelf, my hand knocks against a small box. The box originally held a pair of aquamarine earrings I received for my birthday. I lost one and the other is in the drawer of my bedside table. Now the box holds a folded-up note given to me by Seth Winthrop. My stomach turns just to think of it, like I swallowed a whole gallon of sour milk.

Downstairs, I find Zack in front of our pantry. "It's like snack mecca in here."

"Just grab a bunch of things," I tell him, reaching past him for the store-brand cheddar crackers my mom likes to tell us will give us cancer, but she buys them all the same, so what kind of message is that? Zack takes three granola bars out of the box and drops them into the reusable shopping bag I grabbed from a hook in the pantry. "Take them all," I say.

"Won't your parents mind?" he asks.

"Maybe. But they mind if we eat the food and they mind if we don't eat the food, so what does it even matter?"

"Okay," he says slowly, and takes down a tin of raspberry candies.

"Except those," I say.

"Really?" he asks, dropping the tin with a clang.

"No. Jesus. What's with the weird food weirdness?"

He glances down at his stomach. "It's not weirdness. Weird weirdness or regular weirdness or any weirdness."

"Sorry," I say.

"For what?"

"I didn't know you had food issues." Another game we used to play while waiting for the bus was Last Meal, and Zack was always the best at coming up with the most elaborate meals. Porcini ravioli with a truffle-oil cream sauce, baguette, spinach and roasted beet salad, and key lime pie for dessert. Or a super-deluxe cheeseburger with gorgonzola, bacon, and caramelized onions with a mint chocolate milk shake. I knew he liked food, but I didn't know he was also weird about it.

"I don't have food issues."

"You looked at your stomach."

"Well, it's big," he says. "It's hard to look anywhere else."

"See. Food issues." I pick up the tin of raspberry candies and drop them in the bag. "We'll be back tomorrow, right? We just drive him down to Pennsylvania and then drive him back in the morning, right?"

"That sounds about right. Sure."

"You definitely want to come with us? I mean, if you say no, we can't actually go or anything, so I hope you won't say no. But I also don't want you to feel like you've stepped into this and now can't get out."

"No, I want to go. For real."

"Good." And I'm glad he doesn't ask me why it's so important to go because I'm not sure that I can explain that this is the first time Charlie has expressed interest in anything other than the TV or the couch or his bed or the cat since December. And, sure, I've been bogged down in my own stuff, and maybe a complete break from our real world feels like it could be good for me, too. So, yeah. I need Zack to say yes to this and not ask too many questions.

Charlie clomps into the kitchen and thrusts a piece of paper at me. "Here," he says. I read what he wrote. It's succinct:

MOM, DAD —
WE WENT TO LOOK FOR ADRIAN WILDES.
BE BACK EVENTUALLY.
C&L

I add a postscript:

Just so you know, for once Charlie was the one who had the crazy idea. I'm going with him because he's acting nutso and someone needs to watch out for him. Ergo [I love throwing in the word "ergo"] while you may feel the need to punish me, please take into consideration my motivations.

And then we leave. Zack and Charlie sit up front. I take the back and sit with my legs stretched out across the seat. I stare out the window, at the trees without their leaves, while Charlie directs Zack to drive south in the direction of the place where Adrian was last seen.

The back seat of Zack's car is foul. Like, third-level disgusting. The armrests are sticky and there's a layer of fast-food wrappers that an archaeologist could mine for information about our declining society. I try to make myself as small as possible, something I've gotten good at, and I pull my sleeves down over my hands so I don't touch anything.

Gwen once said that if I got a ride in with Zack my stock would rise. Not as much as hers did for getting a ride from Katie Archer, a senior girl who lived on her street, but it would definitely get a kick from not riding the bus. If she saw Zack's car, she might reevaluate.

"Do you guys even know where you're going?" I ask.

"Ninety-five runs all the way from Maine to Florida.

We'll take that to Pennsylvania and figure it out from there," Charlie says.

"Um, actually, I think we might want to cut off before then," Zack says. "Ninety-five through New York City is a no-go."

They start talking about highways and side roads and all of it just kind of glosses over me and then I realize we're driving past Gwen's neighborhood. It's this new development right by the highway. They planted like a million trees between the highway and the houses so the people who lived there didn't have to see the four-lane road, and people who live there still want the town to build a sound-canceling wall. I mean, buy a house by the highway and what do you expect?

We breeze right by the development and Zack pulls the car up onto the highway. The little sedan shudders and shakes as we get up to speed.

"High-quality piece of machinery you've got here, Zack," I tell him.

"Miss Ruka gets where she needs to go."

"But does she get where we need to go?"

I look out over the trees and tell myself I can see Gwen's pool, but it could be any of a dozen pools in that schmancy neighborhood of McMansions.

Stupid pool.

Truthfully, that day at Gwen's pool wasn't the first time Seth and I spoke. And it certainly wasn't the first time I noticed him. The amount of time I spent noticing him before I actually interacted with him is pathetic. I noticed the way he slung his messenger bag across his chest so that it crossed right below his breastbone, which protruded just enough that I could see it beneath his T-shirt. I noticed that he was left-handed and wrote with his arm curled around the paper. I noticed the day that he stopped to help Tyler O'Leary, a kid so out there that even the nice kids didn't pretend to be nice to him, when Tyler dropped his pencil case and sent stubby colored pencils rolling across the floor. I noticed the way Seth looped his arm around Remy Yoo's waist back when they were still dating. And then one day, it seemed, he noticed me.

BEFORE

May

It was spring and Gwen and I were looking at a sign for the freshman car wash. It was printed on fluorescent pink paper. They used Comic Sans font and a terrible clip-art picture of a dirty, broken-looking car. CAR WASH was in all caps, and the rest was in lowercase, and I wondered which of my horribly sad classmates had made it.

"So what do you think?" Gwen asked. She wanted to go, and she wanted me to suggest we do. She wouldn't actually say this out loud, but I knew it was true. Gwen wanted it both ways. She wanted to be a joiner, to be one of those golden Type-A over-achievers, the kind that teachers like and boys like and coaches like and everyone likes except maybe themselves. But she also wanted to be outside edgy, on the fringe.

"I don't know," I said. "Seems like a lot of work, but I guess it helps our class?"

"The thing of it is—" Seth appeared and started talking as if we'd been in conversation for minutes, days, weeks already. As if the million conversations I'd had with him in my head were real. "It's just a way to get girls to dress in bikini tops and short shorts and spray water at each other. It's disgusting, really."

"Sure," I said. I was the opposite of Gwen: I didn't know what I wanted. I just knew I wanted none of those things she strived for. I guess I wanted the spaces in between. I wanted to just exist. Even before everything with Seth, I wanted to just be in the background, to be not too much one thing or another.

"Have you ever been to one?" he asked. He spoke to just me, that's what it felt like. Gwen might as well have not been there.

I shook my head.

"My mom brought her car when my brother's class did it," Gwen says. "She says they did a terrible job and she had to bring it to the regular car wash after."

"Just you wait and see. It's all old men who come. And middle-aged men. And young men." Seth leaned in closer to me. "Mr. Whitehall went through three times when our grade did it. Even Mr. Tompkins got his car washed."

"Maybe his car was just dirty," I said.

"Maybe. Or maybe that whole geeky guy is just an act."

"Or maybe he is a geek and this is, you know, his—" And

this was when I actually turned away from the poster and looked at Seth Winthrop. He had his thumb looped through the strap of his messenger bag and I couldn't quite see his breastbone, but I knew it was there and I wanted to run my hand over it to know what it felt like.

I had been watching Seth Winthrop for most of the year. Now here he was, two inches away from me, and I was acting like a relatively sane person even though I felt like falling right back against Gwen and having the floor just swallow us up.

"His what?"

Except I couldn't make a sex joke like I would with Gwen or Hannah. I couldn't talk like that to Seth. So I said, "Maybe this is the only way he has to spend his weekend."

"Huh. You're a freshman, right?"

"Yes."

"We both are," Gwen said.

"Are you going?"

"We haven't decided yet. But given your description of it—"

"Oh, don't let me dissuade you." He smiled at me, wide and toothy.

"It just sounds a little gross," I said to the floor.

"True, but if you want to fight a problem like sexism, you have to stare it right in the face."

"That makes sense," I said as I tried to figure out what he meant.

"So you'll go?"

"I guess so. Maybe."

19

"I hope so," he said. Then he smiled and I knew he knew what it did to me. "Because my car is really, really dirty."

He wasn't even around the corner of the hall before Gwen started giggling. "Oh my God, Lexi, you should see the way he looked at you!"

"What?" I asked.

"If you hadn't been looking at the poster half the time, I mean, seriously, Lexi. I was invisible, and normally that would really bother me, but it was actually just so intense I am vicariously on fire for you."

"Really?" I asked.

"Really," she said, throwing her arm around my waist. "And we are so going to that car wash!"

We did go to the car wash, and it was as awful as Seth had promised. And he didn't show. So I was all cold and wet and sticky with soap and didn't even get to see him. I didn't have another conversation with him for three months—that day at Gwen's pool.

BEFORE

August

We sat in the pool chairs with their plastic padded seats. At first my legs were tucked up under me, but then I stretched them out across his lap and he put his hands on my bare calves like it was the most natural thing in the world. All I could think about was how he had used those hands to save the mouse and it wasn't gross at all—it should have been gross, right? I thought they were tender and caring hands, and I couldn't believe how perfectly they curved around my calves. We were like a sculpture, I thought, chipped out of marble.

"The problem with musicians like Adrian Wildes," he said, "is that they spawn the knockoffs. I mean, the dude can play a guitar okay I guess, but he should be like the guitar player in a band. Like he should be a Jimmy Page, I guess. Just go out there, rock the guitar, and get out of the way."

"Right," I agreed, still looking at his hands. He kept his fingernails trimmed neatly: no ragged edges, no loose cuticles. The only boy fingers I'd had much of a chance to look at were Charlie's, and he was a nail biter. Seth was not a nail biter.

"But when you start thinking you can sing and write and, like, have the stage presence or whatever."

"Right," I said again. Maybe there was a hint of calluses on his palms, but they were the nice kind of calluses. Once at the movie theater, this man grabbed my arm and his hands were so rough and raw I thought his dead dry skin might peel off. When I shook my arm free I went into the bathroom and scrubbed and scrubbed and scrubbed. Seth's hands were nothing like that, nothing you wanted to shake off.

"And anyway I don't trust anyone who would date that chick from that crappy show. What was it? She's hot and all, but, well, I'd rather date a girl like you."

21

My body grew warm, and I guess I just wasn't smart enough then to see he was insulting me.

NOW

Zack is listing the things he knows about Adrian Wildes: "He was born outside of Poughkeepsie, and his family moved to Narragansett, Rhode Island, when he was a baby. His real name is Adrian Pincetti. He auditioned for *The Mickey Mouse Club*, but was not accepted, something he considers the greatest bit of bad news he ever received. He got his start on YouTube. His idol is some blues guitarist that no one has ever heard of—Smoky Walker. He's won six Grammys, and his top-selling single was 'Nothing.'"

"How do you know all this?" I interrupt. "I thought you said you had no man crush on him."

"Wikipedia," he says. "And I said I had no big, gay crush on him, to use your totally dismissive terms. That is categorically different from a man crush, which I may or may not have on Adrian Wildes." He turns back to Charlie. "As for his personal life, he has been linked romantically with a series of celebrity women, most of whom are widely considered to be less intelligent than he is. Except, of course, for Alana Greengrass, the love of his life, so to speak, whom he met when he had a cameo in her movie about the country music scene: *A Beat of My Heart*."

"Terrible movie," I say at the same time as Charlie says, "I saw that with Penelope."

He looks over his shoulder at me. "I didn't think it was so bad."

"Is that what Penelope told you to think?"

He turns his head back to the road, which is flying by. Zack is a fast driver.

"Anyway," Zack says. "I just wonder if instead of heading to where he might have last been seen, maybe we should try to anticipate where he'd be going."

We've been driving down 95 for about an hour and are well into Massachusetts. Charlie tugs on the chest strap of his seat belt, which makes a creaking, sticky noise. "That could be anywhere. We need go to where he left his bus."

I look inside the bag of snacks, which is on the seat next to me. If we're really going all the way to Pennsylvania, then we will need to ration this a little. I'm starting to hope, though, that this trip won't go that far. That I can get us home before midnight. "I agree," I say. "I think we need a better plan. Mom and Dad are going to try to be all cool about this, but you know they're going to be flipping out inside. We should try to get home as soon as we can."

"If they say they're cool, they're cool."

Mom and Dad haven't said anything yet. They might not even realize we're gone. It's only one o'clock. Dad might be home in an hour or two, but Mom doesn't usually get home until four, even on the days she doesn't teach. I twist my finger around through the straps of the bag and try not to let the little worm of guilt make its way inside. This is the right choice. Going with Charlie is the right choice for sure.

Zack scratches his head. "I guess I'm just saying that he left, you know. He *left*. So he must have been going somewhere. Unless, well, you know—"

"He didn't kill himself," Charlie says, as if they are close personal friends and he knows exactly what's going on in Adrian Wildes's mind. I, for one, don't care where we go. I'm just along for the ride. Which would make Seth laugh, if he heard me say it. Which in turn is funny because I would have followed Seth anywhere.

Charlie pushes all the buttons for Zack's presets, but we've driven out of range and all we get is fuzz. So he starts turning the dial back and forth so fast. The voices zip past like they're riding bullets.

"Enough!" I say.

"I've got it," he says, and takes his hand off the dial.

". . . the latest on the Adrian Wildes story right after this," comes the DJ's voice before cutting to a pop song that was super popular when I was in eighth grade. Gwen, Hannah, and I used to dance to it in her kitchen while we ate cookie dough right out of the tube. Hannah wouldn't eat the cookie dough at first. She said we'd get salmonella. But Gwen pretended to check Google and said that packaged cookie dough didn't actually have raw egg in it, so it was safe.

Zack taps his fingers to the beat as he drives. "Best pop song ever?" I ask him.

"Ever?" he replies. "You really expect me to pick just one. I mean, there are so many factors to consider. Memorability of lyrics, danceability of beat, not to mention the performance."

"Well, it's obvious you've given a lot of thought to it—"

"I mean, of course I have an ongoing list, but I usually organize it by decade and—"

"One song, right now." I feel myself grinning.

"How about of the last ten years?"

"Ever. One song."

"Aghh—"

"Come on, Zackster —"

"Let him be," Charlie says between his teeth.

"It's a simple question," I say. "Right, Zack?" But I know for Zack it isn't. He's a ranker and a sorter, and not a one-and-done kind of a guy.

"No, it's—"

Charlie presses his fist against his window. "You always have to just push and needle and, like, claw under everyone's skin and—"

"Beyoncé!" Zack cries out. "'Single Ladies.' It has to be, right?"

"See, so simple." But the game isn't fun anymore.

The DJ comes back on. "Adrian Wildes," he says. "Okay, let's get to the bottom of this. He was last seen at his tour bus north of the tiny hamlet of Frenchtown, which is west of Bethlehem, Pennsylvania."

"Hamlet?"

"Shut up, Lexi, I'm trying to listen," Charlie says, and turns up the volume.

An old car passes us filled with teenaged guys with scruffy hair and beanie caps. One of them turns to look at me and I sink down in the back seat. I can't stand the weight of his eyes on me, not even for the half second it takes for the car to pass us.

"Since then authorities have searched a ten-mile radius, including the nearby Delaware River, but so far there has been no sign of him. His publicist released a statement thanking fans for their concern and asking for thoughts and prayers."

"Ah, yes, the always-powerful thoughts and prayers," I say.

"Fans have been leaving comments on Wildes's YouTube videos, especially the early ones that made him a star. A search party will comb the woods around where the bus last stopped with the hopes of finding Wildes or some sign of his whereabouts. And now, back to the music."

"That wasn't much of an update," I say.

The song is by one of Adrian Wildes's old girlfriends—like a blink-and-you-miss-it, barely together girlfriend, but she milked it into two songs, and this is one of them. It's about how she knew what he was up to all along, that she was no fool. But I figure she is a fool for falling for him in the first place. She said she just wanted to take a chance, because you have to keep falling if you ever want to fly or something asinine like that. But it seems like if you just keep falling and falling and falling you aren't going to start flying. Eventually, you won't get back up.

Charlie doesn't say anything. He stares out the window. He

is probably imagining where Penelope is at this very moment, and who she is with. He will calculate that it is three hours earlier in Walla Walla, Washington. He will picture the sun glinting off her dishwater blond hair while we are surrounded by gray mist. He will picture the perfect boy who is making her laugh. The perfect boy with straight white teeth and wavy hair. The boy doesn't have a goatee and Penelope doesn't care. Charlie shifts in his seat, frowning. It's a sucker's game, this imagining, and we both know it.

There's a minivan in the lane next to us. We take turns pulling ahead as the traffic inches forward. In the middle row of seats there's a little girl. She waves to me and I wave back. Then she flashes a peace sign which I also return. Each time we pull up alongside each other, a new gesture. Of course it devolves rapidly and as we putter up next to the minivan this time, I see her face pressed against the glass, nose pushed back, mouth open, cheeks puffed out like some kind of demented deep-sea fish. It's the ugliest thing. I try to ignore her, but she becomes insistent, crossing her eyes. I wave her away with my hand like I'm swatting a fly and she presses her palm to the glass. I'm not sure what she expects me to do. I frown and shake my head. Game's over, little girl. She slaps the other hand against the window. I turn away and when I look back she's sneering at me. I casually give her the finger, barely even lifting it all the way, at the precise moment her mother turns around. Her mother registers shock, then her eyes narrow. I watch her explain to her husband at the same time I'm pointing at the little girl, trying to shift culpability. The father is shaking his head and actually wags his index finger at me.

Charlie looks from the card and back to me. "Lexi, what did you do?"

"Nothing. She started it."

"What did you do?" he asks again.

"She was making an ugly face. I gave her the finger."

"Jesus, Lexi."

"What?" I demand.

Charlie is mouthing "Sorry" to the parents in the minivan while turning his finger next to his temple, the universal sign for crazy, which is pretty funny considering how he's been spending the last few weeks.

"I have to pee," I announce.

"Hold it," Charlie says.

"I can't."

"There's an exit up here," Zack says, sliding over a lane behind the minivan. "Maybe it will give traffic a chance to ease up."

I shift in my seat. Now that I've said it, the need to pee is overwhelming. "Drive in the breakdown lane."

"That's for breakdowns," Zack says.

I roll my eyes. "It's an emergency. Seriously. I will pee all over your car fire-hydrant style."

Zack hesitates, but then drops into the lane, which gets us to the exit quicker. At the bottom of the ramp I see a Total-Mart. "There," I say.

"No way," Charlie says. "I'm not patronizing that store. Do you know the way they treat—"

I interrupt. Anti Total-Mart was one of Penelope's big things and I've heard it all before. "I'm not going to buy anything. I'm going to use the bathroom. I'll pee on the floor if that would make you feel better."

"It's not going to make me feel better. Why would that make me feel better? It's not like the CEO would have to clean it up."

Zack is wisely ignoring our conversation. He turns into the parking lot and finds a space near the entrance.

I run through the sliding doors with Charlie and Zack close behind me. Inside, we are greeted by an old man. "It's so you feel eyes on you," Charlie whispers. "So you don't steal anything."

"Bathroom?" I ask the old man.

He smiles and says, "Back corner," pointing to the far end of the store.

"They want you to have to walk by more things. To tempt you to buy. This whole place is set up to get you to purchase cheap crap that you don't really need."

I start hustling toward the back of the store even though I want to tell Charlie that for someone so concerned about the workers' rights, he's being awfully rude to the greeter.

The bathroom is plain, sanitized, boring, but it is a bathroom, and I am relieved.

I wash my hands with the foamy soap and then dry them in one of those super powerful hand dryers that make your skin move and show all your veins and bones.

Back in the store, I can actually look around. We never go to this kind of place. Mom and Dad agree with Penelope that these big box stores are bringing about the death of small town America and that they signify all that is wrong with modern society: everything has to be quick, cheap, and easy.

But the store itself doesn't seem so bad. It's bright and there are colorful displays of things like volleyballs and archery equipment. I try to imagine myself with a bow and arrow like something out of a fantasy novel. It doesn't quite work with my old sweat shirt and stained jeans.

I jam my hand in my pockets and feel a wad of paper, which I pull out, wondering if it's maybe a note from Gwen or a test from the fall, but instead it's the *Good Feelings Book* that Seth got me. What it drums up in me is, of course, the opposite of good feelings—that was his point, I think—and so I push it back into my pocket and try to forget about it.

I pass the toy section, where there's a little kid having a full-on meltdown over some Matchbox cars. They're on sale two for a dollar and the kid just wants one, but his mom keeps telling . him no. The dad is standing next to them, scrolling through his phone. The mom is trying to explain in this rational voice that he has enough cars at home. I'm thinking that the car is only fifty cents. I pull the wad of money out of my pocket and walk out of the aisle then around and come up behind them. I drop a dollar, wait a beat, and then pick it up. "Excuse me," I say. "Is this your dollar?"

The mom turns around. Her face is tight around the

eyebrows and the lips. I feel the tension in my own face and try to relax it. Hannah's yoga teacher says you should relax your tongue and that will relax your face, because of course Hannah does yoga, and of course she's always talking about her stupid, traitorous tongue. "Um, I don't think so," the mom says. "Did you drop a dollar?" she asks her husband.

He kind of grunts, and I'm thinking that maybe those sitcoms aren't all that wrong. Maybe there are couples that exist in a constant state of antipathy. This makes my stomach drop. "It was on the floor back there," I say.

The boy is watching this conversation from the seat of the cart. More precisely, he has his eyes trained on that dollar bill.

"It's not ours," the mom says.

"Not mine either," I say with a shrug. Then I hand the dollar to the little boy. "Guess it's your lucky day, buddy."

Before the mom or dad can say anything—though, in all honesty, it would've been the mom because to talk the dad would have to take his eyes off the screen—but, anyway, before she can say anything, I stride down the aisle away from them.

It's so easy to do a nice thing every once in a while.

Seth would think I was being sweet and stupid again, but it's the truth. A simple little truth that no one bothers to remember.

I pass through the cosmetics. There are mirrors everywhere, and images of models look down at me with their perfectly smooth, rosy skin and dewy eyes. I run my hand across my own face. My chin is littered with small pimples. I pick up a bottle of concealer and wonder briefly if it would actually help me, and then remember my promise not to buy anything here.

When I find Charlie and Zack, though, they are the ones who have made a purchase. They are sitting in the so-called café, Charlie with a hot dog and Zack with a soft pretzel, each with a slushy, and are poring over a stained and ratty map. "No slushy for me?" I ask.

"Get your own," Charlie replied.

"I thought we weren't supporting the patriarchy or whatever," I tell him.

He ignores me and points to a spot on the map. "Narragansett, Rhode Island. That's where he grew up." Zack circles it.

I look down on the map, which has several small circles around towns in the Northeast. "What are you doing?" I ask.

"Circling key places in Adrian's life," Zack says.

"Zack's right. He's probably not where they last saw him, not anymore. He's probably gone to one of his important spots."

Zack has his phone open and he's looking at the Wikipedia article about Adrian. "We've got where he was born, where his grandmother lives, where he went to college."

"What is that thing anyway?" I joke. "It looks like Google maps, but on paper."

"You're like one of those fish with the glowing light only you're entranced by your own light and just swimming in circles," Charlie tells me.

"What?"

"You're pathetic is what. It's a map."

"I was joking," I say. "Of course I know what a map is."

Charlie just raises his eyebrows at me.

"Where'd you even get it?" I ask.

"It came with the car," Zack says. He taps his pen against the map.

"What about where what's-her-name lives?" I ask. "The love of his life?"

Zack nods and circles New York City.

"We should go there," I say, because then at least this trip could get interesting.

Charlie shakes his head. "She's on location in India."

"Boston," Zack says. "He used to busk in the subways there."

"He's got that song about Burlington, Vermont. About building a little farmhouse and having a quiet life. Maybe that's what he's doing," Charlie suggests.

Zack's pen hovers above Vermont, searching for the city. I put my finger down right over the B. "But we're not going there," I say. "Boring. And in the opposite direction."

"This isn't the road trip of fun places that Lexi wants to go," Charlie says.

"It's not? When are we going on that trip?"

"We have a mission."

"Aye, aye, captain."

"What about that amusement park?" Zack asks, still deftly ignoring our bickering. I know I wouldn't want to go on a road trip with me and Charlie, and I figure it's only a matter of time before Zack calls the whole thing off.

"Shangri-La?" Charlie asks.

"Yeah. Where's that?"

"Pennsylvania, I think. But it never opened."

Zack checks something on his phone, then looks back to the map. He circles a tiny town that seems closer to New York than any city in Pennsylvania. Far. If we go that far we're definitely going to need to find a place to stay for the night. The wad of bills in my pocket suddenly seems smaller.

They look at the map. "Burlington makes a lot of sense, if he just wants to disappear," Charlie says.

I groan. I didn't leave one tiny, snowy college town to go to a slightly larger, snowier college town. "Right, but it's also kind of obvious. I bet people are already looking for him there."

"So then why don't we just keep heading south," Zack says. "Narragansett is the closest."

They nod and it's agreed without any input from me. I would have told them it seems unlikely that he'd be going home.

We walk back toward the exit, and the old man tells us to have a nice day. "You, too," I say, because I realize that maybe being the greeter at this store is not how he intended to spend his last years, and because my brother was a jerk to him, and because I bet a lot of people are jerks to him.

We get back into the car, with Charlie driving now. I think maybe I will get to sit in the front, but Zack flips the front seat forward, then steps aside so I can crawl back into my cage in the back seat. "How gallant of you," I say.

"No problem," he replies.

"An hour and a half until Narragansett," Charlie announces as he backs out of the parking spot.

Whoop-de-freaking-doo.

TWO

Once upon a time, in a great and beautiful kingdom, a princess was born. The kingdom was built upon a cliff that looked out over the blue, churning sea. The view was so magnificent that no man could go to the edge of it without throwing himself from it.

NOW

I keep thinking about the old man working the door at Total-Mart. I bet he wears a hat. Maybe a wool fedora or one of those ones that buttons in front. I bet he opens doors for people. I bet he has a handkerchief.

And there he is stuck at the door of Total-Mart, greeting people who either ignore him or make snide remarks like Charlie did.

"You were kind of an ass to that greeter, Charlie," I say.

"Lexi Green, champion of the downtrodden," he replies.

"I just think a little chivalry could go a long way, that's all."

BEFORE

September

Seth picked me up at 6:20 a.m., just when he said he would. His hair stood up like he was a scarecrow and his straw was escaping his brain.

We drove in comfortable quiet, the radio tuned to an old jazz station. He parked out behind Ruby's, and before he got out of the car he said, "In old days—not like olden times, but our grandparents' times—a girl would know to stay in her seat until the guy came around and opened her door for her."

"There were all sorts of rituals," I said.

"Do you think it's silly?"

"Yes," I answered. Who needed some guy to throw his coat down in a puddle?

Seth rubbed his hand over his hair, smoothing down the curls. "Because of course I know you can open your own door. I just think those things were kind of nice." He smiled down at the steering wheel, sheepish. "Standing up when a lady leaves the table. Taking off your hat at all the right times. You open the car door for a girl, and then she gets in and reaches over to unlock your door for you. Gentle things. Polite things."

"I guess I'd never thought of it that way." So when he got out of the car, I waited while he walked around and opened my door. He took my arm and we walked toward the diner. "It is nice," I said. "It makes me feel special."

"See? Nothing wrong with feeling special. We should all try to make each other feel more special."

"What else did people do back then?" I asked as we slid into a booth.

He said, "Guys ordered for girls at restaurants, I know that."

"Like chose for them?"

"No. Well, maybe. But you should choose for yourself."

I knew what I was going to get, because it's what I always get at Ruby's, but still I looked at the menu. The waitress, whose hair was an impossible shade of orange, came to our table. Seth flipped over his coffee cup to indicate he wanted it filled, which she did, then turned to me. "You, hon?"

"No, thanks."

"She's more of a hot-chocolate gal," he said. "With whipped cream." I don't actually like hot chocolate all that much. Not at Ruby's, anyway; it was more sweet than chocolate. But maybe this was his way of saying he saw me as sweet.

"Of course. Be right back."

When she left, I said, "I usually get the egg sandwich."

"A classic choice," he replied. He was holding his coffee cup in one hand, the other arm draped across the back of the booth. "Remy always got that, too." His face darkened for minute, then a smile cracked his face. "I'm glad you don't think this is all hokey."

"Nothing hokey about good diner food."

"I meant you and me, sitting here, opening doors—all of that. You can be a feminist and still want to be treated right.

I mean, it's just chivalry. It's been around since the middle ages."

"Right," I agreed, but I wondered if being around since the middle ages was a good thing.

He leaned across the table, eyes wide. "It was a whole code of conduct, you know. And it wasn't just about being good to women. It was about looking out for other people."

"I see," I said, and decided that in homeroom I'd ask Ms. Blythe to help me find a book about chivalry so I could have something good and real to say to him about it later, instead of just nodding my head. "You know, I've changed my mind. I think I'm going to have the chocolate-chip pancakes."

The waitress, Alison, returned with my hot chocolate, and Seth said, "I'll have the egg sandwich with sausage and the lady will have the chocolate-chip pancakes. And we'll share a coffee frappe."

"What a gentleman you are!" Alison said. I wanted her to be beaming, to be looking down at me like, *What a lucky girl you are!* But her face was drawn and she only looked down at her pad. When she turned to go, the old hag shook her head.

NOW

"'Anyone lived in a pretty how town,'" Charlie mutters as we drive through the streets of Narragansett. We came in on Route 1A and passed through a quaint, touristy downtown—gack—before starting to drive along the water.

The houses are big and set back from the road, but land-scaped so that you can see just how grand they are. Some of them have brick pillars or stone statues or topiaries. The houses are not ostentatious. They are refined. Like little old ladies sitting on pink pincushion chairs.

"No one who created anything of any artistic substance came from a place like this," I say.

"Because you've had such a trying life," Charlie replies.

"Can you imagine?" Zack tucks his hands behind his head like he's reclining on a fainting couch. "You could have a different room for every day. I bet the floors are marble."

"You didn't strike me as the lap-of-luxury type," Charlie tells him.

"Maybe not permanently. But for a week or two? Not so bad." He checks his phone. "Left up here and then a right."

The houses on this street seem even bigger, clad in weathered gray shingles, with circular driveways to show off all their cars. We've barely gone down the street when we see the line of cars and news vans. There's a cluster of people outside one house with an iron gate and a driveway of crushed stone. Charlie pulls the car over to the side of the road.

"I'm guessing he's not here," I say.

We get out of the car anyway and walk down the street to the crowd. There's a police officer by the gate trying to look stern. He's got the aviator sunglasses on and a thin little moustache which I think makes him look more silly than imposing.

A news reporter is filming a segment. "We're here outside of the childhood home of rock musician Adrian Wildes. Wildes disappeared yesterday, wandering away from his tour bus. He has not been heard from since."

She is wearing a little black skirt and a shimmering red low-cut sweater. Her hair is perfectly coiffed, no frizz at all. I hate her. I hate her and her typical mix of sex kitten and innocent wide-eyed, wowie-isn't-it-sad-that-this-douchebag-is-gone attitude. I mean it's like she came from the local news anchor factory: perfect and perky and just sympathetic enough, but not, like, overly emotional—she feels your pain *and* she'll be there in your moment of trouble.

"The bus was en route to Hartford from Philadelphia, and had taken a side trip so that Wildes could photograph a river that had flooded its banks after excessive rain." She pauses to adjust her own umbrella.

Hannah once confessed that she would like to work on the news. Maybe as a weatherperson since she liked science. Gwen and I had stifled our giggles. "What?" Hannah asked. "It's just so random," Gwen told her. "But I'd bet you'd be really good at it." And she probably would be, with her yellow hair and big eyes. If a storm was coming, she'd let you know just how bad it was going to be, and you would trust her. Trusting Hannah, though, is a mistake.

The reporter goes on: "His family has issued a statement that they appreciate the outpouring of support and that they hope his fans' prayers will be answered and that he will return home soon. This is Allie McMaster in Narragansett."

She drops her microphone to her side and the cameraman lowers the camera. "Good," he says.

"This story is shit," she replies.

My thoughts exactly. Shit story about a shitty musician who should probably just stay lost.

"He's probably high in some hotel room with some groupie," she goes on.

"You'd like to be that groupie, I'd bet, Allie," the cameraman tells her.

"Up yours," she says. She pulls a pack of cigarettes from her bag and lights one, dragging deep. "You know, when I was a little girl, I wanted to be a war reporter. I mean, like, really little. I saw all that shit about people embedded in Iraq, and I was like, 'That is for me.'" I can't stop listening to her, this woman under the shell. "So I go to journalism school—and I went to a good school—and all along I'm like, 'Foreign correspondent, foreign correspondent.' And my professors would smile and say, 'But you've got just the right presence for an anchor. Go for it. Go for it. Admit that's what you want. Everyone wants to be an anchor and you actually have the face for it.' And I'd be like, 'F you telling me what I want. Because I'm pretty I can't do serious work?'" Her voice is at a lower register now and she gestures widely as she speaks.

"Honestly, Allie, I didn't mean to open this can."

She picks at a stray bit of tobacco on her tongue. "Well, you did, and now I've started, so shut it." She sighs. "Whatever, my story's over. Here I am. Not even an anchor, covering some crappy story that isn't even a story. In Narragansett. I work in freaking Narragansett. Breaking news, there was graffiti on a stop sign. We interrupt this program to tell you that the tree lighting ceremony will begin at six forty-five rather than six thirty. I might as well go work for *Inside Edition*."

"You won't be here forever, Allie," the cameraman says.

She sighs again. "Let's get some color commentary." She looks past him right at me and says, "You."

"Yes?" I ask.

She puts on the fake smile and says, "How'd you like to be on TV?"

I shake my head.

"Come on, hon, everyone wants to be on television."

I almost say, *Who are you to tell me what I want?* But I don't. I look over my shoulder at Zack and Charlie. "My brother and my friend," I say. "It was their idea—"

"Sure, you can all be on. No problem."

"That wasn't what I meant, I—"

"Boys," she trills. "Come on over here. I just want to do a quick little interview."

The guys come over, and she introduces herself. "Allie McMaster. Channel Eight News. I'm covering the Adrian Wildes disappearance and I'd love to get your opinion on it." She draws out the word "love." She's wasting her time if she thinks flirting with these two will get her anywhere. Charlie's too wrapped up in Penelope, and Zack's, well, you know.

She sets us up in front of the fence, me in the middle with

the boys on either side. She stands next to us at a funny angle, then nods at the cameraman. "I'm here at the home of Adrian Wildes. With me are three of his biggest fans." I grimace; she goes on. "Where were you when you heard about the disappearance of Adrian Wildes?"

"At home," Charlie says. "In New Hampshire."

She makes her eyes wide, but surprise is as hard to fake as a real smile. "You came all the way from New Hampshire?"

The interview is full of these banalities. Favorite song. Ever seen him in concert. I imagine people seeing us on television back home, even though this is a local station. We're like semi famous. I grin and then it occurs to me that people could see it online or something, and then I think of Seth seeing me here like some crazy fangirl.

The reporter's cigarette has smudged her lipstick. I know she is disgusted with us. I want to tell her: *this is not me.* But I am here, aren't I?

"And you, Lexi, where do you think Adrian is?"

I don't have time to think, only speak. The microphone is practically touching my lips and I can hear Charlie breathing next to me his low wheeze of a breath. "Someplace no one will find him," I say. "I think he's gone."

BEFORE

September

The first weekend after the pool party, Seth took me to the beach. Summer was holding on and the ocean was a cool, dark blue. The wind blew off the ocean and filled our noses with the salt air. "I think I'd like to live on an island someday," I told him. "Not a terribly small island with only one house or anything like that. But like a little island town that you have to take a ferry to get to."

"Me, too," he agreed. "And definitely a bigger island."

"When I was little I read this book about a girl who had to take care of a lighthouse. Abbie was her name. Her dad was the lighthouse keeper and he went to the mainland and then this big storm blew up and she had to save her mom and sisters. She watched over this lighthouse for weeks and kept the light burning." Our teacher had read it to us, and then Gwen and I had read it over and over and acted it out, only in our version we were twins and we took care of the lighthouse together. We'd stand on top of the climbing structure at recess and pretend to be lighting the lamp. We'd call out to other kids to look out for the shore.

"I think I read that, too."

"I loved it, but I'm definitely not interested in waiting out storms on a small island. Like, I'm not sure I'm that hardy."

"Small islands are creepy," Seth said. "My family did this

weird overnight, like, commune thing on Isles of Shoals. Appledore, I think. I kept sneaking off and looking at the rocks and after three days I felt like I had been shipwrecked and that no one was ever going to save me. The only thing that kept me going was that I heard that Blackbeard had buried his treasure there."

I'd heard this story, too. Blackbeard visited the islands off our New Hampshire coast frequently, it was said. Once he was about to be captured, and so he slipped away. He left behind his wife who wandered the island saying, "He will come again." After her death, her ghost was supposed to continue the cry. "Did you see the ghost of Blackbeard's wife?" I asked Seth.

But before he could answer, there was a sudden hush and then a panic. A little girl was caught in the current and couldn't make her way back to shore. There was this whole dramatic rescue, and I found myself clinging to Seth's hand while the lifeguard swam out with her red tube and then dragged the girl back to the beach. Another lifeguard gave the girl mouth-to-mouth while the first sat panting, her head on her knees.

I wondered what it would be like to save someone. To have them be gone, but then to bring them back.

It wasn't long before the news crews showed up, and soon everyone was an expert. There were people jumping up to be interviewed who hadn't even been there. "It was so scary," they gushed to the camera. "My heart was beating a mile a minute." People walking by in the background jumped up and down and waved, calling on their cell phones to the people back home.

"So stupid," Seth said.

"So stupid," I agreed.

"They should actually do something to get recognized themselves, not jump in on someone else's story."

"Right," I said. "Totally."

"I almost drowned once, you know."

I turned to him, eyes wide, imagining his skin pale, his eyes with dark circles, the way the girl's were. I tried to imagine his mother, never without her heels and hoop earrings, running to his side and folding his wet body into her arms. "You did?"

"It was up at Lake Winnipesaukee when I was like nine. We went out on my dad's friend's speedboat and I went tubing and the thing flipped over but I was, like, stuck to it and no one noticed right away. They thought I was messing with them. So then they stopped the boat and they had to fish me out."

I could feel the water pounding against my face, my ears, my body bouncing behind the speed boat, the whole world black. My heart ricocheted and I ached as if I'd actually lost him. "What did it feel like?"

He shrugs. "I dunno." He threw his arm over my shoulders, bare except for my skinny bathing suit straps. "Kind of crazy. I was totally dizzy when they pulled me out and my nose felt like someone had driven a turbo jet up one nostril and out the other. You should have seen the snot rockets."

"Gross," I said, and pushed him away.

NOW

In the car again. It's Zack turn to drive. I'm not sure how they've worked out the schedule, or if it's just an unspoken thing. The one thing that's clear is that I get the stinky, stuffy back seat. Always.

We're driving on Route 1, still in Rhode Island, which seems impossible given that it's barely even a speck of a state. The road veers up to and away from the ocean so that sometimes there's just trees and then all of a sudden this big, blue-gray swath of seawater so vast it seems it has no end.

I don't really know what the plan is and the guys aren't talking. Charlie is mad about the way I acted with the reporter, what I said about Adrian being gone, and maybe Zack is, too. I can feel the anger coming off my brother in waves. When we were little and he'd get like this I knew to steer clear, but where can I go when we are trapped in this tiny little car?

Burlington is in the total opposite direction, so I know that's not our destination. If we keep going this way, we could be headed toward New York City. Suddenly that idea seems more frightening than exciting. How will I keep track of Charlie in a city that big? Anyway, the sun is already setting and New York must be hours away.

I contemplate the likelihood that Seth will actually see the news story. I guess it's possible that the story could get picked up nationally, but, then, it's not much of a story. I wipe away the fog on the window. There's nothing to see outside anyway.

Just gray highway. Everyone always makes road trips sound like these super glamorous funfests: top down convertibles, driving along the coast. But this is nothing like that. The car is small and rumbles funnily and it smells awful. Underneath the fast food and the menthol cough drops, it smells like wet dog.

Zack turns on the radio and someone is playing the guitar. It isn't until Adrian Wildes starts singing that I recognize the song. It's an acoustic version of my absolute least favorite song of his: "Lexi." It isn't just because the girl in the song has the same name as me—which does suck, by the way. Ever since it came out, when I tell people my name, they say "Oh, like the song?" But worse than that is the girl is so pathetic. She's all sad and damaged, and that seems to be the reason he loves her.

I reach between the two front seats and snap the radio off with such force that Zack says, "Hey now, watch the knob. That is one fine piece of car stereo equipment and I wouldn't want you to break it."

"It's a crappy song."

Charlie sighs or groans or otherwise registers his complete disgust with me through a heaving noise.

"It is," I say. "One of a long line."

"You don't like Adrian Wildes anymore," Charlie says. "We get it. Seth totally ruined him for you."

"Actually, now I'm talking about a whole genre of songs. The Damaged Girl song. She's so crazy, sexy, sad, and lovely, and he just can't help but love her."

"I'm not sure that qualifies as a genre," Charlie says. "More like a trope."

"Whatever, dropout. It's like those movies, too. These girls are so messed up and the guys act like it's the best thing ever. If your life is in a rut, she shakes it up. If you're depressed, she'll snap you out of it."

Zack glances at me in the rearview mirror, but keeps silent.

"The thing of it is, if an actual girl—not a song girl, but an actual girl—has actual problems, and she talks about them, the actual guy flips out. It's like, 'Oh, this is getting a little heavy,' and he's gone."

"Ah," Charlie says.

"What?" I demand.

"We're not talking about song girls. We're talking about you and Seth. Again."

"Screw you," I tell him.

"What are those problems you have?" Charlie asks. I can't see his face, but I'm sure he's sneering. "What's the litany of troubles that ails you? Aside from Seth, I mean, because it would seem that he wasn't a problem until you started talking about all those other woes that plague you."

"Screw you," I say again. I look out the window at the skinny pines that seem to stretch out for miles. Charlie is the king of sorrows, I guess. No one else could possibly have troubles, not compared to him. But he doesn't know my problems. He doesn't know problems period. So Penelope dumped him. Big whoop. It's nothing compared to what Seth—what happened between me and Seth.

"It's a hero thing," Zack says.

"What?" Charlie asks.

"The songs—those girls. You think you can save her. You want to save her. And in a song you can."

"So you're saying it's a big fairy tale for everyone?" I ask. "The crazy girls and the loser guys get to live out this alternate reality?"

"Sure," he says. "Though maybe not in such a negative way."

I tap my finger on top of the lock for the door. "Either way, I still think it's stupid."

"Of course you do," Charlie says.

When Seth and I first broke up, I used to check my phone all the time. It was gross, really. I disgusted myself and everyone around me. Not that there was anyone around. Gwen was gone. And Hannah, of course. Charlie was still at college then. Seth's friends went with him. So I only had myself to disgust, but I disgusted myself plenty.

And now it's like a habit. I remember that I have a phone— that it exists at all—and I have to check it. So when I see the man in the car next to us holding his phone in one hand and trying to steer with his elbow since he has a soda in the other, I think of my phone. I mean, first I think, What a douche, but then I think of my phone.

I'm trying to break the habit, so I don't take the phone out right away. Instead I count one, two, three in my head, trying to get all the way to seventeen. I count to seventeen seventeen times.

I'm up to my thirteenth time when Zack says, "Aw crap," and then starts shifting over to the right lane. He takes the next exit all the while muttering, "Oh crap, oh crap, oh crap."

"What?" I finally ask.

"Oil can, oil can," he says, and I guess he's trying to sound like the Tin Man, but he really sounds like a robot in a sci-fi movie with bad special effects.

Once we are off the exit, he pulls into the parking lot of an office building.

Every single person coming in or out of that building is holding a phone.

Zack gets out of the car, pops the hood, and heads around to the trunk. "Miss Ruka leaks oil. We've gone a long way without giving her a top off."

"Move it, Charlie," I tell him.

"Why?"

"So I can get out."

"Why?" he asks again.

"To stretch my legs. To make a break for it. To rob this building full of office peons. What do you care?"

"I care because it inconveniences me."

I roll my eyes and don't say anything, but instead crawl in between the front seats and out through the driver-side door. Then I flip Charlie the bird.

A woman is standing in a little courtyard pacing while she talks on her phone, which is about the last straw for me. I pull out my phone and notice two things: I am at 25 percent battery and I have seven new voicemail messages, all of them from my mom.

"Calling the parentals," I announce.

Charlie doesn't respond.

"I don't understand." Mom's voice wavers up and down and I know she is trying to control it. She is trying to sound like the professor she is, perhaps trying to get one of her lazy-ass students to clarify a point. "You went to search for who?"

"Adrian Wildes. He's a singer. He left his tour bus and no one knows where he is."

"Your father doesn't understand either."

I don't fully understand myself, but I don't want Mom to think that both Charlie and I have totally lost it. She doesn't deserve that. "It's kind of like a social-media thing, I guess. And Charlie thought it would make him feel better."

"He said that?"

"Yes," I lie. "He got up off the couch and said, 'This is something I need to do. To feel whole again.' And so I said, 'Well, I think Adrian Wildes is a steaming pile of crap, but if that's what you need to do to feel better, then let's ride, brother.'"

"I know you are lying to me, but are you also making fun of me?"

"No, Mom. And it's not a complete lie. That's what he said in body language, and that's how I feel about Adrian Wildes."

She sighs. "Oh, Lexi."

"What?"

"Are you sure you're okay?"

"I'm fine," I say. "Just looking out for Charlie."

"Lexi," she says again.

"Isn't that funny, Mom? I mean, like, who would have thought I'd be the one looking out for Charlie. For anyone?"

"You're a responsible girl deep down."

"Everyone is responsible deep down, Mom."

"Where are you now?"

I hesitate.

"Lexi."

"Rhode Island, I think. But maybe Connecticut."

Nothing. More nothing.

"Mom?"

"I see."

"What's wrong with him, Mom?"

"There's nothing wrong with Charlie."

I look over my shoulder. Charlie is sitting on a bench outside the office building. He's staring out at the road, his head twitching back and forth a little as he watches the cars go by. "Okay, sure," I say. "Listen. We have to keep moving or we'll never get back."

"Get moving where?"

"Right now I think we're going toward Pennsylvania. That's where he was last seen. We have a few clues. We aren't totally winging this. And there are three of us, and Zack is a junior, so—" I'm not sure how this bit of information is supposed to help my case, except that Zack is older than me, so at least that's something. "And he's super responsible," I go on. "I remember in middle school he was Citizen of the Month like six times."

"When will you be home?" she asks.

"We'll have to stay somewhere tonight, I think," I tell her.

"Where?"

"I have money. We can stay in a hotel or something. We'll be okay. I won't let Charlie decide to sleep under the stars or anything."

"And then you'll come back tomorrow?"

I hesitate. "Yes."

"Lexi?"

"Yes. I will do my best to get us back home tomorrow, okay? I mean, I think we could turn around now. We might never find this guy. But it's a little hard with Charlie."

There's a buzzing on the other side of the line.

"Mom?"

"I want updates, Lexi."

"Yes, ma'am."

"Enough."

"You got it, Mom. Updates and no booze or drugs or hookers."

"You aren't reassuring me."

"I'm with Charlie and Germy Zack Donovan. We are the least appealing group of people ever to hit the open road."

"You're very appealing, Lexi."

"Let's have the self-confidence talk when I get back, Mommy Dearest."

I look over at the car, where Zack is struggling with a funnel and a can of oil. "Gotta roll."

"I love you, Lexi. Tell Charlie that, too. I love you both."

"Moon, stars, and sun," I say. "Got it. Love you, too."

October

When we started our poetry unit and had to bring in a poem we liked, Gwen chose an Adrian Wildes song. I wasn't sure if she did it to push my buttons (who can push your buttons better than your maybe former best friend?) or if she really, really loved it, but she sure did analyze the crap out of it. "You can see in verse three that he is making an analogy between the twisted tree trunk and the man's conscience. This is augmented by the off rhyme and the alliteration."

Gack.

Good old Dewey DeWitt, our million-year-old hippy English teacher, said, "You know, that is a really astute observation, Gwen. And did you also notice that the word 'soul' is misspelled as its homonym, 'sole,' which of course could be a comparison between the soul as in our spiritual being and sole as in the bottom of our foot. But it could also be a reference to his own name and the unusual spelling of 'wild.' It's risky to assume a poet—or any artist—is creating autobiography, but in this case it seems clear that Wildes is saying that he is the man with the twisted tree trunk soul."

"Or," I said, "maybe he just can't spell."

Gwen rolled her eyes at me.

Dewey DeWitt said, "That is not a very helpful contribution, Lexi."

So I put my head down on my desk. Dewey DeWitt didn't say anything.

It's a cry for help! I wanted to shout. *I am a good student and a good kid and now here I am facedown on the desk. Aren't you going to do anything?*

Tooley spoke from behind me. Mike Tooley, but we've all called him by his last name so long I've almost forgotten he has a first. "I kind of wonder, well, if he's the twisted tree, then, isn't that a lot of self-hate?"

"Yes!" Dewey said enthusiastically.

Gwen said, "I think he's really digging deep and examining himself. We all have dark parts and I think it's very brave of him to take a close look at his."

I turned my head to the side so I could see my notebook. In the margin, I drew a picture of a girl with curly hair, like Gwen. She had a big smile on her face and wore a triangle dress like the women on bathroom signs. I started drawing her deep, dark core: a black spiral. I pressed so hard I tore through the page, but I kept spiraling out until the whole girl was covered in black ink.

Gwen's Black Sole, I wrote underneath it. Then I raised my hand.

"Yes, Lexi?" Dewey DeWitt said. And I've got to hand it to

him: he had a hopeful look on his face even though my cheek was still on my desk.

"A sole is also a fish," I said.

"Lexi—"

"Wait," I said. "And the song is talking about the tree growing down by the river—which is twisting, too, by the way. A twisted river and a twisted tree, and this poor little sole. That's what he says, 'Poor little sole all alone, all alone.' So maybe he didn't misspell it, and maybe it isn't a reference to his own name. Maybe it's a fish swimming in the twisted river by the twisted tree. This poor little fish-soul trying to make it when everything else around her is twisted and bad."

Dewey DeWitt didn't say anything at first. He didn't move, either. Then he stepped around my desk so he's in my line of vision. I sat up, and I didn't turn away. "Well, I'll be," he said. "That's almost brilliant, Lexi."

I smiled at him, but all the while I was looking past him, at Gwen, whose dark little sole was puffing out of her nose.

When I told Seth about it later, he laughed. Then he said, "I think you're giving Adrian Wildes way too much credit."

"Maybe," I said.

"Definitely."

"Probably," I agreed.

NOW

Zack and Charlie are still looking under the hood of the car when I get off the phone with Mom. Like Charlie knows anything at all useful about cars. They have four wheels. They take you places—but only if you get up off the couch and get into them.

There's a sidewalk leading away from the office building, which is weird because the road is a four-laner, dotted with strip malls. It's like some planner said, "We should have a walkable downtown," and thought that putting in some sidewalks would automatically solve the general laziness of the population. I wonder if I am the first ever person to walk down this sidewalk. Like, maybe the city council will all jump out with balloons and give me the key to their city, whatever that means.

Instead what happens is someone yells at me from the road. "Nice tits!"

I cross my arms over my chest. Snap my head up. It's a truck, big and black, and a boy is leaning out the open window. He has on a camouflage baseball cap that hides all of his hair. "Nice tits!" he yells again.

I want to yell something smart back at him. Something that will make him never call out a window again. I want to nonchalantly raise my middle finger at him. I can flip off a little girl, but not this douchebag? I want to yell out, "Is that the best you've got? 'Cause I've gotten it a lot worse!" I want to do anything other than the nothing that I do.

The truck peels off, the black cloud of diesel exhaust behind it making me cough. "Asshole," I mutter under my breath. Too late. I'm always too late with my words when it really matters.

When I am sure the truck is gone and not turning around to come back and yell at me some more, I pivot and start walking back toward Charlie and Zack. The hood of the car is closed and Zack is leaning against it. Charlie is in the passenger seat and even from this far, even through the glass, I can tell he's annoyed with me. Well, screw him. He never has to worry about being yelled at just for walking down the street. Just for existing.

"You okay?" Zack asks.

"Sure," I tell him.

"That truck—were they talking to you?"

"Yeah." I wave my hand, like it's nothing. "Stupid bro-dude. Catcalling. I let out an impressive string of profanity in response. Your ears would've bled."

He looks at me, looks ready to say something, but then Charlie beeps the horn and I climb back into my cage in the back seat.

THREE

*Once upon a time, a princess was born in a kingdom on
a cliff. The view was so magnificent that no man could
go to the edge of it without throwing himself from it. The
king was losing his finest knights and soldiers to the ocean.
The only way to break the spell of the cliff was for a man
to resist its pull. The only beauty more powerful than that
of the sea, the king reasoned, was that of his daughter, the
princess.*

NOW

Adrian Wildes has a video about a road trip. It uses, like,
every filter you can find on your phone's camera, so the
characters in it are all glossy and golden and windswept. The
woman trails her arm out of the car and her hair blows into
her face. It's Alana Greengrass, Adrian Wildes's girlfriend at the
time, and she is absolutely beautiful: long, highlighted hair, eyes
perfectly lined. If the back seat windows in Zack's car actually
went down—which they don't—and I held my hand out the
window, it would probably get smacked off by a passing SUV.

And if I let the wind ruffle my hair, my lungs would fill with diesel exhaust. Alana Greengrass manages to appear sad and pensive and poignant all just by looking into the distance. And the road trip is intercut with all these kissy-kissy scenes between her and Adrian. The song washes over them:

> You always said that when you left
> You'd be good and gone
> And gone for good.
> So let's go together, baby.
> Let's be good and gone from here.

And all the while you assume he's the one who is driving the car, but then the end reveals that it's some other guy and that guy and Alana Greengrass literally go driving off into the sunset together. It was before Alana and Adrian broke up for real, but not too long before. And of course everyone talked about how they knew things were going bad and the video was their swan song, not that I cared at all. I only noticed because Alana Greengrass got totally slammed like it was all her fault—she was too clingy, too distant, too flirty with other guys, too reserved. And Adrian Wildes just walked away, slipping her off like an old coat.

Within three weeks he was dating that pop star. That lasted a month. And again the girl was the one with troubles—couldn't hold a man. I thought that was just being a celebrity, but when Seth left—well, it didn't take him long to find someone else.

To find Hannah.

Anyway the song is maybe three and half minutes long, which is about as long as the road part of a road trip can be interesting.

Really it's just the three of us in this little box rolling down the road for hours and hours and hours. Days, months, years. That's what it feels like.

Zack has three empty (mostly empty) fast food cups in the back seat, one of which is sticky around the edges. There were seven pennies stuck into a divot in what I think is supposed to be an armrest. I pocketed those somewhere between the Total-Mart and Narragansett. The seat belt in back on the driver's side doesn't work. There's a spring or something in my seat that manages to poke into my ass no matter which way I sit.

Super glam, right?

And on the radio, it's all Adrian Wildes, all the time. Here are the songs we hear over and over:

> » "Nothing" (Of course: it was his number one hit and,
>   also even though Charlie couldn't control what came
>   on the radio, it still felt like he was doing it on purpose.
>   Like he had some sort of sixth sense and could tell it
>   made my skin crawl.)
> » "Barnstormers"
> » "All Along the Watchtower" (Cover. This led to lengthy
>   discussion of which of the versions of this song was the
>   best, which I stayed out of because I didn't know half

the bands Zach and Charlie were talking about, and, anyway, the original is always best, so I said it was Jimi Hendrix, and Charlie said, "No, dumbass, Bob Dylan did the original," and that's when I shut up.)

» "Open Up Your Heart"
» "Ain't No Plan"
» "Sweet" (A duet with Alana Greengrass, before every-thing went sour, of course, and it kind of killed me that I liked this song even a little bit.)
» "Two Fer the Road"
» "Hallelujah" (This one was a cover, too, and I guess this one breaks my original-is-best rule, because Jeff Buckley sang it best even though it's a Leonard Cohen song. And if you're impressed that I know who Leonard Cohen is, you can thank Seth since Leonard Cohen is just about the only non-YouTube musician that Seth has any respect for.)
» "Clear Eyes, Full Hearts" (This is a song about a televi-sion show about football in Texas. Really.)
» "Topeka"
» "Bartleby" (And this one is about some Herman Mel-ville story, at least that's what Charlie said. I thought Melville only wrote about the stupid whale, but evi-dently he had boring things to say about other boring topics that would inspire boring songs.)
» "Generations Lost"
» "Too Too Far"

- » "Sweet Obsessive"
- » "Truth. Love." (Punctuation his. Poser.)
- » "Hold On Now" (Another duet with Alana Greengrass, when the end was coming.)
- » "Green Witch"

And all the while I am jealous of Alana in the video. Because she is glowing. Because her hair snapping into her face doesn't seem to bother her. Because she has somewhere to go and someone to go with.

"It's getting late," Zack says. "What do you say we stop for the night?"

"That makes sense," I say. "Especially since, you know, we don't actually have a destination."

"We're going where he was," Charlie tells me. All I can see of him is his hair puffing up above the headrest, so he must be slumped down in the chair. The Charles Green slump: it's legendary.

We've snaked through Rhode Island and we've just gotten back onto 95 in Connecticut and it seems like the cars are zipping past us at alarming rates.

"We could stop, take another look at the map, come up with a plan," Zack says. "My cousin goes to college around here. Connecticut College. We can stay with her for the night and then in the morning we can get going toward Pennsylvania again first thing." His voice is gentle, and I remember once when we were in middle school this stray dog wandered by us at the bus stop.

It was all mangy and had stuff oozing out of its eyes. My heart had raced and I was sure this dog was rabid and was going to attack us. But Zack had just spoken to it in that soft, easy voice, and it curled up right by our feet and when the bus came, Zack told the bus driver, who called animal control. That's the voice Zack is using to talk to Charlie.

Charlie doesn't answer, and I don't want to sway him by saying that I think stopping is a good idea, so I keep quiet. In a few miles, Zack gets off the highway, and we're back on quieter roads.

The campus feels like a movie set: huge stone buildings, some of them draped in ivy. There's a big quad in the middle with the remnants of snow dusting it that are somehow not dingy and gray like the snow everywhere else. Zack parks in a visitor lot and then leads us to one of the drabber buildings. At the security desk he says, "My name is Zack Donovan. I'm here to see my cousin Kristy Donovan. She isn't expecting us."

The security guard doesn't say anything. He picks up the phone and calls up, says "Zack Donovan is here," to whoever answers. Then he hangs up and says, "Wait."

So we wait. I realize that Charlie smells like fried food and I wonder if that's his constant smell now, or if it came from Zack's car. And if it came from Zack's car, does that mean I also smell? I am trying to inconspicuously smell myself when a girl skips down the stairs. She has on pajama bottoms and a T-shirt with a picture of the girl from *Phineas and Ferb* on it. "Zack!" she says, and wraps her arms around him. "I thought that's what the guy said, but I didn't know you were coming, so I thought maybe I'd heard him wrong."

"We're on a road trip and we need a place to crash."

"Oh, Zack! That is so you!" She smiles, and then turns to look at me and Charlie. "I'm Kristen."

"I'm Lexi," I tell her. "And this is my brother, Charlie."

"Okay, you all just need to sign in. We'll find you places to crash, okay? Have you eaten? You look hungry."

I write the time, 6:07, and then all our names onto the little book. First Charlie, then Zack, and then me. For myself, I write Alexandra Green, which is my full name, though no one ever, ever calls me that. But maybe when I go to college, I will change that. I will stop being Lexi, and I will be Alexa. Or Xandra. Or Allie, like the reporter. I trace over the A and actually feel my heart lifting a little bit: maybe changing things is as simple as changing what people call you?

Kristy leads us upstairs, but instead of going into a dorm room, she takes us into a kitchen at the end of the hall that opens up to a room with some couches. "Sit, sit. I'll make you noodles in a bag."

Charlie flops onto a couch, and Zack starts to help her, but I'm stuck somewhere in between. I just stand by a dented table while Zack and Kristy chatter.

"You're on a road trip? Oh, wait, it's your February vacation, isn't it? Well, that's cool. My mom never would have let me do that."

"It wasn't exactly a planned event," Zack says. "And I didn't exactly ask for permission."

Kristy stops moving. "Wait, what? Does your mom know you're here?"

"Not really, no."

She shakes her head and pulls her phone from her pocket. "Call home now before I am killed from a remote distance."

Kristy watches as Zack dials. When he says, "Hey, Mom," I whisper, "Tell her to tell our parents we're fine."

"Connecticut," he says. "With Kristy. Kristy, my cousin. The perfect one who gets straight As and never does crazy things like leave suddenly on a road trip."

Kristy rolls her eyes. I point at myself.

"Lexi and Charlie Green are fine if their parents are wondering." He is quiet for a while, nodding his head. Then he says, "Charles Green and Alexandra Green, I think."

"Wait," I say. "Did your parents ask for our names to report us to the police?"

Zack holds up a hand.

"Do they think we kidnapped you? That is hilarious! It's your car. Oh—wait, do they think we carjacked you?"

"It's fine, Mom," Zack says into the phone. "It's a spur-of-the-moment thing. You're always telling that story about how you drove to Lollapalooza and scalped some tickets and—"

Zack nods a few times.

"His parents are pretty strict," Kristy says. "They're going to flip."

"Mom, you need to chillax. I'm seventeen years old. And I'm

with Kristy. Kristy!"

"Did he just say 'chillax'?" Charlie asks from the couch.

"No, Mom. We're not coming home right now. That would be foolish. We've been driving all afternoon and now you want us to drive home in the dark?"

"It's a word," I say.

Charlie lifts the top half of his body up so I can see his face, which is showing a mix of disgust and disbelief, but maybe also a hint of a smile? That could just be a smudge or something. "No, it isn't," he says.

"It's vernacular," I tell him, pulling out one of Dewey Dewitt's favorite vocab terms.

"We'll be home tomorrow," Zack says into the phone. He's turned so his back is to us now, his shoulders all scrunched up. "I promise."

"It's a made-up word," Charlie says.

"It is of dubious word-ish-ness," Kristy says.

"Word-ish-ness is also dubious," Charlie says, and this time I am pretty sure he is actually smiling, and there is a possibility he is smiling at Kristy. She's kind of cute, I guess, with her hair dyed a not-quite-natural red and her perky boobs. She is wholesome. And responsible, that's what Zack said. Wholesome, responsible, and perky—in other words, the exact opposite of Penelope. I am taking this as a good sign, but then Charlie droops back onto the gray couch.

Zack clicks off the phone and hands it to Kristy. "The only thing that kept my parents from calling the Connecticut State

Police is that I have landed here at the home of angel Kristy Ann Donovan, top ten of her class in high school, owner of an impeccable driving record and a varsity letter from the drama department."

Kristy punches him in the arm. "Oh, sure, lay it on thick, cousin. Know what I hear about? 'Zack makes his family dinner three nights a week. Zack has a store on eBay and has sold enough memorabilia to fund his own college education.' When are you going to be an Internet millionaire?"

"I'm not an Internet millionaire. Yet."

This detail about Zack's internet entrepreneurship is interesting, but I am distracted by something sticking out of the wall: a phone charger. I step over and hook the end into my phone. It buzzes to life: a message from Mom, a text from Dad. Dad doesn't really like texting, but he likes talking on the phone even less. The fact that he wrote to me means it's something major. Something important. I open the text:

be safe

Be safe. It's what Dad always says to us. We're going out to catch the bus to school: "Be safe!" Going on a ski trip with friends: "Be safe!" Running toward the biggest roller coaster at Six Flags, the one with a nine-paragraph-long warning message: "Be safe!" No matter the degree of actual danger we are encountering, that's the message.

I guess it's one less word than "I love you," and more or less says the same thing.

He never told me to be safe with Seth, which is weird if you think about it. There's this whole idea of the dad who meets the potential suitor with a shotgun. The dad who is waiting up in the living room with just a single table lamp to a cast an ominous glow on his face. But it was never like that with Seth and Dad.

BEFORE

November

They only met once, Seth and my dad. We'd already been dating almost three months by then. Seth came over after school. He drove us and we went into the kitchen to cook some bagel bite snacks in the toaster oven. I squirmed a little because I was all embarrassed by them, like they were little-kid food. We brought them into the living room and sat on the couch—this was before Charlie moved back home and set up permanent residence. Seth slipped off his shoes and pulled up his legs to sit crisscross applesauce. He was wearing his feminist T-shirt. His sister who went to Barnard got it for him in the school store. *Not afraid to say the F-word.* It was purple and the bottom hem was unraveling, and I desperately wanted it.

We had the television on but weren't really watching it. Dad came in from a run. He had on old sweatpants that rode up around his ankles, and his gray hair stuck out from behind the headband he always wears on his jogs. He stopped in the middle of the room, between us and the television. "Hello there, young sir," he said. And he chuckled. Then he looked at me, then looked away just as quickly. I think maybe he wasn't prepared for this state of affairs. Like he knew Lexi growing up and getting interested in boys would come eventually, but he still wasn't quite ready for it.

"Hello, Mr. Green," Seth said. "I'm Seth."

"Seth!" Dad said. "Call me Philip."

Seth smiled and said, "Okay."

Then Dad smiled back and said, "Well, off to the shower. Don't want my stink to ruin a moment."

I bit my lip to keep from groaning, and then Dad disappeared up the stairs.

"I guess that was only mildly mortifying," I said.

"He seems nice," Seth replied.

"He is nice. Anyway, I like your shirt."

He looked down. "Yeah? Me, too. You'd look good in it. That's kind of your look, isn't it? Disheveled professor's disheveled daughter."

I blushed hard, but how could I tell him that I spent twenty minutes this morning looking at a stack of choices before finally deciding on a Quidditch team T-shirt.

"That came out wrong. I like you this way. I mean, this is what I like about you."

"You like that I'm a mess?"

"You're not a mess. You're beautiful. What I'm saying is, more girls should be like you. More girls should care about the things that matter and not give a fuck about the things that don't."

"Remy is like that," I said. I wrapped the purple thread from his shirt around my finger.

"Remy? I guess so."

There was a scented candle burning on the coffee table. Apple pie. My mom bought it from one of the neighbor kids who was doing a fund raiser.

"I thought she was right, at Halloween. The way she dressed and what she said—" The tip of my finger turned white as I cut off the circulation to it.

Seth sighed. "Are you and her going to be BFFs now?"

"Yeah, sure." I laughed. "We're going to get one of those necklaces and we'll come to school in matching outfits, but pretend we didn't plan it."

Seth rolled his eyes.

"Remy hates me," I said.

"She doesn't hate you," he told me. "She hates me."

"She hates me because I have you and she doesn't. It's that simple."

He looked down at my finger and unwrapped the thread. "You shouldn't do that to yourself."

"It doesn't hurt."

"Still, you shouldn't." He put his arm around me and I leaned into him. It was the smell of the shirt I wanted, the smell of him. "And girls shouldn't be that way to each other. All competitive. It's society that does it. It makes you hate each other, when really you should be supporting one another."

"Well, sure," I said. "Capitalism is based on women hating themselves and each other."

He had the string then and wrapped it around his own index finger, though not tight enough to press into his skin. "You two would actually get along if you gave it a chance."

"Do you want me to be friends with her?"

"I don't know. Maybe. Probably not. It could be awkward. But she's smart and she would be a good friend to you."

"I have friends. I have Gwen and—"

He rolled his eyes.

"Anyway," I said. "Remy hates me."

"Let it go," he said, and I realized that he thought that Remy hating me—which really I was not sure she did—I realized that this was something he thought I should not care about. This hatred between girls was petty, beneath me.

Maybe he was right.

Maybe.

But I would still box her up and send her to Timbuktu if that were an option. On a more charitable day, I might send her off to that Oberlin conservatory she wanted to attend—Ohio was far enough away. I would vanish her from the school any way I could if it meant that Seth would never realize that she was about a thousand times cooler than me.

I unwound the thread from his finger, then laid our index fingers side by side and wrapped the purple thread around them both. I made sure not to do it too tightly. I didn't want it to hurt him. "I think in some cultures this means we're married."

"Don't be a cultural relativist," he said. But he didn't undo the thread.

"Ah, but what you don't realize is that I meant cultures in other realms. Fantasy worlds where a thread has the magic to bind two people for life." I grinned up at him like a dork. I felt the dorkiness all over my face and my body.

Maybe that thread was magic, because the dorkiness spread from me to him and he kissed me right on the lips, right in my living room even though my dad could have walked in at any time. He kissed me like he really was bound to me, and I to him.

NOW

"I thought I smelled noodles in a bag!" A boy pushes through the door of the kitchen. He is Asian American, with shaggy black-brown hair and an easy smile. He's followed by a freckled and pale-skinned girl who has her long red hair in two braids like some kind of Pippi Longstocking or something.

"My cousin and his friends showed up," Kristy tells them. "I'm feeding them."

The boy looks over at me and Charlie on the couch and waves. I wave back. "I'm Lexi," I tell them.

"Troy," he says.

"Annie," the girl pipes in. She talks in a baby voice. I hate when girls talk in a baby voice.

"Hold on," Troy says. He goes back through the door, leaving Annie frozen. I wonder if she's his girlfriend or just wants to be. I wonder if that's how I looked whenever Seth left a room. I dig my fist into my thigh.

When Troy comes back he has a big bottle of red wine which he pours into paper cups. "We've gotta offer a drink to our new friends."

I grab a cup before anyone can say anything about it, but when I take a sip it tastes sour and sweet, nothing like the stuff my parents get. "Mmm," I say. "Interesting."

"Ha!" Troy laughs. "It's from the bottom row of the bargain shelf." He smiles at me. I glance over at Annie. She's watching the television which isn't turned on, probably only because Charlie hasn't found the remote yet.

"So where are you visiting from?" Troy asks.

"New Hampshire."

"New Hampshire? You just popped in from New Hampshire? How long did that take?"

"They're on a road trip," Kristy explained. "How cool is that?"

"What's the destination?" Troy asks.

I glance over at Charlie who still appears comatose. Zack answers for me. "You hear about Adrian Wildes?"

"How he threw himself in that river?"

I see Charlie tense.

"Well, that's one theory," Zack says. "We're thinking he

might have just gone off somewhere and we're trying to find him."

"Huh," Troy says.

"I don't think he killed himself either," Annie says. "He's not that kind of guy."

This causes Charlie to sit up. "What kind of guy is that?"

Annie leans against the counter, her paper cup of wine close to her lips. "I'm not saying he wouldn't want to kill himself, or that there's a certain type of person who's suicidal or whatnot. He just seems fairly responsible, you know? Like he'd tie up loose ends before he did anything?"

Charlie lies back down. "Maybe," he says.

"Charlie's really tired," I explain.

"Noodles are done!" Kristy takes down a stack of dining hall bowls from the cupboard and starts scooping short, flat noodles covered in some sort of pinkish-red sauce into them. "We're kind of noodles in a bag aficionados here. This is my favorite kind: Parma Rosa."

"Noodles in a bag and cheap wine," Troy says. "We're super classy around here."

When I sit down on the couch, Troy takes the seat next to me. Annie hesitates and then sits down by Charlie's feet. "So you're in high school? What grade are you in?" Troy asks me.

Troy is so close to me that I can feel his leg brush against mine. I scoot closer to the arm of the couch. "Sophomore. Zack's a junior." I scoop up a big mouthful of noodles and jam it into my mouth. I make sure a few noodles hang out so I am as unattractive as I can be. They're still hot, though, and singe the roof of my mouth.

"What about you, Charlie?" Annie asks. I don't know if she is trying to be nice or to make Troy jealous or what. Charlie, pulling himself up to sitting, says, "I go to Essex College."

"Oh," Annie says. "I applied there, too."

"Yeah?" Charlie asks.

"Yeah."

It's a totally scintillating conversation, right? But I mean, I guess it's good that he's talking to someone even if he did leave out the detail about not actually going to school anymore.

I drink some more of my wine. I can feel that it's making my face hot and pink, but I don't care.

"So why Adrian Wildes in particular?" Troy asks.

"It's not like we had a whole roster of missing pop stars to choose from," I retort.

He doesn't even seem to notice the glint in my voice. "Right on," he says.

I kind of wish I had given Charlie a chance to answer, though, because I'm still wondering what we're doing out here chasing someone who doesn't want to be found, assuming he's even still alive. Which is a big assumption.

"Adrian Wildes isn't a pop star," Charlie says. "He plays his own instrument. He writes his own music. It has riffs and depth and substance."

Kristy swallows a bite of noodles, "He played here once like ages ago I guess. But he signed the wall in the green room of the

77

theater. People touch it now before they go onstage for luck." She glances over at Charlie. "I have a work-study job in the theater."

"What are they hoping will happen?" I ask.

"Fame, I guess." She shrugs. "It's actually getting a little faded now and there's this big debate about whether someone should go back over it with a Sharpie or something. There's been a real push to get him to come back to campus and sign it again, but now, well . . ."

Her voice trails off and Zack and I look over at Charlie whose mouth is set in a thin line. I don't think he's taken even one bite of his dinner. Zack says, "When we find him, we will bring him here directly, Sharpie in hand."

Troy bends over and picks up the giant bottle of wine and tops off each of our cups. "To Adrian Wildes!" he says.

We all toast and I drink a big gulp and he fills my cup up again. People keep coming in and out of the common area. Some stay and talk, and others just pass through. I learn that Kristen is double majoring in economics and French and wants to work for the United Nations after she goes to the Peace Corps. Troy is majoring in philosophy, of course. He keeps moving closer to me and touching my leg while he talks, and I keep pulling away. My face burns and I'm not sure if it's the wine or him, but I feel like I want to run outside and suck in cold air. Why do boys always think they can just come into your space like that? Like your body is just a thing that's there for them. I tried to say something about it to Seth once, but—whatever. That's over.

Troy thinks that I would probably like to major in philosophy, too, and then he spends a whole lot of time trying to figure out whether if I came to Connecticut College, he would still be there. "Well, you're a sophomore and I'm a sophomore, so, unless you're on the five-year plan, then, no."

"Ha!" He laughs. "This is why I'm not a math major. Also, wine." He holds up the bottle and starts to pour more in mine, but I shake my head.

Charlie is snoring on the couch when Kristen says, "You know, we should all probably turn in. Zack, you can crash in my room, and Charlie, you can go with Troy, and Lexi can go with Annie. Does that work for everyone?"

"Well—" Troy says, but Annie very quickly says, "Yes, that's great." I can't help but smirk. Having me in her room is better than having me in Troy's, I guess.

When we get to her room, she takes out a new toothbrush and a nicely folded towel. "Do you want to take a shower? You can borrow some pajamas if you want. You can wear my flip flops, too."

She shows me where the women's bathroom is. There are three shower stalls. One of them has a huge wad of someone's hair, so I pick the middle one. Annie gave me her shampoo, too, which is the same kind that Gwen uses. It's weird. I don't think I could have told you what kind of shampoo Gwen used, but as soon as I smelled it it's like we were curled up on her couch together watching a movie.

I don't want to miss Gwen, but I do.

I stay in the shower a long time. It feels like I haven't showered for days, like we've been on this road for a week at least, rather than just a few hours. Back in Annie's room, she's already in her bed. She's laid out this kind of foam folding chair thing and even put clean sheets on it.

"Thanks," I say. "This is really nice of you to share this—whatever this is."

"It's a futon chair," she tells me. "But people call them flip and fucks." She blushes as she says it. She starts undoing her braids and her red hair is in waves.

"Wait, what?"

"Gross, right?"

"It doesn't even make sense. If I came here to sleep with you, we would be in your bed, wouldn't we?"

She doesn't say anything. She looks down at her hands where she stretches a hair elastic. "Are you, like, I mean, are you hitting on me?"

"No. I mean, no. I'm not a lesbian, even if my brother thinks my taste in music leans that way."

"Neither am I," she says. Her voice is rounder now, and lower, not the baby voice she used all night.

"I thought maybe you liked Troy," I say.

She gives a half smile. "I did when I first met him. He is kind of cute, right?"

"Sure."

"But it turns out he flirts with everyone. I mean *everyone*. So you feel all special when you're with him, but then you see him

80

with another girl, and it's like, 'Oh, that's just how he is. I'm not special at all.' I'm not even sure he realizes he's doing it. Like, if you had tried to hook up with him or something, he would have been shocked and said, 'But you're only sixteen.'"

"Actually, I'm fifteen."

"He would be horrified."

"Is that why you won't sleep with me?" I joke.

She smiles. "Exactly. If you came to school here and I was still here—oh, wait, I can actually do basic math."

I smile up at her. Her hair is all down now and fanned around her and I think I understand why she wears it in braids. It's a little bit too beautiful, too stunning. It's like all anyone would see of her. "You have a nice voice," I tell her. "Why do you use that baby voice?"

She looks out the window toward the lights of a building across the quad. "Your brother and Zack made me nervous."

"Zack and Charlie?"

"Boys always make me nervous. It's like, every time I meet a new guy, I can't help it, but my brain is like, Maybe he's the one. Maybe, maybe, maybe. It's pathetic, I know. I mean, I'm nineteen. It's too early for true love to come walking through the door. But I can't help but get my hopes up, you know? And then that voice comes out."

"Well, I wish you had said something because Zack is gay and Charlie is—heartbroken."

"Do you have a boyfriend?" she asks.

"Not right now, no."

"I've never had a boyfriend."

"Really? But you have such great hair."

She laughs at this, big and loud. Then she claps her hand over her mouth. "Is that all it takes?"

"The harder part is finding a good guy. I don't actually believe in True Love if you want to know the truth."

She doesn't say anything. She just looks at me.

I say, "I guess boys make me kind of nervous, too." My stomach tightens with anticipation. I've never really talked with anyone about this. Never said it out loud. I mean, Charlie would tell you that I've bitched a thousand and one nights about Seth, but that's different. I've never said the whole story of what happened, not to anyone. Annie has a poster of Van Gogh's night sky on her ceiling and I stare at the swirls. "It's just that you can never tell with them. They can seem so nice and normal and thoughtful, but underneath it's something else. Or how they act with their friends and how they act with you. Like you were saying with Troy—it's hard to know who he really is, who he really cares about."

"So you're saying all guys are like that. It's just variations on a theme."

"I guess so."

"So maybe you do believe in true love," she says. "And what you don't believe in is the possibility of non-loser guys."

"Have you met any yet?"

"No," she says. "But I have to believe they're out there, right? I mean I haven't ever seen a moose or an elephant in real life, and I believe in those."

BEFORE

September

The bulletin board outside the art room was decorated with some of the best work from the year before. Hannah dragged us down to show us because there was a picture she painted of an egg sitting in a porcelain egg cup. It was really good, actually, in the sense that all the details were just right. The egg looked like it had weight. The cup looked like one fall to the ground and it would smash into a million pieces. But I wasn't sure why she painted an egg in a cup. Weren't paintings supposed to have meaning or something?

"It took me, like, half the semester," Hannah said. "My parents are going to frame it."

"Cool," I said, but couldn't muster much enthusiasm.

"It's really good, Hannah," Gwen told her, sounding much more sincere than I did.

I scanned the rest of the board. My eyes were drawn to a small sketch of an empty chair. Seth did it. Seeing his name, *Seth Winthrop*, beneath the picture made me all warm and fuzzy like I'd transformed into a little kitten in a basket or something totally cute-explosion like that. I knew better than to show that side to Gwen and Hannah, and, anyway, right next to Seth's was a self-portrait by Remy Yoo. She'd drawn herself staring right out of the picture, right through me. She had harsh bangs and a hint of a smile that said *I am better than you.*

"Bitch," I murmured.

"Who?" Hannah asked.

But Gwen saw what caught my eye. "Give it a rest, Lexi. They broke up last year."

Hannah caught on. "It's a really good self-portrait."

"But, like, of course it's a self-portrait, right?" I could just picture Remy staring at herself in every mirror she passed. Staring, staring, staring because she was so beautiful and had, fine, distinct features and that dark, dark hair. Nothing washed out. Nothing soft.

"Um, I think that was an assignment," Hannah said.

I turned to look at her. She stood with her feet together like ballet first position and she was sucking on her lower lip. She looked like somebody's kid sister visiting from the elementary school. "What's your deal?" I asked. "You guys friends with Remy Yoo now?"

"No," Hannah said quickly.

But Gwen said, "I'm not *not* friends with her."

"You should be," I said.

"Why?" Gwen asked. She stood with one foot out to the left, a hand on her hip. Snob stance, that's what we called it in middle school because all the too-cool popular girls stood that way while they made fun of the lesser girls. So, yeah, of course she stood that way now.

"Because she's Seth's ex. Because she treated him badly."

"Did she treat you badly?" Gwen asked.

I thought of the funny looks I'd gotten from Remy in the halls. Not daggers. More like raised eyebrows, impenetrable and unknowable. It's like she knew something I didn't. Like she was holding it over me. "Yeah, sort of. She looks annoyed every time she sees me."

"Of course she's annoyed. You're dating her ex. You won, Lexi. Isn't that good enough for you?"

"Excuse me?"

"Have some grace, Lexi. Don't be a sore winner." Her voice was a mix of pleading and exasperated, like I was on a ledge ready to jump, and this was her last-ditch effort to save me, but part of her kind of wished I would just jump so the whole thing could be over with.

"Screw you," I said.

"Screw you, too," she shot back. Then she pivoted on her heel. She grabbed Hannah, who was blinking like a baby bunny, and dragged her down the hall.

I spun back to the bulletin board. There was Remy Yoo staring back at me, her pencil-drawn eyes flashing. And when I turned to go down the hall, away from where Gwen and Hannah went, there was the real Remy. She stood by the water fountain clutching her water bottle in two hands. "Lexi," she said.

"What?" My voice fought to escape my throat and it sounded garbled and coarse.

"Do you think we could talk sometime?" She took a step toward me.

"Were you listening?" I asked.

"Listening to what?"

I couldn't tell if she was lying or not. I shook my head.

"Whatever. Never mind."

I strode down the hall. Remy stepped into my path. "Lexi," she said again.

I pushed past her. I didn't mean to, but I bumped into her, my elbow hitting her arm. The water bottle fell and its top spun off, spreading water down the hall. "Shit," she whispered.

I kept going. I walked away while the spill slicked the tiles behind me.

NOW

In the morning, I wake up before Annie. I leave the pajamas she loaned me behind and slip back into my jeans. I take a clean shirt from my bag and put my old sweat shirt on over it. I take the toothbrush with me.

She has a whiteboard on her door. I draw a picture of an elephant, and then give it antlers like a moose. I write: *You're more likely to find one of these, but I wish you luck. You deserve it.*

I find Seth and Charlie out in the common room. Zack looks well rested and like he took a shower, too. Charlie doesn't. We step outside into the cold morning air, and Charlie says, "I looked at the campus map online. The theater's over there."

I know what he wants to do, although I don't know why.

We crunch across the frozen snow toward the theater. It's a big stone building with columns built into the face of it. The ground out front is wet with melting snow, and, when I slip a little, I grab on to Zack to steady me.

I figure the door will be locked, but when Charlie pulls on it, it opens, and we all step inside. It's mostly dark, with just one light on down a distant hallway. "Creeptastic," I say.

"I think it's kind of peaceful, actually," Charlie says. His voice doesn't have the edge I've come to expect, but he also isn't really looking at me or maybe even talking to me. It's like his voice is just floating out there for no one to hear.

Charlie opens another door which goes into the theater itself. It's a little weird to be in here with no one else. The darkness is intense, and I take out my cell phone—all charged up now—and use the flashlight to guide us down the aisle. I think of Seth and how I once told him to try out for the play, how he acted like it was the worst possible thing I could have asked him.

At the end of the aisle, Charlie hops onto the stage. Really. He just kind of jumps and twists and lands sitting on the edge of it like it's the most natural thing in the world. I find the stairs on the side and go up those, followed by Zack. Charlie is already making his way backstage. He finds a wall of light switches and flicks a couple, lighting up different areas of the theater before he finds one that brings the backstage into a shady sort of half light. I turn off my phone.

The light makes a crackling noise, and it's easy to imagine the whole thing blowing out, sending sparks and glass raining down on us. Zack and I follow Charlie as he walks the perimeter of the area. He opens one door, peeks in, and then shuts it before I can look in after him. I feel like if I speak, the whole theater will collapse around us. Like it is made of fabric or air and will just drop, and the world around us will be gone, too. It will be just us afloat.

"Here," Charlie says, and pushes open a door. It's a dressing room, messy, with a large mirror that, in this scant light, looks like a puddle hovering in the air. Zack turns on a light and then the mirror is just a mirror, reflecting us back at us. Charlie turns his head.

The signature isn't hard to find. It's right by the door and, like Kristy said, it's fading a little, mostly around the W of his last name. Charlie stands and stares at it a long time before he says, "It's just the past."

I don't know what he means by that. I know he didn't think we would find Adrian Wildes here curled up in the dressing room. But what did he expect?

We're crossing back over the stage when Zack stops. "When I was eleven, my mom signed me up for this boys pageant thing."

"There are pageants for boys?" I ask.

"Yeah. They're—something. Anyway, I had to perform for the talent section, you know. I wanted to sing. But my mom said my voice was 'not from the angels.'"

"Where was it from?" I ask.

He shrugged. "So instead I decided to do magic tricks. I was The Great Zacktini! I had this toy magic set and I practiced and practiced, but when I got up on the stage, I just flubbed. Like big time. Dropping the balls and the scarves and everything. It was a disaster."

"It sounds a little cute, maybe."

"Oh, yeah, the audience thought it was hilarious. I should have hammed it up like I was doing a comedy routine, not a magic act. But instead I just got more and more flustered and then I started to cry a little. But I stayed up there. I finished the act. I got Most Spirit at the end, which I think is actually a step below a participant's ribbon."

The whole time Zack is talking, Charlie is pacing around the theater. Then he sits down on one of the chairs in the front row. So I go and sit next to him. "Sing now," I say.

"What?" Zack asks.

"Or do some magic. But I'm guessing you don't have your magic kit with you, so sing."

He shakes his head and gives a little smile. "Nah."

"Come on," Charlie says. "We'll be the best audience you've ever had."

"The only songs I have in my head are Adrian Wildes songs, and I know how Lexi feels about those."

"It's fine," Charlie says. "It won't kill her."

"It won't," I agree. I kind of want to hear Zack sing. I wonder if he's really terrible or if his mom was being mean or what.

Zack looks down at the floor of the stage, but then he starts singing, kind of quiet and low. I recognize the song pretty quickly—"Topeka"—but Zack sings it differently.

You blow across me
Like a Topeka tornado.

And all I can think is,
How'm I gonna save you
From the storm inside?

Adrian Wildes's voice, when he sings it, is full of sorrow, but Zack sings it more with guilt and anger, his voice scratching over the words like boots over ice. And maybe his mom is right and his voice doesn't come from an angel, but as he's singing, I find myself loving the song with every word he sings.

When Zack finishes, Charlie says, "I gotta piss."

"So polite," I reply.

When he's gone, I say, "You know, if we were ever going to find Adrian Wildes, it'll be by looking someplace no one else is looking."

"I don't think we're going to find him," Zack says.

"Then why'd you come?"

"I told you, my parents—"

"They're fighting?"

"They *aren't* fighting. They aren't talking They aren't anything. It's the Cold War up in our house. Mutual assured destruction."

"So coming along with me and Charlie has been a real break from all that, huh?"

He smiles down at the stage. "What about you?"

"I'm not sure how familiar you are with Charlie's general demeanor lately, but he's been on the couch for weeks, and frankly wasn't Mr. Get Up and Go before that, and now he's suddenly raring and ready to go."

"But that's a good a thing, right?"

"Were you not paying attention during the suicide unit in health class—the sudden energy and euphoria—"

"I wouldn't exactly call Charlie euphoric."

"You haven't seen him this last month. The only bigger sign would be if he had started giving away all of his possessions. He is on the edge, and I need to stay with him."

My stomach sinks then as I realize I have just left him alone. Going to the bathroom is a classic escape move in cop dramas. But then Charlie is walking back across the stage. He claps his hands together. "We need to regroup," he says, and pulls the old folded map from his back pocket.

"So, I was thinking in the bathroom—"

"Spare the details," I interrupt.

He doesn't even bother to roll his eyes. "We've been to Narragansett, right?" he says, putting his finger down on the map. "That's where he's from. And here's Philadelphia, that was his last stop. And then he was on his way to New England for shows in Hartford and then Boston, right?" He put a second finger on Hartford.

"Okay, sure?" Zack says. "We knew all this."

"But he went missing on the Delaware River near Bethlehem. That's totally out of the way if the bus was going to Hartford."

I look where he's pointing. He's right: the spot on the map is nowhere near 95 or any of the other highways you would take to get from Philadelphia to Hartford. "But he asked to go see the river, right? It's his tour, so maybe they had to go where he wanted."

"Right. I think we need to try to get on the road he was on."

"What do you mean?"

"Follow the Delaware River north, and look where it gets you." He traces his finger up the map along the blue line that narrows as he goes north. It's so thin I can barely see it, but then it widens again as it curves up along the border between New York and Pennsylvania and leads right into one of the circles he and Zack had drawn earlier: Shangri-La, the abandoned amusement park. "I think that's where he was heading. We start there. If we don't find him, then we follow the river south and we're bound to run into him." He traces his finger south until it gets to Trenton, New Jersey. "If we haven't, we can get back on ninety-five north there."

"That almost sounds like a plan that almost sounds like it makes sense," I tell him.

Zack raises his eyebrows at me, and I think he's asking if I'm still just playing along. I don't know. Charlie's fingers traced miles and miles of driving, but at least we're moving in some sort of rational direction.

Charlie clumsily folds the map. "Three hours to Shangri-La!"

And with that, we head to paradise.

FOUR

Once upon a time, a princess was born in a kingdom on a cliff. The view was so magnificent that no man could go to the edge of it without throwing himself from it. The king was losing his finest knights and soldiers to the ocean. The only way to break the spell of the cliff was for a man to resist its pull. The only beauty more powerful than that of the sea was that of his daughter, the princess. And so the king issued a proclamation: any man who could go to the edge of the cliff and resist its pull would have his daughter's hand in marriage.

NOW

*M*y phone buzzes. We must be driving through a service bubble because my phone buzzes again and again as a slew of messages are delivered.

Gwen, 9:17 a.m.: Do you have the English homework?

Gwen, 9:19 a.m.: It's just I left my notebook at school.

Gwen, 9:23 a.m.: DeWitt didn't put it on the portal. Again.

Gwen, 9:28 a.m.: I tried to call Torrance or Jude, but they didn't answer.

Gwen, 9:29 a.m.: And Hannah, well, you know what she's up to. ;)

Gwen, 9:37 a.m.: Listen, you don't have to be a bitch about it. Just let me know if you have the English assignment.

Gwen, 10:03 a.m.: So maybe the Hannah comment was a little uncalled for. And calling you a bitch.

Gwen, 10:04 a.m.: Calling you a bitch in the text above, I mean. Still not sure about past instances. :D

Gwen, 10:05 a.m.: That was a joke, in case you weren't sure.

Gwen, 10:13 a.m.: I'm trying to make a move here. Like an opening parlay.

Gwen, 10:14 a.m.: Are you going to ignore me forever?

Gwen, 10:37 a.m.: Just called your house. Your mom told me you went to look for Adrian Wildes. WTF?

Lexi, 10:39 a.m.: It was Charlie's idea.

Gwen, 10:40 a.m.: You should've called me. I would have gone, too.

Lexi, 10:41 a.m.: It wasn't exactly planned.

Lexi, 10:42 a.m.: Anyway, my phone is about to die.

Gwen, 10:43 a.m.: If you find him, give him a big, fat kiss for me.

Lexi, 10:44 a.m.: Definitely not.

I have the English assignment. I could tell her. I already did it. It was a textual analysis of the opening chapter of *The Catcher in the Rye* because of course Dewey DeWitt loves good old Holden Caulfield. But there's three days left of vacation and she'll figure out what she needs to do.

Also, my phone has a good charge on it for now, so I lied about that. But then, she lied about coming with us. She never would have come, and probably would have mocked me openly. Maybe that's all we do now—lie, lie, lie. I wonder if you can lie yourself back around to the truth.

I pick up my phone again and send a message to my parents: **On the road again. Heading to Pennsylvania. All limbs still attached. No new tattoos.**

The phone is warm in my hand, like a stone that's been sitting in the sun. At the start of the school year my parents read this article about how kids shouldn't have their phones in their bedrooms at night because they were staying up to all hours and also maybe radiation. So they bought this fancy charging dock and put it in their bedroom and I bitched and complained about it. But it meant that when Gwen stopped texting me, I could pretend it was because she knew I wouldn't answer in the night.

My mom texts me back: **No NEW tattoos?**

Lexi, 10:56 a.m.: Oh. You didn't know about Charlie's tramp stamp?

Mom, 10:57 a.m.: Lexi, that is not funny.

Lexi, 10:58 a.m.: It's really very tasteful as far as tramp stamps go.

Mom, 10:59 a.m.: I wish you wouldn't use phrases like "tramp stamp."

Lexi, 11:00 a.m.: It is a very tasteful lower back tattoo.

Mom, 11:01 a.m.: ROFL

Lexi, 11:02 a.m.: Literally?

Mom, 11:03 a.m.: Just stay safe, okay?

Lexi, 11:04 a.m.: Of course.

And then I add the emoji of two girls and a heart which I guess is not meant to be a mom and her daughter, but I think she'll get the point.

"Jesus Christ, Lexi, can you at least mute your phone?" Charlie sighs from the front seat.

"For your information, I was texting Mom and letting her know that we weren't eaten by wolves."

"You could be texting from inside the wolf," Zack says.

"I don't think I would fit inside a wolf," I say. "And if I could, and if I had my phone, I would not lie and tell my mother I was okay. I would say, 'Help, help, I'm in the belly of the wolf!' And then a kindly woodsman would come and chop me out."

"You are so messed up," Charlie tells me.

"Hey that's a nice glass house you have there. Want me to gather some stones for you?"

The car makes a clunking noise and gives a little shimmy like it's tired of hearing me and Charlie argue, too.

"We're going to need to top off the oil again soon," Zack says. "We're also going to need to fill the tank."

My phone buzzes one more time. I think it's going to be from Mom, one last plea for us to stay safe. Instead it's from **Gwen:** When you get back, maybe we could talk.

I want to respond, but we drive around a corner and down a gentle hill and my service cuts out.

BEFORE

October

Gwen and I met at Ruby's before school. It was a couple of weeks before Halloween, and Seth and I still hadn't figured out what famous couple we wanted to be. Ruby's was already decked out with tiny fake pumpkins on each table and a mannequin dressed like a witch behind the counter. Gwen and I chose a booth near the front—a two-seater—and the stuffing in my seat is pushing out of the pink vinyl. She got a grilled muffin and I got their egg sandwich and I had ketchup on the corner of my mouth, edging toward my cheek, but she didn't tell me that and I didn't notice until second period when I went to the bathroom. Instead she said, "I never thought you'd be the kind of girl who got a boyfriend and just disappeared."

I held up my hand right between us. "I'm still here." I smiled. She didn't.

"We've had to reschedule this three times."

"That's because my mom's on this, like, no trans fat thing. She thinks Ruby's is a hellhole. I think it's an oasis, actually. The mythical place, not the band."

"I'm aware." She had asked for a separate cup for the frappe we ordered to share, and now she poured in her half. She took the only straw and sipped in hard. "The Harvest Fest is in town this weekend. Sophomores are doing a booth with face painting for kids. You coming?"

"I'm not a very good artist," I said. The truth was, Seth and

I were supposed to be working on a video this weekend, and maybe going into Portsmouth.

She stirred the frappe. We used to always share the same cup. First we'd drink the plastic cup down to the bottom, then we'd dump in the extra that they always served to you in the metal frappe-making cup and drink that down, too. So fast sometimes we'd give ourselves headaches.

"It's really thick today, don't you think?" I asked, and slurped some out of my plastic cup.

"Banal," Gwen said, looking past me toward the window. Then this kick to the gut: "Turns out you're as bad as your brother."

I had the egg sandwich in my hands, mouth open, ready to take a bite. "Excuse me?"

"You heard me. You're making small talk about the thickness of Ruby's frappes, now? Oh, okay, nice chatting with you, Penelope."

"Take that back," I said.

She smirked. "No take backs."

"I'm not like Charlie and I'm definitely not like Penelope."

She looked out the window behind me. "I think the frappes are actually just the same as always. And the weather is really lovely. And did you catch the latest episode of *America's Funniest Home Videos*? I think the ones where the guys get hit in the crotch are hilarious, but you also can't beat a good old-fashioned dog-falling-down video."

"Stop it."

"Then again, I also do like babies being surprised by their world." She still wasn't looking at me. Her pale cheeks flushed pink.

"Stop it."

"Did you hear it's going to be an exceptionally cold winter?"

I put my egg sandwich down on the plate that showed signs of wear. The egg was sliding out to the side, taking the ketchup with it.

"What do you want, Gwen?"

"This is an ultimatum." She stirred her straw through her half of the frappe, and it left a rivet behind it. It *was* thicker than normal. "You stop being a fucking succubus and spend some time with us."

"Or what?"

"Or you won't be spending time with us."

"No one likes an ultimatum."

"No one likes to be ditched for a guy, especially a guy with YouTube aspirations."

If I'd been able to be honest with myself or if I had known then what Hannah and Seth were doing—maybe even at that very moment—maybe I would have acted differently. But I doubt it.

I let the YouTube comment slide. I let it all slide. "You're right. I guess I was just excited. It was so new and—"

"I'm not looking for an explanation."

"Do you even want to spend time with me?"

"I think so."

99

"You're not sure?"

"I haven't seen you in three weeks. Maybe you really have been turned into a pod person."

"I haven't."

"We'll see."

The waitress came over, looked at our plates, and said, "Gals, you're going to be late for school."

"Can we have our check then, please?" Gwen asked, all sugar again.

How would I rewrite this now? She was right.

She was right about all of it and I was stupid.

Later that week, they made us fill out a survey during homeroom. Ms. Blythe, my homeroom teacher and also the librarian, perched on the edge of a table next to her coffee. "To be perfectly honest, I'm not sure these surveys are truly ethical. There's nowhere here telling me to tell you that you don't need to participate. Only to instruct you be perfectly honest. What is perfect honesty, anyway?"

"So we don't have to participate?" Tooley asked.

"I'm certainly not going to make you," she said. "Then again, it does gather useful information."

She passed each of us a folded paper with bubble dots like a standardized test. We scrambled to find number two pencils. Ms. Blythe had a bunch of golf pencils near the computers for writing down the call numbers for books. They made me feel like a giant. *Argh*, I growled in my head at the pencil.

The questions at first were simple.

How often do you smoke tobacco cigarettes?

Never. I filled the bubble in edge to edge. In fact, I had smoked two times in my life. Once as an eleven-year-old, then again the summer before my freshman year, both times with Charlie. I hated it both times. The first was exploratory for both of us. *Just what are these cigarettes like? Will we die instantly?* The second time was a pre-Penelope attempt at edginess. That was one good thing she squashed.

How often do you chew tobacco?

Eww. Never.

How often do you smoke marijuana (cannabis)?

Tooley laughed. "Ms. Blythe, some of these scales don't go high enough."

"Silent survey taking."

Next it went into questions about alcohol. I hesitated over the questions about frequency, then chose two to three times per month.

Approximately how many alcoholic beverages do you consume in a session (party, etc.)?

I chewed on the edge of golf pencil. It was woody and gritty all at once.

"Will you join me for an alcoholic-beverage session?" Gwen whispered.

"A party or an et cetera?" I whispered back, peeking at her from the corner of my eye to catch a sly smile.

I lightly colored in the circle for one to two and noticed that she chose five to six. Was that true?

Next were questions about diet and exercise. Easy.

Then: *Are you sexually active?*

Without meaning to, I wrapped my arm around the survey like I was afraid people were going to try to copy off of me.

Yes.

If yes, continue to question fourteen. If no, skip to question sixteen.

14. What age were you first sexually active?

The choices went all the way down to seven. Seven! I filled in fifteen.

How many sexual partners have you had?

The choices went up to "More than ten." I colored in the bubble under the one.

Okay. Done with that. On to question sixteen with the virgins.

But, no.

Have you ever been pressured into sexual activity?

Yes

No

Not sure

How could you be unsure?

(No, thank you.)

Well, there is pressure and there is force. Charlie would probably say that they were not the same thing physically speaking, that force is directional and pressure is—pressure. So, yeah, maybe Seth pressured me. There wasn't anything inherently wrong with that. He was just letting me know what he wanted. I could've said no.

Gwen flipped the page.

Screw it. I colored in No. Ms. Blythe had said this survey wasn't even ethical.

The questions moved back into safer territory.

Have you witnessed an act of physical violence in the last year, such as one student shoving another?

No.

Have you been in a physical fight in the last year?

No.

Is there an adult at school you feel you could trust to talk about a troubling issue?

I glanced up at Ms. Blythe. She was standing back at the circulation desk of the library, flipping through a magazine.

Yes.

When we finished, Ms. Blythe picked up a piece of paper and read, "'We understand that some of the questions in this survey might have made you uncomfortable or raised concerning issues for you. Your school guidance counselor could help you—'"

Gwen snickered and Tooley said, "Mr. Wilkins, right on. Roll that cadaver out of storage."

"Michael." She cleared her throat, then continued: "'We have provided informational brochures which cover the topics in this survey. We ask your teachers to dispense them to all of you at this time. We ask each of you to take one for reasons of privacy.' So here you go." Ms. Blythe passed the tri-fold brochures around in a stack. We each took one dutifully. I flipped through. They were printed in purpley-pink ink on gray paper so the stock-image teens—smoking pot, hugging a bottle, kissing—were all purple hued. *Drug Use: Flying High to Rock Bottom. Alcohol: How Much Is Too Much? Sex: Saying Yes or Saying No.* I shut the brochure and shoved it into my bag.

"Was that so traumatizing that you need to keep your brochure, Lexi?" Gwen asked.

"I just think it's funny. And anyway I don't want Ms. Blythe to get in trouble."

The bell rang and we all started to leave. Most kids threw their brochure in the recycle bin. Ms. Blythe gathered up the surveys while I stood in the doorway.

"Everything okay, Lexi?"

"Sure." I hooked my bag onto my shoulder. "They asked if there was an adult in school we could trust, and I thought of you."

She smiled. "Thanks, Lexi. That's nice of you."

I waited for her to ask me if there was something I wanted to talk to her about. I left this big garage door wide open. She didn't ask.

"Anyway, you were right," I said.

"Was I?"

"It's hard to be perfectly honest."

NOW

"Wait," Zack says. Charlie is driving. He doesn't slow down at all. "Wait," Zack says again. "That sign says Guilford. There's an exit for Guilford in three miles."

"What's so special about Guilford?" I ask.

"Adrian Wildes spent a summer there. It was the hometown of Smoky Walker. Adrian came here before he was famous and spent a summer working in one of the fish restaurants during the day and playing with Smoky Walker at night. But here's the really important thing—Smoky Walker came here to *escape*. It's this quaint little seaside town and he came here to get away from everything."

Charlie glances over at Zack. "Really?"

"We need to get off here. I didn't realize how close it was to New London." His voice rises with excitement, and I think maybe he is actually on to something. Like if Adrian Wildes is actually hiding out somewhere, this place could make sense. The two of them could be in some hole-in-the-wall joint playing blues guitar and drinking cheap beer and just communing or whatever it is guys do when they're trying to be all deep.

I guess that's what Seth thought he was doing when he went to stupid cons and waited for hours to get some YouTube guy to sign his laptop or whatever. Jamming. Shooting the shit. Riffing off one another and just, like, you know, spinning ideas. *Creating.*

"Does Smoky Walker still live here?" I ask.

"He's dead."

Well, that deflated my hope balloon real fast.

But Charlie is crossing over into the exit lane, his blinker flashing right, right, right, so I guess this is the next stop on our search for the magnificent Adrian Wildes.

"Smoky Walker isn't here anymore," I say.

"But Smoky Walker was his *mentor*," Zack says, spinning around in his seat. "Smoky Walker was who and how and what Adrian wanted to be. If this is where Smoky came when he wanted to get away from it all, then this is where Adrian would come." He's nodding as he speaks, or maybe that's the car bouncing. His cheeks, ruddy most of the time, are getting brighter and brighter red, like there's dye spreading out over his skin. "This is the best lead we've had."

"I like it when you talk about it like that," I say. "Like we're detectives. It almost makes this whole mess fun."

Charlie barely slows down as we get off the highway and onto the side road.

"It was one of the first settlements in the United States," Zack says, pointing at a sign as we breeze past it.

"Any other totally not at all interesting trivia about the little hamlet?"

"You don't need to be snarky," Charlie tells me.

"I don't? I thought that was my role here. We've got the depressed guy, the gay guy, and the bitch. Did I audition for the wrong part? Is this role actually for a perky girl with bouncy hair and bouncy boobs? Because I don't have either of those, but

I guess I could stuff my bra."

"You need to shut up," Charlie says.

"Oh! I got it! I'm playing the girl in the background. The one who doesn't actually say anything, just comes along for, like, extra scenery, I guess. Just sit here and look pretty. Sure, fine."

"Who said you were pretty?" Charlie snaps back.

I don't know why Charlie and I ramp up like this, but when we do, I can't stop. Zack breathes out slow and low. "So, how about them Red Sox?" he asks.

His words just hang in the air, like I could reach out and pop them.

Charlie pulls off the exit and into the town. The downtown area is built around a village green with little shops and cute streetlights. "It looks like a TV town," I mutter. "It's not real."

No one answers. Charlie parks the car and we get out. Zack is on his phone, scrolling through whatever information he can find. "The restaurant Adrian worked at was closer to the ocean, but I think we should go to this bar that Smoky used to play in."

When we get to the address, there's no bar. It's been turned into a coffee shop. There's a plaque out front that says:

**PREVIOUS SITE OF GUS'S JOINT
SITE OF NUMEROUS PERFORMANCES BY
LEGENDARY GUITARIST
LEWIS "SMOKY" WALKER**

The plaque is small, and the copper is seeping green. Someone has jammed pink-gray gum on top of it.

"Still," Charlie says. "I mean, maybe?" I can feel the hope oozing off him. What I can't tell is why it's so important to him to believe that Adrian Wildes is still okay—is still alive—and that we're going to find him.

Zack smiles at him. "Anything is possible, right?"

The coffee shop has a bar with stools right when you come in, but no one looks up at us. There does seem to be a little stage in the back. Maybe it's left over from the Smoky Walker days, but I bet now it's used mostly by the moody teens of greater Guilford to pour out their angsty feelings or their rage or whatever else they have inside them that they think someone else will care about.

That's what Seth was always trying to figure out—what could he say that someone else would care about? What he could say that would spike up his views. But he never thought of anything, and that's why he only ever created that one, ranting video. He talked about it and talked about it and talked about it. How great it would be. How he'd be the next big thing on the web. How he'd be kissing Essex good-bye and not letting the door hit his ass on the way out.

So I guess I shouldn't be so hard on those people who actually say something.

We're all standing just inside the doorway, twisting our heads from side to side like this is some sort of word search and if we just look closely enough the people will suddenly clarify themselves right in front of our eyes and one of them will be Adrian Wildes.

Zack leads the way into an area with two mismatched couches and a dinged-up coffee table. He leans right over the couple sitting on the blue leather couch and says, "Look, here he is."

He's right. It's a picture of Adrian Wildes holding a guitar. Next to him is a man who I can only assume is Smoky Walker: large and black and ecstatic looking. Both of them are bathed in a silver light that makes them glow.

"There's one over here, too," Charlie says.

But they're just pictures: the real person is nowhere to be found. I think for a minute that maybe they are all hiding him: the barista and the customers. Maybe they saw us coming and Adrian dove behind the counter and they are all just waiting for us to leave so he can come back out and go back to his sulking escape from reality. But there is no tension in the air. Just the smell of coffee and innocuous music.

"Can I help you?" the barista finally asks. His hair is clipped close to his head and he has gauges in his ears and a tattoo that creeps around his neck. I kind of want to stick my finger through the gauge hole and tug just to see what it would feel like. Actually, I wish he would take the ring out so I could feel the inside of his ear.

"We're just looking," Charlie says.

"Did Smoky Walker really play here?" Zack asks.

The barista shrugs. "That's what the plaque says. That's not really my jam, though." He picks up a cloth and starts wiping off the espresso machine.

"What about Adrian Wildes?" I ask.

The barista actually scoffs. "Sorry, sweetheart."

"Oh, it's not me who's interested. My dipshit brother here is on a quest. He's like Don Quixote tilting at pop stars."

The barista only shakes his head, which makes me think he's not a very good alt-rock-hipster if he doesn't know who Don Quixote is.

"We just thought he might be here since his idol was Smoky Walker," Charlie explains.

"Smoky Walker is dead," the barista says. "So he wouldn't have anyone to see." He speaks slowly, like there is something wrong with my brother. And even though I'm the one who just called my brother a dipshit, this still makes me angry.

"Yeah, thanks for the update," I say.

"If you're not going to order something, I'm going to have to ask you to leave."

"We don't want any of your shitty, overpriced coffee," I tell him. I pivot to go, and thankfully, Charlie and Zack are right behind me. I don't know what I would have done if I had stormed out of there and they had stayed behind.

"He could have at least been half-assed helpful, don't you think?" I say.

Zack turns to Charlie. He puts his hand on his shoulder. "Come on. Let's drive out to the ocean, okay? We can find that restaurant."

Charlie's face is dark again, like a micro-storm has blown in off the ocean and settled right there over his high forehead, dropping rain and hail and gusting wind across him. That's the way he is now, I think, either a lake so still you aren't sure it's real or an ocean all churned up during hurricane season, and I'm not sure which is scarier.

"Hey." A voice comes from behind us. There's a white teen-aged guy striding toward us. He's wearing a beanie and his hair curls up underneath it at the back. Hockey hair. There's a girl behind him, lanky and pale and a little greasy looking, and a few steps behind. "Hey," he says again. "You really looking for Adrian Wildes?"

I square my body. I don't need some hockey guy and his greasy girlfriend coming out here to tell us we're being pathetic and that Adrian Wildes is gone, gone, gone. But the boy is smiling and he says, "He did come by here a few months ago. Before his tour."

"Really?" Charlie asks, stepping toward them.

The girl twists her hair around her fingers. The boy's shadow cuts straight across her face.

"Yeah," the guy says. He tugs on his beanie. The hair curling out from under it is blond, but his eyebrows are thick and dark. "We were down by the water. We saw him skipping stones."

"You don't really expect us to believe that, do you?" I ask.

"Lexi," Charlie says, but the guy just looks confused.

"A lot of people do it," he says.

"We've got really smooth stones on our beaches," the girl

adds.

I want to tell her that all beaches have smooth stones. It's because of the ocean, all the rough edges get smoothed away by tossing and turning around. It's like sea glass. It's like what happened to Charlie with Penelope.

Charlie says, "Show us."

"Charlie, he's not there now. We should get back on the road."

But Charlie is laser focused again. We are going to the beach to see where Adrian Wildes may or may not have stood. And that's that.

We all cram back into Miss Ruka. Of course the couple is in the back with me. The boy sits behind the passenger seat and the girl is half on his lap and half on the middle seat. I remember cramming into Seth's friend Torrance's car. Gwen sat up front with Hannah, the two of them belted in together. Four of us sat in the back and I had to sit on Seth's lap. "There's no seat belt for me," I said. "Don't worry, Lex," he replied. "You've got me." That was when we still all hung out together. Before it was just Seth and me, me and Seth.

They lead us out of town and it occurs to me that this could all be some elaborate setup. Like we could get all the way out of town and then they'd pull out a gun. No, probably not a gun. A knife. I look at the lanky girl. She's wearing an oversized army jacket that probably belongs to the boy. The sleeves are so long her hands don't peek out. There's lot of room to hide a knife.

"My name is Jacob," the boy says. "This is Caroline."

"You live in this town?" I ask.

"Yeah," the boy says. "It's okay. Kind of bougie, you know, but it's not so bad."

"The ocean is pretty," the girl says.

"We live by the ocean, too," I say.

"Cool," Jacob says. I see him squeeze Caroline's leg. It looks like he's squeezing pretty hard and I wonder if she likes it. If it's reassuring to her. Or if it feels like something else entirely.

"We're not right on the ocean," Zack says. "Technically our town is on a bay."

"We're on the bay that leads to the ocean," I tell them. "So practically the same thing."

"Uh-huh," Jacob says.

"Did you talk to him?" Charlie asks.

"Adrian Wildes? Nah. He was way in his own world. Also, we were, um, a little—we had our own thing going on." He pinches his forefinger and thumb together and holds them up to his lips. "It was super windy that day and we were having trouble getting things going, you know."

I check Caroline's eyes. They don't look red rimmed or anything now, so being high wouldn't explain her near-comatose state. "You can sit down in the middle if you want," I tell her.

She gives a half shrug and then curls her body more into his and away from mine. And it's not like I want to be wedged into the back seat with her, but it's also not like I am gross and germ infested or anything. Sitting on him is just unnecessary.

"We're good like this," Jacob says. "Right, baby?"

Baby?

"So, Caroline," I ask. "Read any good books lately?"

"What?" she asks.

"Lexi," Charlie says with a warning tone from the front seat.

"I'm just making small talk," I say.

"The road's gonna kind of split and curve up here. Follow the curve."

"Got it," Zack says.

"So, have you?" I ask.

She does that half shrug again. "We're reading *Pride and Prejudice* in English class. I guess I like it."

"Really?" Jacob asks. "I always felt like that was just something they included so there could be a book by a woman. I didn't even finish it."

He's older than her, I realize. "I liked it," I say. "I thought it was really clever and even though it's old a lot of the stuff she talks about, it matters today—like keeping up appearances and the social roles and all that stuff."

"Yeah," she says. "Plus all the back and forth with Darcy and Elizabeth, and with her sister and that awful guy—"

"Wickham," Zack says. "What a tool."

"Right." Caroline giggles.

"Up here," Jacob says. "We were just past those sand dunes."

Zack pulls the car off to the side of the road. It's a blank stretch of beach in front of us, but off to the left is a strip of shingled cottages. You'd think none of us have ever gotten out of a car the way we trip over one another. Zack gets out first and flips the driver's seat forward. Charlie holds still and looks at the ocean. So Caroline has to lean back toward me to let Jacob get out, and when she does her elbow goes into my side, which doesn't hurt, but she apologizes like she slit my throat. Finally they get out—him pulling her by both hands—and Charlie still hasn't moved, so I climb out the driver's side, too, right into a wall of cool ocean air. My nose starts running and I tug my little hoodie closer around me.

"You coming, Charlie?" I ask.

He clicks off his seat belt and gets out of the car. He has on a waffle-weave shirt, but that's it. He shivers a little, but doesn't look for anything to keep him warm, doesn't even put his hands in his pockets.

Caroline follows Jacob, a couple steps behind. I see her watching him, watching the way his body moves, and I wonder how long they've been together. Is this still new? Is that why she's disappearing into him? And it's not like this should be a hard question for me to answer. I mean, I mastered the art of disappearing into a guy, didn't I? Still, I can't look away and I can't make sense of what I'm seeing. Is this what we looked like to other people? Is this what *I* looked like? The girl behind the boy? The silent girl? The girl afraid to have an opinion of her own?

Charlie stands at the top of the dune, looking out over the water. I'm not sure what this is supposed to tell us about Adrian Wildes. He was here a couple of months ago. So what?

"So, you guys have any grass or anything?" Jacob asks.

Caroline looks hopeful. Stoned or looking to be stoned all the time. At least she has an excuse for her behavior.

"Nope, totally clean," Zack says.

"That's cool," Jacob tells him. Caroline chews her lower lip.

"You think he was staying in one of these houses?" Charlie asks.

"Yeah, rumor is it's that one," Jacob says, pointing to a white house with heavy green shutters over the windows, all tucked up for winter. "Someone saw a light, but I don't know."

Charlie heads for the house, and so I follow with Zack right behind. Jacob and Caroline hang back. "Did you lock the car?" I whisper to Zack.

"What? No, why?"

I glance over my shoulder.

"Oh, come on, Lexi, they're just a couple of stoners."

Charlie climbs the steps of the house, his feet clomping on the ice that covers the wooden stairs. I grip the handrail tightly so my feet don't slip out from underneath me. There's a big wraparound porch and I can just picture some old rocking chairs out here, maybe Adrian sitting in one and playing his guitar while Alana Greengrass reads in another chair beside him.

The door is locked, of course, but Charlie pulls on it gently at first and then roughly.

"No go," I say. "Too bad, so sad, let's get going."

He doesn't hear me, or pretends not to. He's gotten very good at both of those things. He walks down the length of the porch, testing each of the plywood shutters. He goes around the corner of the porch. I look over at Zack. "So, what, we're breaking and entering now?"

"None of the windows are going to open," Zack says. "Just let him walk around a little and then we'll go."

I lift my hood up over my ears. When we left New Hampshire it wasn't too cold, but now the temperature seems to be dropping. My dad would be able to tell me exactly why, with a lengthy explanation about jet streams and cold fronts and on and on. I wish I had thought to bring my winter jacket.

"Back here!" Charlie calls.

I take a step toward Charlie's voice, and slip on a patch of glare ice. Zack catches me by the arm, his grip sure and firm. So I keep holding on to him as we walk around the porch. It must be nice to be so solid, to know that you are usually the biggest guy in the room. That has to feel safe.

Charlie stands by a window, holding up the plywood. "This one just lifted right up," he says. "Check the window."

"We can't break into this house, Charlie," I tell him. "We don't even know if it's Adrian Wildes's house, and that wouldn't excuse it even if it were."

"He might be in there," Charlie says.

The house is dark. Nothing stirs. "If he's in there, he's probably—"

"He could be sleeping or hurt," Charlie says. "It's like a wellness check that police do."

"Except for the part about us not being police officers."

He sighs and turns to Zack. "Just hold this shutter up for

me." Zack, the traitor, takes the plywood from Charlie's hands. Charlie bends over and tugs on the window. It opens smooth and easy and Charlie steps up and over the sill and into the house.

"You going?" Zack asks.

"Are you?"

I've followed my brother this far, and I figure I can keep using the my-brother's-keeper defense. My parents might come bail me out for that. Maybe. I think about texting them. Breaking into a house now. NBD.

"This is not a good choice," I tell him. When we were little, and we did something wrong, our parents would say, "Was that a good choice or a bad choice?" Any time they asked the question, you knew the answer was "bad choice." But I step over the sill. I'm not as tall as Charlie so I have to straddle it for a moment before my right foot touches down on the floor inside the house. Zack climbs in behind me, letting the shutter down gently.

"My first felony," I say. "How about you?"

"Second," he says. "Well, third, but I don't really count the thing with the dog." He smiles and puts his hand on my shoulder.

We've entered into the living room. There's an oval, braided rug in the center of the room with an oval coffee table right on top of it. On the coffee table is an oval tray with three crystal wine glasses on it. All the ovals make my head spin.

Footsteps fall above us. I turn to Zack. "Adrian?" I whisper.

He shakes his head. "I think it's Charlie."

We head toward the hallway where we can see a twisting staircase headed upward. There's a little table at the bottom of the stairs, with framed pictures of older people on it. The pictures look like they were black and white but have been tinted with pastels in that strange way that makes everyone look overly rosy cheeked. None of them look like Adrian Wildes. "We've broken into a stranger's house," I say.

"Adrian Wildes is a stranger, too," Zack says. He's got his hand on the stairway railing. "Charlie?" he calls.

"Up here," Charlie replies. His voice hitches as if the words are stuck.

Zack takes the steps two at a time, but I linger. The light in the house is strange, seeping in around the edges of the boarded-up windows. It's just enough to see, but dark enough for shadows to hide.

Adrian could be upstairs. Dead. And if he is, I realize, I don't want to find him.

Instead I find Charlie lying on his back on a twin bed. The windows up here aren't boarded up, and more light filters in through the gauzy curtains. There's a lacy coverlet over the bed, like something our grandmother would have in her guest room, and a small wicker table with a white lamp on it. Charlie looks like a smear of coal against all this white. He doesn't move and it's like he and Adrian have blended in my head or something, because I lurch forward and call out, "Charlie!"

He lifts up his head.

Not dead.

He points past us and I turn and look at the bureau. On top there's a lace doily—another thing our grandmother would have—with three old bottles, one green, one clear, one purple. Next to them, in a tiny heart-shaped frame, is a picture of Alana Greengrass. I almost don't recognize her because it's not like a magazine picture. I pick it up to take a closer look. She isn't wearing any makeup and her hair is blowing in front of her face. She smiles like she's looking at the one person in the world who matters to her at all. And I realize that person is Adrian.

"He was here?" I ask.

"There's some shaving stuff and a toothbrush in the bathroom," Charlie says. "In the master bedroom, there's some of his clothes."

"How do you know they're his?" I ask.

He doesn't answer, so I go into the room myself. The picture is still in my hand and so I slip it into my pocket. Hanging in the closet is a big, bulky fisherman's sweater. He was photographed wearing one like it a lot after he broke up with Alana Greengrass. But that was almost a year ago. If this is his sweater, and it is his house, we still don't know when he was last here. What matters is that he's not here now. Which I guess is why Charlie is catatonic on the bed in the other room.

I close the master bedroom door behind me when I leave the room. In the small room, Zack is sitting on the bed next to Charlie. "It means we're on the right track," he's saying. Which isn't true, not necessarily, but I don't say so.

"We should get going," I say.

The boys don't move, but I can't stand to be in this house another minute. It's all the sudden too stuffy, too hot, too awful. "I'll meet you back at the car."

I know I should stay with Charlie. I mean, he's up there lying on that bed like he's had a stroke or something. But I can't. I can't breathe.

Down the stairs and out the window. I don't know why it was so hard to breathe in there. It's like Adrian's sadness has gone through the whole place. I could smell it. I recognize that stench from Charlie and from me. Utter, utter heartbreak that seeps up through the pores and sours everything around it.

I'm careful on the porch, but once I get onto the sand of the beach, I start to run. The cold air hurts my lungs, but I have to get that smell off me.

Up over the dune and then I see Caroline standing outside the car tapping her foot and looking from side to side. It's odd. It's like she's playing lookout or something, and where is Jacob anyway? The front windshield is steamed up, but through it I can see a lump of a shape moving around. Jacob? What's he doing in the front seat? It's like he's looking for something under the steering wheel.

As soon as I have that thought, I realize what's going on: he's trying to hot-wire the car. Why anyone would want to steal crappy old Miss Ruka I have no idea, but it looks like that's what he's doing. "Hey!" I yell, and start running down toward them. "Hey!"

Caroline looks up. "Jacob!" she says.

A muffled "What?" comes from inside the car. I'm almost back to them now.

"Jacob!" Caroline says again. Her voice thin as a reed.

"What?" he replies. His voice is louder and annoyed.

"What are you doing?" I demand.

His head pops up. I can see it through the foggy windshield, just a hazy gray shape, but I can imagine his face: surprised and annoyed and maybe a little scared.

"Are you trying to steal the car?" I ask. I speak to Caroline because Jacob, shitty coward, stays in the car.

She looks over her shoulder, back toward the house.

"What the hell? It's a crappy car. Why would you steal such a crappy, gross car?"

"Because we need a car," she says. Her voice is as dull as radio static.

Jacob finally opens the door and slowly, slowly eases himself out.

I watch Caroline's sleeves. If they are car thieves, then maybe my hidden knife theory isn't so crazy after all.

"We just need to get out of town," Jacob says. He's holding up both his hands, but he's not the one I'm worried about.

"So ask us for a ride," I tell him.

"Do you have the keys?" he asks. He steps closer. My mouth goes dry.

"No," I say. I stick out my chin.

This is a bad choice, I think. Confronting a junkie is pretty much always a bad choice.

Another step closer to me. "Just hand them over if you do."

My gaze flicks from him back to Caroline. "Why do you need to leave?" I ask her.

"We just do," she says. "This town—we need to get out of here." She shakes her head.

Jacob takes another step. My lips are paper. My breath shallow and ragged. What will he do to me? How much does this car mean? He is bigger than Seth, taller and heavier looking.

"We're taking this car," he says.

"No, you're not." The words just come out. He's not expecting them. I can tell by the flicker in his eyes. He hasn't thought this through, I realize. Neither of them have. I look at Caroline's twitching hands. Do they think they're going to drive someplace and sell the car? "You should go," I tell them.

Caroline puts a hand on Jacob's shoulder, but he shrugs her off. "We need this car," he says.

"You can't have it," I tell him. "It's not yours to take, okay?" Tears well in my eyes. "You might think you need it, but we need it, too, and it's ours, so just get the fuck out of here before Zack and my brother get back."

He takes another step forward and I push him. Hard. He rocks back into Caroline who tries to catch him, but they tumble backward together.

"Lexi?" Zack calls from behind me. "Lexi, what's going on?"

Jacob and Caroline scramble to their feet in front of me. I want to push them down again. Again and again. I am angry and sad and it's all mixed up inside of me so my fists are clenched and hot tears burn my cheeks.

"Lexi?" Zack asks when he gets up alongside me.

"They were trying to steal the car," I tell him.

Zack looks at them. "Get in the car, Lexi." His voice is calm. "You, too, Charlie."

I pop the driver's seat forward and crawl into the back seat. Charlie takes the passenger seat. Anger radiates off of Zack.

He sits in the driver's seat and starts the car with the door still open. "I suggest you get out of our way."

He slams the door shut and spins the car around. We fishtail back and forth, and then he hits the gas. Miss Ruka sputters and coughs, then we peel off down the road. Jacob slaps the hood as we go by, but that's it.

"We're just going to leave them there?" Charlie asks.

"They were going to leave us," I reply. "Is the car okay?"

"I think so," Zack says. "But as you know, she is a very delicate machine."

I spin around and watch Jacob and Caroline get smaller and smaller until they're just little specks on the horizon.

FIVE

Once upon a time, a princess was born in a kingdom on a cliff. The view of the sea was so magnificent that no man could go to the edge of it without throwing himself from it. Many great men were lost, and so the king issued a proclamation: any man who could go to the edge of the cliff and resist it's pull would have his daughter's hand in marriage. Princes and commoners, old men and young, wise and foolish men, they all traveled from near and far to test their will, but not one could pass the test. Each man who ventured to the edge of the cliff threw himself into the sea.

NOW

Zack and Charlie's windows are down even though it's cold out. It's like the air inside the car has turned so stale it could suffocate us and we would just be this drifting car. They'd never be able to figure out what happened to us. They'd think it was a group suicide.

My heart, though, is not still. It's pounding. What would

Jacob have done if I had not pushed him? And if Zack and Charlie had not shown up? Would he have scrambled up and punched me? Thrown me to the ground and patted and pawed at me looking for the keys I didn't have? My body shakes.

"What do you think they were on?" I ask.

"I don't know," Zack says.

"But they were on something, right?"

"Or wanted to be," Charlie says.

We learned about what addiction can do to you in school. To your body and your brain. Jacob would've hurt me. Badly. For the stupid car that I didn't even have the keys to, he would've hurt me, because his brain was telling him that made sense. If Charlie and Zack hadn't come. It will always be like this. I will always be at risk. Because there will always be someone bigger and stronger than me. And that's what was burning me and making my heart race, my pits sweat.

We're back on the road to Pennsylvania, to the abandoned amusement park. It'll be three hours or so before we get there. Then, what, another eight or so home? I pick up my phone wondering if I should text my mom now and let her know that it'll definitely be another day. I will leave out the part about someone trying to steal our car. But I don't get to make that choice because evidently the cheap-ass cell phone plan my parents got for us doesn't work in the rest of the country.

I'm trying not to think any more about Jacob and Caroline back by the ocean. It's not like I feel bad for them, not really. I mean, they tried to steal our car. And Jacob was going to—I don't know. I don't know. But seeing Caroline there, twitching and blind with whatever it was she felt for him—maybe I could feel a little bad for her.

"You think they'll call someone to come get them?" I ask.

"What does it matter?" Charlie replies.

"I don't know. I just—" Then I shake my head because it's all too mixed up and I'm not sure what it is that I want to say.

I pick up the bag of snacks. The boys hit it pretty hard on the way out of New London, but there's a couple of granola bars left, and those raspberry hard candies. I tear open a granola bar. It's the hard kind and crumbs get all over me even though I am taking tiny, careful mouse bites. I feel bad for half a second but then realize it will be the freshest, healthiest thing in Zack's car.

"Hey, your cousin Kristy said you like to cook," I say.

"Yeah?" Zack responds.

"But this car is like fast-food city."

"I have a taste for the finer and the lower things in life," Zack responds. "Some days you just can't beat processed bun, orange cheese, and gray meat."

"Some days it's porcini ravioli, somedays it's a super-deluxe cheeseburger," I say, thinking of our Last Meal game.

"What kind of cooking do you do?" Charlie asks, and I think maybe I should write it down because it's the first time in months he has expressed interest in something other than himself, Penelope, or Adrian Wildes.

"Italian. Some French. I really like making soup. Last Christmas I got an immersion blender and it changed my life."

"What's an immersion blender?"

"It's like a blender but it's a stick so you can put it right into the pot. My soup game upped like seven levels with that thing."

"You should have me over for soup," I tell him.

"I didn't know you liked soup."

"Everybody likes soup."

"Penelope doesn't like soup," Charlie says.

"Penelope is a goddamn moron," I say. I really don't mean to. It just kind of blurts out. But honestly, I mean, who doesn't like soup? Like, at all? She had to make that choice. Like, she was sitting around and said, "Hmm, what's a strange food quirk I could have? Drink milk like a cat? No, too weird. And some guys don't like cats. Soup? I could eat only soup. Oh, no—*no* soup. That will make me unique!"

"Yeah." Charlie sighs. "Probably."

But it doesn't feel like a victory. It feels like being pulled under muddy water at night. And even though it's true that Penelope is a moron, I wish I hadn't said it because hearing Charlie admit it is somehow a thousand times worse than hearing him go on about how great she is. Like, he knows. He *knows*. And somehow that is worse for him. Knowing how awful she is, but still wanting her? That's the actual worst.

BEFORE

October

Remy Yoo—the evil ex—was at the sink when I came out of the bathroom stall. She was washing her hands with about six pumps of the pink, industrial, powdered soap—enough to take off a layer of skin. But her hands were perfect. Her fingers were long and slender, the nail beds perfectly round. She played the clarinet, and I guess she was really good. It was easy to see why when you saw those fingers. I was entranced by them, the nimble way they moved, and of course I couldn't help but picture them dancing over Seth's skin. Seth and I had been together a month and a half, but he was with Remy for almost eight months, and my time with him seemed frail in comparison. He'd told me how it was with her, the way she trampled his heart. She sounded like a total Penelope.

"Do you have epilepsy or something?" she asked me.

"Huh?"

"You're staring at my hands. Not moving. Like you're having a seizure."

"Just waiting for you to move."

She stepped aside so I could wash my hands, but only if I stood right next to her.

So this was what it came down to? A turf war in the second floor girl's bathroom? Fine. I could stand my ground.

I stepped forward, turned on the hot water. The soap was gritty against my skin. I hated school bathroom soap and school bathroom smell. Even more, I hated standing next to Remy Yoo, so close I could feel her breath.

"I suppose you figured out that I followed you in here." She pulled a cosmetics bag from her backpack and started applying black eyeliner to her lids.

"It occurred to me."

"I just wanted to know if you're okay."

"Okay?"

"With Seth."

I smirked and turned off the water. I had to reach past her to get a brown paper towel. She didn't flinch. "We're super," I said.

"I dated him last year."

"I know."

So this was where she staked her claim.

"Do you know why we broke up?"

"I don't have time for your sad saga."

"It's not a saga. It's a simple story, really. He wanted to have sex and I didn't."

I crumpled the paper towel and tossed it into the wastebin. "So he broke up with you and now you're ready to screw him and want him back?"

"That's not exactly—"

"Sorry, Remy, you had your chance."

She put her hand on my arm—wrapped those perfect fingers around my bicep. "I know, okay. *I know.*"

We stared into each other's eyes—hers golden brown and lively, but not flashing, not angry. She looked sad. They were mother's eyes. Worried eyes.

I shook off her arm. "You don't know anything." I yanked open the bathroom door and then added, loud enough for it to echo down the hall: "Bitch."

A head popped out of one of the alcoves. Zack Donovan. "Lexi?" he asked. I kept walking.

I guess I should have warned Hannah. I guess that's how

these things work. She wouldn't have listened, though. She wouldn't have listened and this time I would have been the bitch.

NOW

I fall asleep. Or something like sleep. It's like I can still feel myself in the car, and even hear Charlie and Zack talking about which kind of SUV is the least douche-y (another word previously foreign to Charlie's vocabulary. Had he let Penelope jab something up his nose in a DIY lobotomy? That would explain a lot, actually).

The car shakes back and forth, and it's like that is shaking the smell of old French fries out of the rugs. Probably from Burger King. Zack seems like a Burger King kind of a guy. Me, I prefer Wendy's. Not that I frequent fast food or anything.

I'm not sure how long it's been when we bump over the rumble strip. My forehead smacks against the cold glass of the window. "What?" I ask. "Are we there?" I don't think three hours have passed with me dozing, and the light still feels like midday light.

When the car stops on the side of the road I ask, "Peeing again?" But then I notice there's a person outside, standing near the car. I can't tell if it's a boy or girl because they are wearing jeans and an oversized hoodie with the hood pulled up. They've got a backpack on and heavy-looking boots. "Wait, are we picking up a hitchhiker?"

"It does appear that way," Zack replies.

"Are you crazy? Didn't you learn this lesson with the stoners?"

"I think maybe they were actually meth heads or something," Zack says.

"You never pick up hitchhikers. They are bound to shiv you."

"Shiving may be a prison-exclusive activity," Zack says.

"Maybe the hitchhiker is an escaped convict. Shiving could be a way of life." I am joking, but my heart is going like tiger in a cage. I've seen the movies. Nothing good ever happens with a hitchhiker.

"Open the door," Charlie tells Zack, who does what he's told.

Zack flips forward the seat, and then the person—a girl, I realize, not much older than me—climbs in. My heartbeat slows a little. Yes, teenage girls can be psychopaths—I mean, of course—but she has a soft face and freckles across the brown skin of her nose and doe eyes. Also I think that Charlie, Zack, and I could take her if it came to that. Unless she has a gun.

I draw my legs into my chest. I'm not going to sit in the death spot with no seat belt. So she has to sort of crawl over me, tossing a button-covered backpack onto the floor in front of her. Once she's settled in, I say, "They picked me up outside Atlanta, and I've been in the back of this car ever since."

Her soft look falters for a minute, but then Charlie says, "She's my sister. She's a liar."

"I can see that," the girl says. I don't know if she means she can see the family resemblance or that she can tell just by looking at me that I am not to be trusted, but either way, I'm not too happy. I look out the window.

"My name is Harper," she says.

"Really?" I ask.

"Really," she replies.

"Like the author?" I ask.

"Like the author," she agrees.

"I'm surprised you knew that, Lexi," Charlie says.

I hit the back of his seat. "Don't use our real names, dumbass."

"Why not?" Charlie asks.

"She's not using her real name. Clearly. I mean, it would be like if someone picked you up and you were like, 'My name is J. D. Like the author. J. D. Salinger.'"

"I would be more likely to use F. Scott."

"I didn't make the author connection," Harper says. "You did."

"Everyone would. How many Harpers are there in the world?"

"At least two," Harper says.

"Where are you heading?" Zack asks.

"New York City," she says. "Which, you know, was clue one that you were lying seeing as how we are heading *toward* Atlanta right now, not away."

I raise an eyebrow. "New York City, huh?"

"What?" she asks. She lowers her hood, revealing a mess of curls. I tuck myself in closer to the side of the car. She smells like the clove cigarettes some of Seth's friends smoke, the ones that are already out of high school and going to Essex College.

"Nothing," I mumble. I zip my hoodie up so it covers my chin.

She swivels in the seat so she's facing me. That broken spring must be digging right into the soft flesh of her butt, but she doesn't seem to mind. Maybe she is like the opposite of the princess and the pea. She twists a curl around her finger, then tucks it behind her ear. "It was obviously something. Just go on and say it."

"Don't mind my sister," Charlie says. He shifts the rearview mirror so he can get a better view of her. "Lexi is angry."

"Of course she is," Harper says.

"Yeah, yeah," I mutter. "If you're not angry, you're not paying attention. Is that one of your buttons?"

Harper stares at me with something like disappointment. But also something else that I can't quite put my finger on. Those big doe eyes are confusing. I wonder if it's hard to go through life with those so-called windows to the soul thrown wide open so anyone can climb in. "I know what you're thinking, anyway," she says. "Small-town girl chasing her dreams to New York City."

She's right. I say, "Struggling on the mean streets, just trying to make it big."

She reaches down and picks up her backpack. The buttons

aren't sayings. They're all different abstract designs in bright patterns that stand out like flowers against the dirty beige canvas of her bag. "Good guess, but New York is actually just a stop along the way. I have a friend there and I'm going to stay with her a couple of days and then I'm going down to Florida. Another one of my friends moved down there and got a job in a restaurant. She says the pay is real good and I'm sick of this winter, so——"

"What about school?" I ask.

She laughs. "Been there, failed that."

"Super cool," I mutter. "The whole car is full of dropouts."

Charlie has been stealing glances at Harper in the rearview mirror, but now he glowers at me. "Where in Florida are you going?" he asks. He's got something stuck between his teeth, but I don't tell him.

"The Gulf Coast. Near Tampa." She chews on the corner of her thumbnail. Charlie takes a ramp onto Interstate 84 and the car shudders as we accelerate. "My friend told me it was eighty degrees and sunny there today. And yesterday. And the day before that." She smiles. "The sun is good for you, you know? That's why we're all pissy up here. Not enough sun. You never hear about pissy people in Florida" She holds her bag in her lap, hugging it like it's her old teddy bear.

"But there are lots of old people in Florida," I say. "And old people are always pissy."

Charlie rolls his eyes, but Harper laughs. It's a deeper laugh than I would have expected from her. "What about all of you?

Where are you going?"

Charlie rubs his forehead right above the bridge of his nose and I wonder if he has the good sense to be embarrassed by our quest. "Pennsylvania," he tells her. "We're looking for Adrian Wildes."

She nods as if this is the most normal thing in the world and I wonder about some of her other rides. Where were those people going and what did they tell her? "What's the strangest ride you've ever gotten?" I ask.

"Well, nothing too weird on this trip yet. I'm just starting out. But once I got a ride with cat breeders. They had the female cat and were going to meet the sire. The cat didn't sound too happy about any of it."

"No one likes an arranged marriage."

"Not even a marriage," Harper says, smiling at me. "It was like an arranged hookup. An arranged impregnation."

"Gack," I say.

"Gack," she agrees.

"Is anyone hungry?" Charlie asks. "I'm really, really hungry."

"Me, too," Zack says.

"Mind stopping for something to eat?" Charlie asks Harper.

Harper shifts in her seat. "Okay, I guess." She glances at me and then back at the road. For all her bravado, she's still kind of scared.

There's a sign for all the fast food places we can pick from: McDonald's, Wendy's, Burger King, Taco Bell. "What do you like?" I ask her.

"It doesn't matter to me," Harper says. We're curling off the highway and onto some little side road.

Charlie pulls into the parking lot of a restaurant called the Chowder Bowl. Charlie doesn't like chowder. He says it's too creamy. "I think it's always good to go to local places," he says.

"Sure, okay," Harper says.

Is he trying to impress her? Whatever, I don't care. Charlie might not like chowder, but I love it.

A hostess seats us at a table near the back. The chairs are shiny, wooden, and round, with bright pink seats. The menus are heavy, plastic-coated ordeals with some sort of ribbon around the edges. They have seventeen different types of chowder: corn, harvest, fish, potato, on and on. They even have three different types of clam chowder: New England, Manhattan, and Rhode Island. "What's Manhattan clam chowder?" I ask.

"It has tomatoes instead of cream," Harper says.

"What? That's not even chowder. That's soup. Next you're going to tell me that Rhode Island clam chowder doesn't even have clams in it."

"Rhode Island clam chowder is made with quahogs and bacon," says our waiter, a twenty-something guy who has appeared out of nowhere. He's wearing a button-down shirt, bowtie, and vest. "Our specialty is the harvest chowder which pairs a medley of seafood with the vegetables of the harvest: winter squash and corn."

"Is this true?" Harper asks, pointing to something on the menu.

The waiter leans over her shoulder. "Yes. If you can stand on one foot, balance a chowder spoon on your nose, close your eyes, and recite the alphabet backward, your meal is free."

"The whole table or just one person?"

"Just the performer," he tells her.

"We're in," she tells him.

"You need to order first. Order and eat and then you do the thing before the bill comes."

"Okay, then. I'll have the harvest chowder. A bowl of it. And I want the roll on the side, and also extra packs of oyster crackers."

The waiter writes it down. "To drink?"

"A Coke."

"We have Pepsi products. Is that okay?" he asks.

She shakes her head. "Um, sorry, no." I think she's joking, but she says, "I'll have an iced tea."

She shrugs off her coat and settles in while the rest of us order. I get the Rhode Island clam chowder, Zack chooses harvest, and Charlie, traitor to the chowder cause, chooses Manhattan.

When the waiter leaves, Harper says, "I am a master of getting free meals. It's an essential life skill." She picks up the soup spoon at her place and sets it on her nose. It slides right off and clangs onto the table.

"I have money," I tell her.

"Yeah, so do I, but free is better than paying, don't you think. Also you guys should order extra packs of oyster crackers. Having some of those in your bag can save you."

A bus boy fills our water glasses, and we all drink. Harper tries again to get the spoon on her nose. I pick mine up. It's wide and flat and I can see why it's so hard to get it to stick. I huff a breath onto the smooth surface, then rub it with my thumb. I put it on my nose and hold it there for a moment before letting go. It stays and I say, "Just a little trick I picked up along the way."

"Isn't that cheating?" Charlie asks.

"What? I just cleaned it off a little," I say with a smile.

"Warm and damp sticks better," Zack says. "Good thinking."

While we wait for our chowders, we practice saying the alphabet backward. "The hard part will be standing on one foot with our eyes closed," Zack says. "That will totally mess up your balance."

"I don't know why you guys are working so hard at this. It's a little humiliating, don't you think?" Charlie asks.

"It's a free lunch," Harper says.

"There's no such thing as a free lunch," Charlie says back to her.

"Sure, sure. No free lunch and no free ride, but here we are."

The waiter places our bowls of chowder in front of us. They are enormous. Bigger than my head. "Can I have some extra oyster crackers?" I ask.

He sighs. "Sure."

"Oh my God," Zack says, letting out his breath. "This is freaking fantastic."

He's right. It's the best chowder I've ever had. It's sweet and salty and slips over my tongue like silk. I feel warm from the inside out.

The waiter finally cracks a smile. "We've won Best Soup/

Chowder for nine years straight. And the seven years before that."

"What happened in the year you missed?" I ask.

"Voter fraud," he says with a frown. "I'll be back with your crackers."

We eat without saying much, like we are starving wolves who have just taken down a deer. Even Charlie seems content. It's hard to be angry when you're eating soup. Unless, I guess, you are Penelope.

"So what's your thinking on Adrian Wildes?" Harper asks.

I zip my lips tight. This is the topic that always gets me in trouble.

Charlie says, "We're going to this abandoned amusement park that he wrote about because we think he might be there."

"Cool," she says.

"You could come," he suggests. He opens a package of oyster crackers.

"I don't think that's on the way to Florida." She speaks down into her soup. "I really just need to get closer to Danbury. I should be able to get a ride to New York pretty easily from there. Also, I'm serious about the crackers. Eat the bread now, crackers later."

"And that's today's Travel Tips with Harper Lee."

She smiles. "What do you think he's doing there? Just hanging out on the carousel?"

"We think he's trying to get away from it all," Zack says.

"Like you," I say.

She swallows. "Me?"

"Yeah," I tell her. "Pack up one life, put it away, and start again. Become a new person."

Putting down her spoon, she looks right at me. "You can't become someone else." She says it so matter-of-factly, like it's the most obvious thing in the world. Like I'm a toddler and she has to explain that we can't go into the television and live on Sesame Street. But isn't that we're all trying to do all the time? Become someone else. Throw off one life and choose another.

"So why do you need to go someplace new?"

"I need to go someplace new because that's where the job is. And because I get itchy staying in one place. Anyway, so, listen, if Adrian Wildes is trying to get away from it all, why don't you just let him get away?"

Zack slurps his chowder. Charlie spins his soup in his bowl. So it's up to me to talk. "I guess we just think he might be in some danger?"

"Okay, sure, I get it." She looks at each of us in turn. "I wasn't sure if this was just like an excuse for a road trip or what."

"More than that," I tell her.

She nods and I wonder what she's agreeing to. "I saw him in concert once," she says. "It was like pre-supercelebrity days and he was opening for this girl group I loved. Opal Essence. Remember them? I'd say I was maybe twelve years old? So, like, when he was just bursting it big onto YouTube."

"Was it any good?" I ask.

"Sure. I mean, I was twelve and he was cute, and the girls in Opal Essence said he was great, so that colored my view a lot." She shrugs. "I guess I can see how he felt pigeonholed. How he was sick of being that person."

"It's gotta feel like an anvil," Charlie says.

The waiter comes back. "Dessert?" he asks.

"Is that part of the free meal deal?" Harper asks.

"If you successfully complete the challenge," he tells her.

"Awesome. I'll have a piece of that lemon meringue pie I saw on the way in."

"Me, too," I agree.

Zack chooses cheesecake, but Charlie doesn't get anything, not even the brownie sundae which is what he always gets and Mom always steals bites from him.

As soon as the desserts come, Harper says, "Let's do this." She stands up, takes her spoon, and places it on her nose. "Come on, guys, all for one and one for all and all that."

Zack and I stand up, too, but of course Charlie stays sitting down. We put the spoons on our noses and close our eyes. Carefully, I lift one foot.

"All contestants are in the proper position," the waiter says.

I want to giggle at that, but Harper says, in a solemn tone, "Ready. Let's begin."

"Z-Y-X-W," we begin, slowly and deliberately. "V-U-T."

"Damn it," Zack says, and then I hear the clatter of the spoon hitting the floor.

Harper and I keep going. "L-K-J." On and on. "H-G-F." All the way to "C-B-A."

"Congratulations," the waiter says in a flat voice. "You each have won a free meal." Harper and I high-five and her eyes are bright and shiny. The waiter takes our picture with a Polaroid camera and says he'll put it on the wall at the front. "Take another," I say.

He glances over his shoulder, then takes another quick picture of us. I watch as we develop. We are off-kilter and fuzzy, but smiling, arms around each other. We eat our pie, gleefully. It is well-earned pie.

"I should make you pay for yours," I tell Charlie when our bill comes. But we both know he doesn't have any money.

"Make sure you tip him well," Harper tells me. "Tip him on what the amount would have been."

I agree and leave one of my twenties on the table.

On the way out, I look at our picture on the board. It is in better focus. Harper and I grin like idiots. Charlie is in the picture, too. Behind us, sitting at the table and staring angrily at nothing.

BEFORE

September

Seth told me that all I needed to do was pretend. "Pretend to be these girls. You *know* them. You can embody them." He set up his camera on a tripod.

Seth had one thing in common with Adrian Wildes: his own YouTube channel. But he wasn't like internet-celebrity-turned-regular-celebrity Adrian Wildes. He was just getting started. He'd only uploaded one video, just some off-the-cuff, slice-of-life observational humor. "The rant is a mainstay of modern comedy," he told me.

He commented a lot, and took part in discussion boards. On line he was StinkySalmon. I was Lexile3000, but I didn't comment or interact much. My favorite YouTuber was a girl named Possum. Just Possum. She always wore hand-knit hats that looked like all different animals—although never a possum. She played the mandolin, which is close enough to a ukulele to be hip, but a thousand times more beautiful. Sometimes she played the banjo or the fiddle. Anyway, some of her songs were silly, but most of them were the funny kind that hid a deep, deep sadness.

It was what Adrian Wildes wished he could be, but he just ended up schlocky. I was clicking through her Tumblr while Seth set up. He looked over my shoulder. "I can't tell if she's pretty or not." We'd been together three weeks. He still felt new to me. It still felt like maybe I shouldn't touch him or else he might disappear into a puff of smoke.

"I think she is," I said.

But what I was thinking was: *Does it matter?* And: *Do you think I'm pretty?* It was like two trains pulling out of the station of my brain and I couldn't decide which one to be on. It shouldn't matter how she looked. This I knew. She was a musician, and her music should be what mattered. And anyway, women are always held to this insane standard about their looks. Like I once read a review of this girl comedian and the reviewer, he actually said that the reason this comic was so funny was that these really crass things were coming out of this tiny, pretty woman. Like if she hadn't been beautiful, her jokes would have been what—boring?

Anyway, I'd like to say that was the train I chose. But all the while I was thinking about how Seth had never told me I was pretty. I clicked on a link to one of her videos.

"Yeah, I guess it's hard to tell with the hats and the makeup. All that makeup."

I looked at the screen. Possum favored red lipstick and cat eyes and sometimes she wore false eyelashes: it was all a sort of fifties glam. "I guess it's for the camera—"

"Girls always think they need to wear so much makeup. There are whole channels devoted to showing you how to do it."

"I know—" I'd actually looked up tutorials on those lips and eyes. I even tried to get the red-red lips she had, but I'd looked like a clown. When I tried to wipe the lipstick off it smeared across my cheeks. I'd had to text Gwen to find out how to take it off. Vaseline, she'd texted back to me and an emoji of a kissy-face. She could do the red lips perfectly. So could Hannah.

"It's utterly ridiculous," Seth said. "And false." He tugged at the neck of his shirt.

"Some girls think it's like an expression of their personality." Without meaning to, I rubbed my fingers over my own lips.

"It's false. It's a false promise. You offer up one thing, but underneath, it's something totally different."

"And underneath all that is what really matters."

And also: *Maybe she is not offering anything up in the first place.*

He turned from the screen to look at me. Possum was still singing, but it was all *oohs* and *ahs* and *la la las*. He got a goopy smile. "That is both the sweetest and naïvest thing I have ever heard. It's perfect."

He put one hand on my cheek and kissed me, soft and sweet.

"Now come on," he said. "We need to get this video done."

"You know, you should get credit for these videos. Like at school. I think Ms. Lynch teaches a video class or film or something. Charlie took it. With Penelope, of course."

"Gack, Penelope Richards."

"Exactly."

"Your brother always seemed relatively sane."

"Relatively."

"But Penelope Richards. Gack."

Gack indeed.

Seth pushed a button on the back of the camera. It was a handheld one, small enough to disappear into his pocket. He'd spent a fortune on it because it had amazing video quality. "Anyway," he said. "All I'm asking is for you to play a role. Acting. You barely even need to say anything. Just put on a costume and make the dumb expressions. I'll be talking, and you'll be like the visualizations of my ideas."

"I'd like to be the visualization of your ideals," I said. But maybe it was too soft for him to hear, because he didn't respond.

"It'll be easy, really. There's the indecisive girl who won't actually speak her mind and just lets you make the decision."

"Maybe she doesn't care about whatever it is?"

"All the time? No."

"So what would I do for that?"

"You just say, 'I don't know. What do you want to do?' See, it's not just that it shows a lack of personality. In part it's not her fault, because society has told girls not to have strong opinions. But that's what we're trying to fight against, right?"

"Sure, okay."

"And then there's girls that undercut other girls. Like Remy," he said.

"Or Gwen."

"Exactly. And again, it's because society pits women against one another, but still. So for that you can just, I don't know. I think maybe you can pretend you're talking to another girl and be like, 'Are you really sure about that dress?' Or, 'Do you really think you're ready for calculus?'"

"I don't know about this, Seth. I've never actually heard any-one—"

"It's exaggeration to make a point."

Hyperbole. Dewey DeWitt's voice rings in my head.

"And we've already talked about makeup. How it's a lie."

"It's just, I don't want it to be taken the wrong way. Like, you want it to be pro women, right?"

He stopped playing with the camera and finally looked at me. "Of course. How could you even question that?"

"I just want to make sure."

"Come on, Lexi, you know me. I'm an actual T-shirt-wear-ing *feminist*. What I'm trying to do is reveal to girls how they've been manipulated and how that impacts their behavior and how we all need to change."

I twisted my fingers together. "I see that. I guess. I don't know."

"What?"

I wanted to tell him that I thought it was off, somehow. That it seemed like it was mocking. But I knew that wasn't his intention. And anyway, he had his mind made up. So I said, "I'm just not a very good actress."

He left the camera and came over to me. He was right in front of me, my eyes to his chin. He put both hands on my arms. "You know you're the most beautiful girl I know." He hesitated. "Have you ever seen a fern unfold?"

"Yes, I think so," I said, though I wasn't sure what this sudden right turn in conversation was all about.

"The way a fern unfolds is the way you smile. I watch you and try to see it happen. It's so slow it's almost imperceptible. But then it takes over your whole face like the fern reaching up for the sun."

I turned my head. His cheeks were flushed, eyes turned down.

"Seth—"

"That was corny, I know."

"No. It was the loveliest thing anyone ever said to me."

He smiled now, quick and full. I leaned over and kissed him, first on the cheek, then on the lips. I could kiss Seth Winthrop for hours, I thought.

He pulled away. "Here's the thing: you get it. You just do. You get what it means to be a full-on, self-possessed girl. You don't take any bullshit, but you still smile like a fern. You aren't like all those girls I'm talking about. That's why I need you in my video."

So I agreed. Maybe it was what he said about the fern, or maybe I really did believe what he was trying to say, but I think it was something else. When he talked about me, I saw myself differently—his way. If I let him record me, then I could see me as he sees me, and that would be a powerful thing.

NOW

A green sign comes into view. "This is it," Zack says. "Where do you want us to drop you in Danbury?"

"The closer to eighty-four the better," she says. "That's where you need to go, too, right? To go into Pennsylvania?"

"You sure you don't want to come with us?" Charlie asks her.

"Tempting," she says.

"We'd drive you right to New York on the way back," he says. All this care for a girl he's barely even met. I mean, I agree with him. We *should* take her to New York. We *should* make sure she gets where she's going. That's just, like, the basic level of decency. But where the hell was all this care when I needed him?

"But if we find Adrian Wildes, there will be all this hoopla, and I really need to get down to Florida before the spring break crowds start coming in March. If I can get those tips, I'll be set through the slow summer."

Charlie nods. So sure he is that we're going to find Adrian Wildes, this seems like a legit excuse.

We drive a little longer until we're right by the on-ramp for the highway. Zack pulls the car into the parking lot of a Gulp 'N' Go. "I need some things," I say as I get out of the car with Harper.

"I'm gonna top off the oil," Zack says.

"And then we have to go," Charlie says.

"I have to tell you something," I ask as we step into the Gulp 'N' Go. The fluorescent lights and all the brightly colored signs and food shock my eyes. The smell of old pizza and hot dogs turns my stomach.

"Shoot," she says as she examines a display of nuts and trail mix.

"I don't think you should hitch all the way to Florida."

"Why not?"

"It just seems dangerous."

"I've got a code," she says. "A set of rules, you know, for keeping safe. It's mostly about the clothes. Schlubby but clean clothes. Manly clothes, you know." She turns to me, "That's why for, like, half a second I thought maybe you really were a hitchhiker when I got in the car."

I look down at myself and realize she and I are dressed in a pretty similar way—faded jeans, T-shirts, and hoodies. "Wouldn't you get more rides with a short skirt and booby shirt?"

She shakes her head and her face grows dark. "Not if you

want to make it where you're going. That's rule one of hitchhiking, okay?"

"Okay," I agree, even though I don't plan to ever need those rules.

"You dress like that, a certain kind of person will pick you up. And that type of person will expect a certain type of payment. And nine times out of ten, that type of person will take it if you don't give it."

I pick up a pack of chips, look at them for a minute, then put them back down. "That's like saying that a girl deserves it if she wears a tight dress to a party."

She shakes her head. "None of us deserve anything. I'm just telling you about the kind of people you meet when you're hitching."

None of us. Us.

She takes out her lip balm and applies it. "People like to categorize other people, right? And the first clue they use is dress. It's wrong, and I fight the good fight, but when I'm out on the road I try to send a very clear message that fits into the preconceived categories. I'm a girl, but I'm a tough girl, the kind who has done this before and will spot your tricks."

"You *are* that girl."

"Sure, that's one part of who I am. But it's not the whole of it. None of us fits one hundred percent into those boxes, right? We all blur the lines. I'm not changing myself, just how people see me."

She chooses a box of granola bars and heads toward the

cold case.

"I don't understand," I say, and my voice cracks. "What's the difference between changing how people see you and how you actually are?"

She pivots so she's looking right at me. Behind her is a case full of milks and juices that come in all different colors and it's like she's standing in front of some crazy stained-glass window. Like this is church. "Lexi," she says. "What happened?"

"What?" I ask, and step back.

"You keep talking about throwing off one life for another or changing who you are. What life are you trying to get away from?"

I scoff and kick the linoleum. "I don't think we told you about our hometown. It's, like, the boringest boring in boringland. And I—"

"Yeah," she says. "Yeah, I wear disguises. And you're right, Harper isn't really my name. It's Natalie. I've got this armor to put on when I hitch, and I guess I have some lighter version of it that I wear all the time, but the trick of it is, Lexi, you have to know who you can trust to see you without it."

She might as well have told me the trick to being rich was knowing the lottery numbers before they were picked.

"You can trust me, Lexi," she says. "If there's anything you want to—"

"You need to go to New York," I say. "And we need to go find stupid Adrian Wildes who is probably dead or drunk but whatever. Anyway, you want a slushy? I'm gonna get a slushy if you want one."

She follows me over to the slushy machine and grabs two cups. "On me," she says. "What flavor?"

"Blue?"

"Good choice."

She fills both of our cups and then we pay at the register.

I dig into my pocket and pull out the *Good Feelings* book. I find one that says *Life's the journey, not the destination*, and then write my address on the back. "Will you send me a postcard when you get there or something? Just so I know?"

"All right, Mom," she says. But she smiles.

It feels weird getting into the car without her. It feels worse to drive away and leave her there sitting on the bench out in front of the store, drinking her slushy and waiting for her next ride. "We should have kidnapped her," I say.

Charlie is driving now, and he looks in the rearview mirror. He slows down. "Maybe—"

But then we lock eyes in the mirror. We can't actually make her come with us. We can't make her take the safer choice. So he keeps driving and I lean back in the seat and sip so hard on my blue slushy that I give myself a brain freeze.

Maybe Zack is right. Maybe all boys want to be a hero sometimes. But I don't think Harper needs a hero. Too bad there's no way to put out a sign: *Good people of the earth: now is the time that I need saving.*

BEFORE

December

When Charlie came home for winter break, it wasn't like he did it with any fanfare. He just oozed back into our life. He was there all the time, in every spare, open space. At the dinner table. In my way in the bathroom when I needed to get ready for school. "Jesus, Charlie," I said, "can you stop picking at your zits so I can brush my teeth."

He opened the bathroom door. "What's up your ass?" he asked me.

I want to punch him. Hard. Right in the gut.

Instead, I pushed past him into the bathroom. *Just three more weeks*, I told myself. Because I still thought he was going back to school. That in three weeks his break would be over and I could go back to pretending I was an only child.

He was on the couch when I got downstairs. Feet up and reading *Real Simple* magazine. "You could drive me to school," I told him. All this week I've seen Remy Yoo dropped off by her older brother and let myself believe that Charlie and I could be like that.

"I could. I could also stick needles under my fingernails."

"Screw you," I told him.

"Jesus, what's with you and the rides? You flipped out when I wouldn't pick you up a couple of weeks ago from what's-his-name's house—"

"Seth." I squeezed my hands into fists. Not now. Not this.

"And now you're demanding rides to school? I walked to the bus stop and so can you, princess."

When we were younger, we used to get into it big-time. Rolling on the floor, punching, scratching fights. Mom and Dad didn't know what to do with us. Now, in my mind, I launched across the room and landed on him and I ripped his eyeballs out.

"Screw you," I said again.

"You were nicer when you were with that guy. Or at least, you didn't bug me all the time. I mean, honestly, Lexi. I'm on break. *Break*. That means I get to rest. I need to rest, okay? You don't need to give me such a hard time about it."

It was like I could actually feel the rage boiling inside of me. My vision blurred. Since Seth and I broke up I had been scrambling to build a wall to hold me up, and here came Charlie just knocking it down, pulling out bricks so the whole thing fell down around me. And I fell down, too.

"Well, you were a thousand times cooler before Penelope came into your life."

"Don't talk about Penelope," he said.

"What? It's true. Everyone knows it. I mean, God, Charlie, you're going to freaking Essex College when you could've gone to Carnegie Mellon. All for her, and now she's gone."

"Lexi!" It was my mom, behind me. She put her hand on my arm. "Come on," she said. "Let's get you to school."

She practically yanked me out of the room. Charlie didn't

react. Mom's face was tense and pale. She brought me into the mudroom and shut the door to the house behind us. It was like I was seven again and I'd really done it.

"He started it, Mom."

"It's okay, Lexi. Just." She sighed and tucked her hair behind her ear. She bent over and picked up a pair of Charlie's sneakers and tossed them into the cubby where he should've put them himself. It's been the same rule since we were born, practically, and he still couldn't manage to do it. "Charlie's going through some things right now."

Charlie and Penelope had broken up three months ago. Seth had just dumped me three weeks before. If one of us should get a pass because we were *going through some things* it was me. I grabbed my coat off the peg by the door.

"I can drive you," she said.

"No," I told her. "I'm fine." Because that's what I had to do. I had to be fine. I wasn't going to be a pathetic whelp picking at pimples and reading home organization magazines. If there was one thing I learned from Charlie, it was how *not* to act when things go bad. I would build this wall back up, brick by brick. I would not be like Charlie.

I will not.

I went into school from the back bus circle. The hallway goes right by the band room. Remy was in there with some of the other band and drama kids who hung out there, mostly juniors and seniors. I knew them all. Our school was small like that. I

could've walked right in and maybe they would've blinked, but
it wouldn't have been that big of a deal. I could've said, "Remy,
can I talk to you?"

Remy looked up. We locked eyes.

I kept walking.

SIX

*Once upon a time, a princess was born in a kingdom on
a cliff. The view of the sea was so magnificent that no
man could go to the edge of it without throwing himself
from it. Many great men were lost, and so the king issued
a proclamation: any man who could go to the edge of the
cliff and resist it's pull would have his daughter's hand
in marriage. Princes and commoners traveled from near
and far to test their will, but not one could pass the test.
The princess could not bear the loss of life another day.
At the break of dawn, she marched out to the cliff's edge.
There she stood, the sun rising over the ocean which
had momentarily stilled. She had passed the test. When
she turned, she saw beside her a bold knight, his armor
glinting in the early sunlight.*

NOW

*I*t's almost two hours on 84 into Pennsylvania. Two quiet
hours where I slip in and out of sleep and think about
texting Mom, but can't quite bring myself to do it, and anyway

my phone is nearly dead from searching for service and I should save the battery in case of emergency. I wish I had thought to get a charger at the gas station. When we get off 84 to take the smaller road out toward Shangri-La, Charlie pulls the car over. *Scenic Overlook*, a sign reads. I have no idea what he's doing. It's, like, suddenly the mission is less urgent, I guess, and we can stop for pretty views. Maybe he's trying to slow things down. Maybe he's realizing what we all believe—that Adrian Wildes is dead. Or maybe he's just weird. Nothing Charlie does makes sense.

We walk up to the guardrail that prevents you from dropping down an embankment into the Delaware River below. We watch the river for a few minutes. It's captivating, really. The way it is the same thing, over and over, but also different every single second. The edges are ridged with ice, and the middle is frothy white.

"This is the river he went to see," Zack says. He doesn't say it, but I think I know what he's getting at: if Adrian Wildes had jumped in, he would have washed up someplace like this: tossed and turned against the rocks and probably bloody and bruised beyond recognition, but most likely found. Unless he got pulled under. Unless his body was trapped below that foam.

"If you followed along the river down to where he—where he went missing, it would be less than fifty miles."

"That's a lot of ground to cover," I say. "Or, I guess, a lot of water." I force a laugh out, but Charlie's eyes are glassy and he doesn't respond. He's leaning hard against the guardrail. I can see it pushing against the flesh of his thighs, leaving stains on

159

his already dirty jeans.

I kind of remember this story we read once—not with Dewey DeWitt, but with my family. Maybe someone made it up, I'm not sure. Maybe I dreamed it. Anyway, it was this cliff out over the ocean. And the view was so beautiful, so mesmerizing, that no one could go to the edge of that cliff without throwing himself from it. The king was losing all his best men to the cliff. But he had something more mesmerizing than the ocean: a beautiful daughter. He proclaimed that the first man who could withstand the cliff should have his daughter's hand in marriage. He thought that if one man could withstand it, it would break the spell of the place. And so man after man came from near and far. Old men, young men, handsome men, and ugly men. But not one of them could resist the draw of the ocean. The princess saw them all. She saw them all dying for her—but she also knew, I think, that they weren't really dying for her. They were dying for her beauty and for her status, which wasn't the same as dying for her. So one day at the break of dawn, she went out to the cliff herself. She looked out at the water, and she felt nothing but calm. The wind whipped her hair across her face. And so she turned. She had withstood the cliff. She had won her own freedom. When she turned, she saw a knight, all in black. He had followed her to the cliff. He had seen her resist it. She smiled at him, but he, in his envy and rage, charged at her. She stumbled backward, down and down and down into the water. She was lost.

I turn to Charlie. "It's like that story, isn't it? The one with the cliff and the princess and the king and the knight pushed her in?"

"He didn't push her. She jumped."

"No. He was jealous that she could do something he could not, and he pushed her."

"If he couldn't do it, then he would have gone in, too—"

"But she broke the spell."

He shakes his head, but he doesn't say anything else about it.

The water sloshes against its banks. A branch is caught up in the froth, crashing against unseen rocks and breaking into bits below us.

Charlie leans forward, and I find myself reaching out and grabbing on to his shirt. He looks back at me with an angry grimace, eyes flashing like stoplights.

"It's not too much farther to Shangri-La," Zack says.

Charlie and I just stare at each other. I wonder if my eyes are sparking, too.

"Let's go then," Charlie says. "If it's not far from here, then let's go."

Neither Zack nor I say anything. I guess we've both realized that this is Charlie's mission now. We just need to follow him.

BEFORE

December

There was a holiday concert at school and Mom said we needed to go. All of us. Gwen was in the chorus, and Mom thought that I should go to support her. "If you leave the door open just a crack, honey, she can come back in."

"The door is open, Mom. She's not interested."

She put her hand on my shoulder. "Just try, okay?" Then she turned behind her and called to Charlie. He'd been home from school for a week and spent most of it on the couch. "It's time to go!"

"Go where?"

"The concert. Come on!" She turned to me. "I think this will be good for him."

I wasn't sure how seeing a bunch of high school kids play nondenominational holiday songs was good for anyone. "Good for his ass, maybe. I don't know how he doesn't have bedsores from that couch. Does he even go upstairs to sleep?"

"Lexi, I understand that you are at the age for pushing boundaries, but you need to think about your use of language."

"Thanks, Mom." I noticed that she did not answer my question.

"It's been a tough semester for Charlie," she said.

And mine had been just peachy.

Dad came into the mud room. "You look nice," he said to me, but before I could answer, he turned to Mom. "Charlie's still on the couch."

Mom sighed. "I'll go talk to him."

"I tried," Dad said.

"Just give me a second," Mom said.

When she left, I asked Dad, "So, what's the big deal? Why does Charlie have to go to this concert?"

He hesitated. "Music is good for all of us, don't you think? It's important to be a part of the cultural community."

I guess this is where I should have realized that something more than just laziness was going on with Charlie. I could've pressed Dad to tell me what Charlie's deal was. But I didn't. "You sound like a brochure," I told him.

"Huh," he said. "Better than an infomercial, I guess." He looked over his shoulder. "I'm just gonna go see how Charlie and your mom are doing."

"I'll be in the car."

We were late and had to sit in pairs. Charlie and my dad sat in front of us by a couple of rows. I could see the backs of both of their heads. They were almost the exact same shape: long and oval. Their hair even swirled the same way: counterclockwise. Charlie's head was not turned toward the stage, though there was a violin quartet playing. Instead he looked to his right. At Penelope Richards. Gack. What was she doing here?

"Mom," I whispered. And nodded my head.

"Oh," she said.

Penelope was with her parents. She had her hair pulled back in a ponytail that swung as she nodded along to the music.

"It's okay," Mom said. "He'll be okay. He's past this."

Hardly past it, I thought, if he was always camped out on the couch. I tried to relax in the folding metal chair, but it was like I had a rifle trained on my back. So I turned around. And there was Seth. With Hannah. Holding her hand. He gave me a tiny, deadly smile.

I whipped my head back around and tried to make my breath come normally. My back went stiff. It was like I could still feel him touching me. My skin itched and I couldn't stop myself from scratching so hard I turned my forearms red.

Charlie spent the whole time looking at Penelope.

I'm surprised we even noticed the music. Then the band began playing and Remy had a solo. She stood in the center of the stage in her black skirt and white button-down shirt. Hers had a little black-ribbon trim around the collar. When she played her face relaxed. Her fingers moved like dancers.

When the song finished, applause broke out and I swallow down tears. Mom said, "I didn't realize you liked Schubert so much."

People were still clapping, but from behind me, I heard Seth's voice. "Slut." I wasn't sure if he was talking to me or if he was talking about Remy, but I said, "Excuse me," and I stood up and rushed out of the auditorium and into the hall.

The band was filtering out and I almost crashed into Julie Wexler. "Watch it!"

"You okay, Lexi?" Remy asked.

Her cheeks were flushed. She held her clarinet in one hand, her sheet music in the other. I'd never learned to play an instrument. Those notes on the paper meant nothing to me, but she could unlock them and bring people to their feet.

I ran toward the door. "Weirdo," Julie said.

"No, she's all right," Remy replied.

I burst out into the cold air and ran to the wall by the front door. I sucked in air like it was water. Still my skin itched and my lungs were tight. I rubbed my hands against my arms harder and harder and harder but all I could feel was Seth's word raining down on me.

I can't be like this forever. It can't always be this way.

And so I kept building the wall around me. Brick by dusty brick.

NOW

It's raining when we get to Shangri-La—the barest hint of rain, but cold, almost frozen rain nonetheless. I wrap my sweat shirt around me and wish I had thought to bring something warmer. There is no sound but our movements: the *swish-swish* of Charlie's coat as he swings his arm, the *thud-flap* of Zack's shoe.

Charlie has parked the car right up by the filigreed gate, so we don't have far to walk. There's a chain on the gate, but we can swing the gate out far enough to slip in. No alarm sounds. No lights flash on. It's like they don't even care anymore.

Shangri-La, A Paradise Amusement Park was only open for two and half seasons. One day the gates were just locked. The owners moved to some little island somewhere and owed all these people money that they never paid. Adrian Wildes sang about it. That's why we're here. I guess he heard about it and stopped to see it when he was on tour in the area, before he made it big. It had a "lasting, profound, deep effect on him," at least according to Wikipedia.

Just inside the gate is the steel husk of a whale, its mouth a perpetual gape. Farther on I think I see the beginnings of a roller coaster, but it's hard to tell. The whole place is in shadows. We walk down a path and I try to imagine it full of people, parents chasing after their kids who are sticky with cotton candy. Merry-go-round music spilling forward. Balloons floating into the air. All I can see, though, is gray sky.

"I don't think he's here," I say. "I don't think there's anybody here."

Charlie shrugs me off and keeps walking. "It's a perfect place for depression."

"We don't know that he's depressed," I say. "Stop projecting."

Neither he nor Zack responds. The path changes from pavement to brick which seems to be glittering. It was meant to look like gold, I suppose, but now it just looks tarnished.

We come to a low, wooden building. There's a lock on the door, but it's been broken and hangs, rusty and off-kilter. Zack picks up a stick and uses it to prod the door open. Inside is only blackness. "I'm not going in there," I say, and back away from the dark.

Charlie pokes his head in. "Adrian?" he calls. "Adrian, are you in there."

No sound. No echo.

"This is stupid," I say.

"You've thought this whole trip is stupid," Charlie replies, which is, of course, true.

"I just don't understand why this is so important to you. We've driven hundreds of miles and you won't even say why you want to find him."

Charlie talks to the wet ground instead of to me: "Don't you ever feel like doing that? Just disappearing?"

"Everyone feels that way sometimes," I tell him, but I think of Harper telling me that disappearing and starting new is impossible.

"You can't just leave your life. Someone has to pull you back."

"Maybe he's done being famous." I'm very proud of myself for not saying that maybe he's done being a douchebag. I guess my lips probably flicked into a smile for half a second, because Charlie turns away. "Maybe he just wants to start a new life," I add.

"Someone always has to pull you back."

"But—"

"He needs to know that someone wants to pull him back."

I know we aren't talking about Adrian Wildes anymore. But all the words I want to say lodge in my throat. I've been trying to pull him back. Or I thought I had. Maybe insulting him as he sat on the couch didn't help, but if I had been all lovey-dovey and sappy, it wouldn't have worked either. Anyway, it didn't matter, because he's walking away from me again.

I back up and keep heading down the path. I'm sick of protecting Charlie. This is a fool's mission, and he knows it. What would we even do if we found Adrian Wildes? Either he doesn't want to be found, or, if he does, it's not by a bunch of teenagers. I kick a rock and it scuttles across the pavement in front of me.

BEFORE

September

Seth took me down to Canobie Lake Park once. I guess this place could have been like that. Maybe it had been nice at one time, but then it got kind of trashy.

We went in the teacups again and again because they were my favorite. We rode until neither of us could walk straight and we ended up falling down right outside the ride, arms and legs tangled together. Then we laughed. We laughed so loud and for so long, rolling on the ground, that a security guard came over and told us to move along.

"We can't," Seth protested.

I shook my head, still giggling too much to speak.

"The ride," Seth gasped. "It has robbed us of our ability to walk. We're going to just have to sit here for a while."

The guard shook his head. "Move along," he repeated.

Seth jumped to his feet, wobbled, and reached down to grab both of my hands in his. He pulled me to my feet, wrapped his arm around my waist, and we stumbled down the path toward the arcade. We watched the people's faces watching us. Most stepped out of our way, sure we were drunk or high or just out of our minds. One woman actually hugged her son close to her legs. But there was this one couple, maybe they are in their thirties. They had two little kids with them. They looked at each other, grinning. The man winked and the woman mouthed, "I love you." And it was stupid, but I thought, *someday, someday, someday. Someday that could be me and Seth.* So I turned to him and say, "I think I love you."

He wrapped his arm around me and pulled me close to him. The world swayed around us.

NOW

I walk away from the boys down a path that is more icy than snowy. My feet slip beneath me and so I am half sliding and half wobbling and probably look like a baby penguin only not cute. But I don't care. Who's going to see me? Charlie and Zack? Who cares?

The path goes through this sort of Middle Eastern area: a cartoon version of it anyway. The buildings have minarets and it looks like at one time they were painted all sorts of bright colors. One has a window that's boarded up, but the board has been broken through like someone took an ax to it and then yanked apart the plywood. I slip over to it and peer inside. Once my eyes adjust to the shadow, I see it's one of those games, the rigged kind. There are creepy clown faces and targets. I shudder and turn away.

I walk toward a Ferris wheel that has tilted slightly. Maybe it's the years of being left alone or the tree that is growing up along a central axis or an ice storm. I don't know. There are lots of ways for a place to fall apart. One of the cars has fallen off and is in a mangled mess on the ground.

I can see why Adrian would want to write a song about this place. The sadness pushes down on you, but there's also this weird sense of hope. Like I can imagine that Ferris wheel straightening itself right back up and spinning to life with that mechanical joyful music. I can imagine the lights and sitting at the top with a boy—not Seth—with his arm around me and looking out over all of the park. It's there, but it's gone.

Harper would like it here. I wish she had stayed with us. We could've gotten her to Florida eventually. Maybe.

The path loops around and I think I must be in the food court. There's a big flat area with metal picnic tables bolted to the cement. There's a roof over it, with one side collapsed by snow.

Gwen likes amusement park food. It's weird because she's so careful about everything. So careful with her image. But get her in front of some cotton candy and her whole face lights up and she digs in with abandon. She says the holy grail is freshly spun cotton candy and someday she's going to have her own machine. And she likes corn dogs, too, and that weird ice cream that is little pellets. I know a million stupid little things like this about her, and sometimes when she was spinning away from me, I thought about spilling them all.

But I didn't.

She said she would've come, but I don't know if I believe her. If I had called and said, "State of Emergency. Charlie is going Code Red. I need you," I don't know if she would have stopped her marathon of whatever Disney preteen show she was sucked into and gotten in the car with us. I used to know that. Even when she was so angry at me and spitting venom. Even then I knew I could still call her and she would drop everything for me.

Now things are calmer, but I don't think I'm on her list of help-at-any-hour friends anymore. And that's like a thousand times worse than her being angry with me.

My phone is heavy in my sweat shirt pocket and I pull it out. The battery is down to four percent, but I have service and I can see I have three texts from Mom:

Mom, 3:17 p.m.: This is your mom. Dad said I should text you to make sure you guys are okay. I said that this was your adventure and that you would tell us if there was a problem. You would tell us if there was a problem, right?

Mom, 3:49 p.m.: I have two scenarios for why you have not answered my texts. One: you are some place without service or your phone has died. Two: you are acting petulantly. I will not allow myself to entertain a third possibility.

Mom, 4:03 p.m.: I am afraid I am contemplating a third scenario.

My phone's battery warning blinks onto the screen. I dismiss it, type a word into a text message, and push send. My phone turns dark and I hope that the message made it out in time.

Lexi, 4:17pm: Safe.

The path takes me all the way around to the front of the park again. There's one bench alongside the path and I sit on it, pulling my knees up to my chest. In the dusk, I can still see Charlie and Zack wandering around. Charlie is stooped, his body changed by his breakup with Penelope. But what about me? I lost someone, too. I lost so many someones that I loved and I still manage to get up every morning and go to school and be a normal person. "What about me?" I yell.

Zack looks up and then trots down the path toward me. "You okay?" he asks.

"Peachy," I reply. "Peachy and plum-diggity."

He sits down on the bench next to me. "Adrian's not here," he says. "I'm not sure he's anywhere."

"You think he's dead?"

"I'm not ready to go that far," Zack says. "Well, maybe not out loud. But I think if he doesn't want to be found, he has the means not to be found."

"What would he be doing?"

"Something else," he says. "Mushroom farming. Custom furniture making. Accounting. Who knows?"

"Harper says you can't become a new person," I tell him. "You can't give up one life and start a new one."

"Wherever you go, there you are," he says.

"What does that mean?"

"It's one of those old sayings. It's like, no matter where you go, no matter how much your circumstances change, you're still you."

I think about this a moment. "What if someone else tries to

change you?"

"You mean like your brother and Penelope?" he asks.

"Sure," I say.

"I guess maybe I think that it doesn't work? Like, maybe we all have a range for our personalities, and they can change you within that range, but not outside of it. I mean, unless we're talking like trauma here. Like a blow to the head or something."

"Because that changes your brain," I say.

"Right."

Zack keeps tapping his foot in a puddle, making tiny splashes. "You used to go out with Seth Winthrop, didn't you?"

I snap my head away from him; it's like he's been in my thoughts, in my memories. "So?"

"So he's kind of cute," Zack says.

"You're not his type."

"That makes two of us, I guess."

I look back at him. His face doesn't look mean, but, still, I could slap him. "What do you know about it?"

He scratches his head. "I don't think you actually want to know that," he says.

"He's not gay. If you think that's some deep dark secret or something—"

"Nothing deep or dark about being gay," he says. "As for Seth . . ."

"I know all of Seth's secrets. That's what broke us up."

Zack nods. "If you could have known at the beginning, would you still have done it?" he asks.

"No. Why would I set myself up for that?"

"So it didn't balance out? The good can't hold up to the bad?"

"The good wasn't really good. He used to—" But I stop myself from saying more.

Zack nods again, then he picks something out of his pocket. "I found it on the ground over there." He hands it to me. It's a poker chip with one red side and one pink side. In the middle it's stamped with gold letters that say *Shangri-La*. "Two sides, right?"

"Right," I agree, annoyed.

"I think that most things don't have two sides like that."

I roll my eyes. "Golly gee whiz, thanks for the advice, Granddad."

He takes the poker chip back and slips it into his pocket. "Never mind," he says, standing up. He doesn't walk away, though.

"What?" I ask.

"What what?"

"What is it? What aren't you saying?"

"Just that in art class, he used to draw you. All the time. One picture after another. Mr. Solloway finally had to tell him to find another subject."

"Seth isn't taking art this year," I say.

"It wasn't this year. It was last year."

The air is still between us. In the distance, I can hear Charlie rustling around. "Screw you," I say.

"What?"

"Why would you tell me that? Screw you!"

He smooths his hands down the front of his shirt as if he's wiping himself clean of me. He turns on his heel and sets back off down the path. I wait a moment, and then follow him, hoping that we are leaving. He catches up to Charlie. They talk. Charlie nods. I hang back. Charlie calls back to me, "We're going. He's not here." I refrain from telling him I knew that all along.

In the car, I put my head against the cool, fogged glass. When I shift my head, my forehead wipes away and I'm left with one clear spot to look out at the silver-black road and the silver-gray night. I wonder what those pictures look like. Are they sketches, the lines still rough? Are they inked with crisp clear lines? How did he see me? How did he put me down on paper?

He never once showed a drawing to me. Never once told me about it. Because, I realize, we didn't match up. The paper version from his mind and the real world me just weren't the same, and so he let me go.

We've driven about twenty minutes when Zack swivels around in the front seat so his face is looking at mine through the space between the headrest and the door. "I just thought you'd like to know," he whispers. "That's all."

Adrian Wildes is actually kind of a good-looking guy. He has that cloud of thick, dark hair, and chocolate brown eyes. And even though it's total cheezeballs—and in a crap song to boot—he has that line about always letting you fall asleep first, just holding you until you slip into sleep. So cheezeballs—but also kind of nice.

I imagine what I'd do if we actually found him. I allow myself this fantasy even though it's outlandish. In my mind, the guys are gone and it's just me and Adrian. And he takes me to the hotel he's hiding out in. It's a nice hotel. The bathroom is huge with a tub with jets and there are thick robes you can put on when you get out. There's a balcony that overlooks a river. And every morning, room service wheels in a cart with fresh fruit and pastries. So we go to his hotel room. And we just talk and talk and I find out he's really not so bad.

"I know I come off as a douche," he says.

"Total d-bag."

"But it's partly a way of protecting myself. I keep the real me hidden away so the public can't take it from me."

"And I suppose you're going to say you only share the real you with a few people and one of those few, rare, special people is me? I'm not falling for it."

"Well, I was going to say that, and it wouldn't be me playing some game. But I'll wait, and you'll see."

So I do wait. We stay in that hotel for days. It's a suite and I can sleep on the couch. He doesn't make a move.

We talk and talk and eat pastries and talk and I realize that he was telling the truth, that he's not a total d-bag.

When we finally come out, I'm Lexi Green, The Girl Who Saved Adrian Wildes. Our picture is in all the gossip magazines.

It would just burn Seth right up.

BEFORE

November

Sometimes when Seth and I were having sex, I closed my eyes and pictured Adrian Wildes instead. Not to get me off. I don't know. He made that sex face when he played the guitar, so it was easy to come up with the image in my mind. I pictured Adrian Wildes, imagined it was him grunting in my ear, and then it was over.

If you close your eyes and keep yourself still, you can transport your body just about anywhere. Any place your imagination can conjure, you can go there. Sun-drenched beaches. Outer space. Under deep, deep water.

You have to hold on.

There might be jabs of pain, of pressure holding you down. But it's all worth it for the journey. All worth it.

You can do anything for seven minutes.

"We should probably use condoms, huh? Or maybe you should go on birth control?"

"I don't think so."

"Yeah. I think you'd need your parents' permission or something. Let's get dressed."

Pulled on underwear. Bra. Sock. Shirt overhead.

"I'm glad you always agree in the end."

Your head popped out of your shirt's neck like a turtle. He put a hand on your shoulder, gently where before it pushed hard into your bone.

"You're so good, Lexi. So, so good."

NOW

The boys have to pee again. "Can you see from the map where the next exit is?" Charlie asks.

"Why can't we just pull over?" I ask. "I mean, isn't the joy of being a guy that you can just pee wherever you want to. Rocket-launcher pee all over everything, everywhere."

"Pee isn't like a rocket launcher," Charlie says.

"Speak for yourself, young man," Zack replies.

"So, pull over and have a literal pissing contest and then we can get back on the road."

"Since when have you been in such a rush?" Charlie asks. "I thought you didn't think we were going to find him and didn't care if we did."

"We're going home now, right? He wasn't there, so we're following the river back to Trenton and then home. Right?"

"Rest stop," Zack says, and Charlie swerves the car over so hard my head hits the side.

"*Sorry, Lexi,*" I say. "That's okay, Charlie. I know you have a tiny bladder. *You're right! I do have a tiny bladder! Thank you for noticing.*"

"Zip it, Lexi."

He pulls the car into an angled parking place. I think about staying in the car, but I know that I should go now, because in an hour I could be the one who has to go, and I don't want to hear about it from Charlie. So when Zack gets himself out of the front passenger seat, I say, "Can you pop it?"

And Charlie of course says, "I thought you didn't have to go."

"I'm being proactive. Maybe you should have done that back at Shangri-La."

It's one of those squat buildings with a few vending machines and the bathrooms to each side. The light above the women's room isn't working. I hesitate. Zack and Charlie head toward the men's room. It's stupid, really, but my feet won't move. A deserted rest stop bathroom. It's stupid. If I yelled, Charlie and Zack would hear me, I think. Maybe. I don't know. I'm just being stupid, but I still can't seem to make my feet move.

"Wait up!" I call.

Charlie looks over his shoulder. "What?"

"I'm coming with you. Want to check out the old men's room, see if it's any different from the women's room."

Charlie shakes his head, but says, "Suit yourself," so I follow them in. They head right for the urinals, weird white sink-ish things against the wall. I go into one of the stalls. The toilet is all silver metal with no tank. I squat above it, but no pee comes out. Of course. I don't want them to hear me. So I start singing the lumberjack song from Monty Python.

"Lexi!" Charlie calls, but Zack joins in.

I can kind of hear the stream of their pee under our singing, but I tell myself that they can't hear me. Anyway, I barely have to go. When I finish, I call out, "Everyone done? Everything put away?"

"Yes," Zack replies. "The anaconda is back in its cage."

I come out of the stall and head for the sink. "Listen, obviously I can't speak for the average homosexual male, but girls aren't really interested in anacondas. Too scary."

"Yeah, yeah, it's not the size of the ship, it's the motion in the ocean and all that," Zack says.

I turn on the tap. Only cold water comes out, and there doesn't seem to be any soap in the dispenser. I rub my hands together hard.

"Lexi doesn't know what she's talking about," Charlie says. He's finished washing his hands, but the hot air dryer doesn't work, so he wipes his hands on his pants.

Above the sink is a mirror. Well, really it's a rectangular slab of metal. I can see myself in it, but no details. I'm just a blur of basic face-like shapes: eyes, nose, pink mouth, swirl of hair. "Give it a rest, Charlie," I say, still looking at my reflection.

"She just likes to talk about sex," Charlie says. "Sex and swearing and whatever else she thinks will shock you."

I bite hard on the inside of my cheek. I can't notice any difference in my reflection, but I am sure my whole body is washing over with purple rage. I turn off the tap and wipe my hands on my own pants. "You're an asshole, Charlie. How's that for shocking?"

"Pretty mild, actually."

"Pretty truthful, though," I reply.

I push past him and step out into the cold night. The air hits the inside of my nose and makes me breathe in sharply, just like I did with Seth. I close my eyes, try to slow my breath, try to forget where I am. Just like I did with Seth.

BEFORE

October

The streets in Portsmouth were crowded with tourists. We ducked into Macro Polo, which was basically a whole store of gag gifts, but kind of upscale gag gifts, if such a thing could even exist. There was fake poop, but also books of hipster haiku. I flipped through that one:

> *The coffee was not cool.*
> *Yet. He drank it all the same.*
> *Being hipster burns.*

I looked up at Seth to read it to him, but he was holding out a tiny booklet to me: *Good Feelings.*

"You need this," he told me. "Because you are so earnest."

I frowned. "I'm not earnest with anyone except you."

He stood so we were right next to each other. He was taller, but still our hips lined up, and our legs stretched to the ground like they were one. He flipped open the book and we read together, "Look up an old friend when you're feeling down." He turned to another page: "Art nourishes the soul like food nourishes the body."

"Gack," he said.

The pages were all perforated so you could tear them out and give them to someone, I guessed to make their day better or something. I couldn't imagine doing that. More so, I couldn't imagine receiving one. What would I do if a stranger appeared in front of me, holding out a tiny slip of paper? I would shake my head and say, "No, thank you."

My stomach dropped and I leaned away from Seth, reaching over the table to pick up a book of funny cat pictures.

Then again, it might be nice to have a little positive message handed to you, especially on a bad day. Just a little thought to show that we were all humans. "An example of the empathetic heart," Dewey DeWitt might call it—that's what he said we needed to bring to each text we read.

"See, what we need to do is write the real truth of things on the back." Seth ruffled the pages with his thumb. "'Home is where they take you in no matter what,'" he read. "I mean, gack, right? Not everyone's home is like that. How would that feel if you had an abusive father and an alcoholic mother? How would that feel if you have no home?"

"You're right," I said. "These are Good Feelings for people who already feel pretty good."

"Come on," he said. He walked toward the register with one

of the tiny booklets.

"Really?" I asked. "Won't that just encourage the company to make more of these ridiculous things?"

"Commerce marches on regardless of what the people want," he replied.

"Well—"

"Anyway, our purchase is barely a drop in a bucket."

"A single molecule of water," I replied.

"Sure," he said.

He bought the book, told the clerk we didn't need a bag, and handed it to me. I slipped it into my pocket. I thought I would never, ever pass one out—not a real one or a mean one. He slipped his hand into mine and we walked back out into the tourist throng.

"Coffee?" he asked.

"Okay."

I liked Breaking New Grounds, but he liked this place with an eastern European name and a weird graffiti mural out front, so we went there. My latte came with an elaborate design in the foam and I was trying to make out what it was when a woman in her fifties came in. She had on high-waisted jeans with an elastic waist. Her hair was cut short and it poofed around her head. She carried a little purse with a huge gold snap. Seth watched her come in and shook his head.

"So I was thinking you should try out for the play," I told him.

"What?" he asked. His eyes were still on the woman.

"The play. They're doing *The Importance of Being Earnest*. It's really funny. And I think you would be great as one of the Earnests. Hannah wants to work on costumes or something, and I thought that could be fun. Or backstage or something."

The woman ordered a mocha with skim milk. "Make it a decaf," she said. "And can I get whipped cream on that?"

"Jesus," Seth muttered.

"What?" I asked.

"What does she think this is? Starbucks?"

I shrugged. "Anyway, so what do you think?"

"About what?"

"About the play."

"Yeah, I think you and Hannah would do a good job with costumes. You don't need to be able to sew or anything, right?"

"But are you going to try out?"

He turned from the woman and looked at me. His eyebrows were knitted together as if he was seeing me for the first time and wasn't really sure what I was. "Why would I try out for the play?"

"Because it's acting. I thought it would be good practice for you. For your YouTube stuff."

"That's not acting," he said.

"It's performing."

He looked back toward the counter. The woman had her drink, the whipped cream piled on like an impossible cloud atop a mountain. The coffee sloshed a little as she sat down at a table and pulled out a home decorating magazine. Seth shook his head.

"You know, I thought maybe if you were performing that might, like—well, it's like Mr. Solloway says: you have to be doing art to do art." I ran my finger around the edge of my cup. "You just haven't put a video up in a while, and I thought that if you were in the play and on stage and performing, then maybe you would start feeling more creative and—"

"That's not the type of performing I do."

"I know, but—"

"And anyway, why are you suddenly so concerned about my video production?"

"I'm not. I mean, it just seems like something you care a lot about."

"I *do* care a lot. And that's why I'm waiting to do something good. I'm writing all the time, you know. Testing out ideas."

"You are?"

"Sure," he said. "I only want to put my best work out there."

"Oh," I said. "That makes sense."

"Of course it does." He put his hand on top of mine. "I've got things under control. And nobody likes a nag." He jerked his head toward the lady with the mocha who was dog-earing a page in the magazine. "What do you bet she goes home to her husband and is like, 'Honey, I really think we need to open up this wall and put in some French doors and the color of the year is periwinkle so let's redo the bathroom.' I bet she even has a honey-do list."

"Gack," I said.

"Right," he agreed. "You know what she needs? She needs a Not-So-Good Feeling reminder."

I wrapped both hands around my paper cup, contemplated the milk foam design some more, then took a sip.

"Give me your book," he said.

"What?"

"Your *Good Feelings* book. Give it to me."

He held out his hand and shook his fingers at me, so I pulled the little book from my pocket (it was warm and dangerous). He took it and turned to the back, where there were blank pages for you to write your own Good Feeling messages. From his own back pocket he took a black fine-point pen and wrote, "Renovating your house won't change who you really are."

I chuckled, but felt heavy stones in my chest and throat.

He handed the book back to me, his thumb marking the place. "Go give it to her."

"I don't—"

"Go on, it's funny. And it is actually a helpful message. If she focused more on herself—"

"But we don't know the first thing about her. Maybe she is just fine the way she is."

He raised his eyebrows. "She is not just fine. Go on."

I took the book from him and stood up. "All right then, but meet me outside." I put the top on my coffee and handed it to him.

"Okay, sure."

He took our coffees and head for the door. I watched his

back. I could see his sinewy muscles through his black T-shirt.

I had my forefinger and thumb on the note Seth had written. As I approached, the woman looked up at me. Her eyes were milky blue and set a little too far apart. Her lipstick left a mark on the edge of her cup. I looked down at the book, and turned back a page. This one read, "You are stronger than you know." I tore it out and handed it to her. She looked down, read it, then looked up at me, perplexed. "Just trying to spread some goodwill," I said, then turn and walked out the door. Seth was waiting for me with the coffee and a kiss on the cheek.

SEVEN

Once upon a time, a princess was born in a kingdom on
a cliff. The view of the sea was so magnificent that no
man could go to the edge of it without throwing himself
from it. Many great men were lost, and so the king issued
a proclamation: any man who could go to the edge of the
cliff and resist it's pull would have his daughter's hand
in marriage. Princes and commoners traveled from near
and far to test their will, but not one could pass the test.
The princess could not bear the loss of life another day.
At the break of dawn, she marched out to the cliff's edge.
There she stood, the sun rising over the ocean which
had momentarily stilled. She had passed the test. When
she turned, she saw beside her a bold knight, his armor
glinting in the early sunlight. He was filled with envy and
rage, and he charged at her. She tumbled backward off the
cliff and down into the water.

NOW

When we get home I'm having Mom and Dad take you
to the doctor to have your bladder checked."

"Are you serious?" I shoot back. "You guys are the ones who have needed to pee every hour on the hour. This is the first time I'm asking for a stop!" My bladder is pressing against all my other internal organs like a drunk trying to get to the bar. "There!" I say. There's a neon light flashing *Open! Open! Open!* I don't care what it is, I'll just run in, pee, and run out.

When Zack navigates the car into the parking lot, it looks like someone's house, a double-wide plopped down on this stretch of country highway. Then the light above the door crackles on and I see a sign: *Sherri's Gentlemen's Club.* I'm guess it's probably like the Knights of Columbus or the VFW or some other weird place for old men to hang out, but I figure if they're really gentlemen, they'll let me use their bathroom. I push on Charlie's seat. "Move it," I say.

"We can't go in there," Charlie replies.

"They'll let me use their bathroom," I say. I push on Charlie's seat again. "Come on!" It's like now that I'm in the vicinity of the bathroom, my bladder can sense it and is pushing against me even more urgently. "Seriously, Old Faithful is about to blow."

"That's disgusting."

"Move!" I bellow.

"I think we should let her go in," Zack says.

"My parents will kill me."

"Our parents are already going to kill us," I say.

Zack opens his door, steps out, then, after a few unsuccessful tries, flips his seat forward. He holds out a hand to me. "Milady."

I take his hand and he pulls me from the car. Maybe a drop of pee slips out. Maybe. I half jog, half stagger to the door. Zack is a few steps behind me, and I hear Charlie get out of his side of the car.

I yank the door open and there's a big man with an impressively long beard blocking my way. "I understand that this place is men only, which, I mean—well, I'm hoping you will make an exception because I really, really, really need to pee."

"How old are you?"

"How old am I? Is this a bar or something?"

"Or something," the man says. He doesn't move, not even a centimeter.

"And I made the mistake of getting a giant slushy. That was a long time ago, and I did go once, but I guess those things have staying power, and I didn't realize we were entering a barren bathroom wasteland. And I just really need to go."

"We could get in a lot of trouble."

"You can escort me straight to the bathroom. I won't try to order a drink or anything. I might not ever—" But then I stop because I notice the stage. More precisely, I notice the woman in red high heels and a red sparkling thong and nothing else who is casually swinging her hips from side to side, a bored look on her face. "Oh."

"Oh," the man says. I think he is smiling under his beard.

"The thing is, I still really need to pee."

He laughs then. "Come with me."

Instead of leading me through the bar, though, he takes me around back with Charlie and Zack trotting behind. He gives three sharp knocks on a yellow door, and someone yells, "Come on then!"

He holds the door open for me. "On the left. You boys wait out here."

"Oh, they don't interest me much," Zack says.

They? I step through the door and seven heads swivel to look at me. Their hair is piled high and they have perfect red lips and perfectly lined eyes. Glitter and sequins and gold hang from clothes racks in between the mirrors. "Hi," I mumble. "I'm Lexi and I need to pee."

"What do you think this is? Pissers Anonymous?" one woman asks.

Another woman puts her hand gently on my arm. "Right over here, sweetheart." She pushes open a small door and I step into the bathroom. There's glitter all over the seat and the floor and I wonder if strippers have more STDs than other people, or if that's just a stereotype or a prejudice. I decide it's better to be safe and hover above the seat. I pee for five minutes. I make sure to clean off the seat when I'm done. I wash my hands and dry them on my jeans.

When I come out, the women are back to getting ready. They are all different sizes and shapes, but I am pretty sure all of them are white. It's hard to tell in the dim light and because they all seem to have heavily dosed themselves in self-tanner. Self-tanner and glitter. Maybe there is some sort of special product that is a mix of glitter and tanner and it is marketed almost exclusively to strippers. Or exotic dancers. Adult performers? I'm not sure what the right word is. Seth always said that pornography was empowering for women. That it allowed them to use their bodies that men were so eager to exploit.

(He said this. He really said this. And I never saw the irony there.)

But these women do not look especially empowered. They look like women I would see at the grocery store, only with fewer clothes and more glitter.

"I've never been in a strip club before."

"You don't say," the woman who laughed at me when I first came in says, and the group around her laughs, too. But the nice lady who showed me the bathroom just smiles.

I look around from face to face to face. This is a tiny town, but there are seven of them. And there were at least half a dozen cars in the lot. Is the stripper to population ratio particularly high?

"My name is Lexi," I say, because I realize that's what you're supposed to do when you meet new people, even if those people are hardly wearing any clothes and you suddenly feel very warm and very self-conscious.

"I'm Jewel," the nice woman says. "Where you headed with those two boys, sweetheart?"

"That's my brother and our gay neighbor," I say.

"One of them's a queen?" the Pissers Anonymous woman asks.

I flush, but say. "Zack. The bigger one. But I'm pretty sure he's not a queen. A bear, maybe?"

This sets the women laughing again. They are like this

happy little family. This is not what the world of movies and television has led me to expect. Strip clubs are always in the city, usually on lower levels. But this one looks like a house. And there the woman is either just background to whatever the men in the show are doing, or she has some sad, sad story and needs to be rescued by the leading man who will love her even though she has this troubled past. This is not that. "Are you all—" I begin. "I mean, this is sort of a strange place for a, you know—"

"A what?" Avery asks.

The woman at the dressing table next to Avery says, "Ease up."

"Why? She's in our space looking at us like she's wandered into a freak show. This poor little lost lamb who's never seen the world—crock of bullshit. She pisses me off."

I know she's right, but I've never thought about strippers that much before, about how someone becomes one.

Jewel puts a hand on my arm. "Don't let Avery bother you. She's mean to everyone."

She sits down backward in a chair that I think might be part of her act. "Anyway, everyone needs a little entertainment, right? Even in little country towns."

"Especially in little country towns," Avery said.

"How'd you end up in this part of Pennsylvania?" Jewel asks me.

"My brother had this crazy idea to go look for Adrian Wildes."

"Oh," says another woman. She is small and her outfit is all black with not even one piece of sequins. "I dance to his stuff sometimes. College boys like it, and college boys tip well."

"Makes their mommas proud," Avery says.

"So you heading up to Winsacondor then?" Jewel asks.

"Winsacondor?"

"The old summer camp. He went there as a kid."

"Yeah, but it closed down," another woman says.

"Closed down and he bought it."

"Really?" I ask. We're supposed to be heading back to where the tour bus last was, but maybe this is the type of clue we've been looking for.

"Sure, two or three years ago. Big news around here."

"Lacey thought he'd come into the club."

"I did not," the small woman says.

"Anyway, it's just another twenty miles or so. The sign is down, but the posts are still there. And the street is Winsacondor Way."

"Thanks," I say.

"Give him a big kiss hello for us," Avery says.

"Yeah, send him down our way, sweetheart."

"Okay, sure. If we find him, I'll do that."

And this makes them laugh and laugh.

I push my way back out into the cool evening air.

"What took you so long?" Charlie demanded.

"I was talking with the dancers."

"The strippers?" Charlie asked.

"Yeah."

"I thought I was going to have to bust down that door and save you."

"Hardly."

"Hardly what. I could save you if you needed it. Remember that time Max Hicks pushed you off the swing."

It was ten years ago. "I'm not the one who needs saving."

Charlie huffs and turns to go back to the car.

"Anyway," I say. "The dancers told me where Adrian Wildes is. If either of you still cares."

BEFORE

October

Seth cupped the beer bottle in two hands so they grew cold and then he put his hand on my neck.

We'd gone through the list of famous couples we could be: Sid & Nancy, Carol & Mike Brady, John F. Kennedy & Lee Harvey Oswald. Then we'd tried more subversive ones: Velma & Fred, Smurfette & Gargamel, Holden Caulfield & Yoko Ono.

In the end we decided that couples costumes were stupid. "We each have our own identity, right?"

"Right. It's not like we're subsumed by this relationship."

So he dressed up as White Trash Guy in a NASCAR T-shirt, ripped jeans, and baseball cap. I was a sexy Muppet. We had seen the costume at Total-Mart and decided it was a totally ironic critique of Halloween as slut fest.

"You mean," I'd said, "the way girls feel like it's their only chance to display their sexuality without judgment?"

"Right. Slut fest. Male gaze. Sure."

Only it seemed the student body of Essex High School didn't get irony, because I was given numerous compliments for how cute and/or hot I looked.

"You do look pretty cute-slash-hot," Seth said.

"Thanks?"

He gulped from his beer, then offered me some. I don't like beer but I didn't want to be one of those girls who only drank froufrou stuff: peach schnapps and whatever else has been raided from the backs of parents' liquor cabinets. So I took a sip. It was cold and sour. "I think that's skunked."

"A sexy Muppet and a beer scholar. This could be love."

I took another sip.

Gwen was there. She dressed as a sexy sailor zombie. The makeup job was impressive—gory and real—peels of fake skin curled off her cheek to reveal pink and red flesh. If anyone was doing a send-up of the sexualization of Halloween, it was her. I'd have told her this if we were talking.

She sat on the porch swing with Ione and Silas. I watched them through the window. They were smoking pot and probably talking about the latest book in the Nightshade Trilogy, or whether they were going to play laser tag this weekend or go to the movies.

"Cute." It was Remy Yoo. "Disturbing, but cute."

"It's supposed to be ironic."

"I know."

Remy wore a tuxedo with her hair slicked back. She was beautiful. I stepped closer to Seth, closing the distance so there was only a hairline fracture between us.

"What are you?" Seth asked her. His voice was edgy and hard.

"I'm in drag." She looked past him as she spoke.

"That's a how, not a what," he said.

"Sure," she said, and looked ready to step away.

I still had the beer in my hand, gripping it around the neck. I took a long drink, then handed it to Seth who dragged a pull as he slipped his arm around my waist.

"It feels kind of empowering, actually," she said. "Everyone knows it's me, but they still look at me different. Give me a little more space."

"Respect the cock," Seth said.

She frowned. Hard. "It's totally ridiculous is what it is," she said. "But it kind of makes me want to come to school like this."

"Nothing would make our faculty happier than to have a transgendered student."

On the one hand, it was hard to believe they dated, the way they were looking at each other with this impossible mix of boredom and antipathy. But the frisson between them—I think that's the right word—it was undeniable. Like if this were a movie, the next scene would be them having angry sex.

"I wouldn't be transgendered. Just dressing like a man." When she talked, she looked at me, not at him.

"A subtle distinction sure to be lost on most of the faculty."

"It would just be a mask," I said.

"Which is no different than how we go through life every day. Mine would just be obvious."

"I don't wear a mask," I said.

"Oh, sugar," she said. And she laughed and laughed. And that wouldn't be so bad if I didn't turn to see Seth smirking right along with her even as he rubbed the back of my hand with his thumb.

NOW

As we walk back to the car, snow starts falling. The big fat kind of flake that you can actually catch on your tongue and it stings you for a moment before melting away.

"How far did they say it was?" Zack asks as he pulls open the driver's side door.

"Twenty miles or so. Not so far."

"In the dark. In the snow. Through the mountains," Zack says. "I'm not sure Miss Ruka can handle that."

"She can't or you can't?" I ask.

"Maybe he's right," Charlie says. He's looking out at the road, where the snow makes rainbow prisms in the streetlights. "Maybe we should tuck it in for the night."

"This is your mission," I say. I know he's right, but I never intended to spend two nights away from home. "Where exactly do you suggest we stay? I mean, I bet I could curl right up on the glitter floor back there, and maybe I could convince them to take Zack, but I don't think they want you at all."

Zack shuts his door and trots back toward the bouncer. He's kind of graceful. He jogs back, the air puffing white out of his mouth. "Guy says there's a motel up the road. They rent by the hour or the night."

"Do you think it would be cheaper if we just did six hours or something?" I ask, perplexed. Charlie and Zack laugh.

"Just when I think you might be turning into a real live girl about town, you say something like that," Charlie says. He flips the seat forward so I can get in back.

"You know, a gentleman wouldn't laugh at a girl for not knowing something. And he would let me sit up front."

"You're my sister, not a girl I'm trying to impress. Chivalry is dead. I thought that's how you wanted it, mini-feminist. And they rent by the hour so people can have sex."

Though the notion of a motel that rents by the hour has never occurred to me, the Sunset Motel looks just as I'd imagine an hourly hotel would. The guy behind the front desk is maybe nineteen and has pimples across his chin and cheeks like an acne beard. He doesn't look at us while he talks. Just rattles off the rates and the rules and makes Charlie sign something since he is over eighteen and the only one who can legally rent the room.

"There's a pool," the boy says as he hands Charlie the key.

"I bet he thinks this is some sort of weird threesome," I say once we step back outside and start walking toward our room.

Charlie shudders and Zack says, "It would actually probably be a normal threesome compared to his usual clientele."

"Gross," I say.

Charlie unlocks the door and we all step through a time warp. The floor is orange carpet with cigarette burns and an ominous stain at the foot of one of the full beds. Each bed has a royal blue coverlet, tan sheets, and two pillows, flat as tortillas. The bathroom mirror is cracked, and the sink and counter is some weird form of white and gold marble that's peeling up at the edges. There are two thin towels, and a toilet paper roll that's nearly gone.

I wish my phone weren't dead so I could take pictures. No one will believe me.

The hourly rate is twenty-five dollars, but the whole night is only fifty-seven, further depleting my stack of cash. I'm not sure how we're going to get home, really. We need to fill up the tank again, soon, and of course we have to eat. Neither of the guys seems too concerned about it. Instead they stand stock-still in the middle of the room. "So," Zack says.

"So," Charlie agrees.

And once again I feel like they understand something I don't. I watch where they are both looking. The beds. Two beds, three people. "Oh for Christ's sake," I say. "It's a simple math problem. I can sleep with you, Charlie, because it's not like we haven't had to do it before. Or I can sleep with you, Zack, because I know you won't try anything. Or you guys can sleep together, but I know you both will be all weird about it, but then try to be not weird. So eliminate that. So we have two choices. And since I know that Charlie kicks, I'm sleeping with you, Zack."

"Okay," Zack says. But he doesn't move.

I flop down on the bed farthest from the door on the side closest to the wall. "If a serial killer comes in, he'll get both of you first, and hopefully be too tired by the time he gets to me."

"That's lovely, Lexi," Zack says.

I notice a phone on the table between the beds. It's the old kind of phone, with big push buttons and a curly cord that hooks the mouthpiece to the receiver. Glued to it are instructions for making a collect call. I pick up the receiver and dial.

A computer instructs me: "Please state your name."

"Lexi," I say. And then, in case it's for some official business, I say, "Alexandra Green."

"Thank you."

The phone rings only once.

"Hello?" My mom's voice is panicked.

Before I can say anything, the computer says. "You have a collect call from—" There is a pause and then my voice: "Lexi. Alexandra Green."

I sound forlorn. Like my voice has been all hollowed out. How long has it sounded that way?

"Do you accept the charges?"

"Yes! Where are you, Lexi?"

"We're in Pennsylvania. We went to a strip club."

"Lex!" Charlie calls from his bed.

"Pennsylvania, you said? You're all crackly?"

"Well, we're in this totally sketchy motel. I think the phone is even older than you."

Nothing.

"Mom?"

"I don't like this."

"I was only kidding."

"Is Charlie there? Is he okay?"

"Yeah, he's fine. I mean, he's a little miffed since they wouldn't let him in the strip club, but he's fine."

"It sounds like you keep saying 'strip club.'"

"We're all fine. Zack, too. Can you call his mom and dad?"

"Can I talk to Charlie?"

"This is like in one of those hostage movies and you ask to talk to him to make sure I haven't actually killed him already."

"Lexi," Mom says.

"Fine, here he is."

I reach the phone out to him, and he takes it. "Uh-huh . . . uh-huh . . . I will."

"Wouldn't you rather talk to me than him?" I ask Zack.

Zack just shrugs, but I can see a little smile.

"I'm sorry about what I said back at the amusement park," I tell him. "It's just that—it's still a little raw. A lot raw."

Charlie hands the phone back to me. "Hey, Mom," I say.

"You should see this motel. The remote control for the television is chained to the bedside table."

"That's great. Listen, you need to keep an eye on him."

"I am, Mom. But let's not forget that he's the older one, so maybe he should get the lecture every once in a while."

"We'll talk about it when we get home."

"Wait, does that mean I'm in trouble?"

"No, honey. Just that we have a lot to talk about when you get home."

"Okay."

"And, honey."

"Yeah?"

"Don't use the pillows and sleep on top of the sheets. If you bring bedbugs home, I will murder you both."

"Aye, aye, captain."

"I love you."

"I love you, too."

The indoor pool is surrounded by all these fake plants that are like palm-tree shrubbery, nothing that exists in real life. The ground around it is all pebbles glazed over with some thick shellac that has taken on the color of boogers. The pool itself is lit with blue and green underwater lights that make it look like a lagoon. But not like a romantic-movie-style lagoon. More like a dank and potentially eel-infested lagoon. I don't know if eels actually live in lagoons. There's a river that runs through our town, the Lamprey River, and sometimes kids jump off the bridge and go skinny-dipping. I did it once. With Gwen, before Seth. We were swimming in the silky moonlight when I felt something both cool and warm brush against my thigh. "Don't try anything, Gwen," I said. Her chin was underwater, and the ripples of the water seemed to be reflected in her big eyes. "What are you talking about?" she asked. And it was like in that moment, perfect clarity. There was a reason this was named the Lamprey River. Lamprey eels. Eels in the river. I scrambled for the edge and climbed out far from my clothes, not caring who saw my naked body. "Eels," I called to Gwen. "Eels!"

"I'm not going in," I say to Charlie and Zack. "I don't have a swimsuit."

"Go in your underwear," Charlie says. "You can be sure that Zack and I won't be looking."

"I might look," Zack says, "but I won't judge."

"What's to judge?" I ask. But my body is not the same since I quit field hockey. It is mine and not mine.

"You always go in the motel pool," Charlie says. "Always." He pulls off his shirt. He has the tiniest tuft of chest hair, and there's something obscene about it. It's not just imagining Penelope running her fingers through it. I look away from him, down at the snot rocks. I hear one splash and then another: the boys are in the water.

I sit on a lounge chair, the straps pressing against my jeans. The guys are just floating in the water, soft swishes of sound.

Fuck it.

I take off my clothes and with three steps I dive into the

water. It's warm and salty. I stay under for as long as I can, blink my eyes open, and I'm staring right into one of the green lights. It's fuzzy, like I'm going into that tunnel of light you're supposed to see when you die.

And then the light goes out.

I sputter to the surface. We are in complete darkness. The smell of chlorine fills my nose and, I don't know, this sounds crazy. It is crazy. But it's like I'm transported. Back to the first time. With Seth. The first time with Seth.

I scramble out of the pool. "I'm going back to the room," I tell them. There's a stack of stiff towels on a shelf. I grab one and try to wrap it around me, but it's too small and as I walk back down the hall, every time I take a step, the edge of my underwear shows. I feel certain that someone is going to come out of a room and see me. Someone will emerge and they will see me and they will know just by looking at me the kind of trash that Seth thought I was.

BEFORE

November

Sloppy Sue's was not really a bar. It had been one, but it had so many liquor violations for serving minors that it was about to be closed down. So they decided to just become a liquor-free club and serve those same patrons. And if those minors chose to sneak in a flask or a bottle of Coke with half the soda dumped out and replaced with rum, well, the owners didn't look too carefully. What they did care about was the music. All the best local bands played here. One legend held that Adrian Wildes had played the club, before he went all commercial. A second legend held that he had come back in disguise, as part of band called Kinky Slide, a band that only ever played one, mythic show. But Seth swore he had been there that night, and no way no how was that Adrian Wildes.

We went to Sloppy Sue's the weekend after Halloween to see Vaginas of Steel, an all-girl punk-rap-ska band from Dover. Seth said they can actually thrashed pretty hard and anyway they were so damn hot in those leather bras and rubber shorts. "It's a statement, right? On the male gaze," he said as he gazed.

The singer had a ring on each finger and bracelets up her arm. She looked familiar, but I couldn't place her. Seth was right up at the stage, which was three feet above the ground, which made him eye level with her crotch.

I had a club soda with lime in a plastic cup. I stood against the side wall, out of the throng of thrashing bodies.

Seth had snuck in a flask and added a heavy dose of vodka to my cup.

The windows behind the band were gray fog.

Vaginas of Steel really worked the crowd, up and up and up, and I wondered what it was like to control a whole group like that. I wondered if the singer even realized her power.

The throng lurched toward me and I made myself as flat as faded wallpaper. The heat came off the crowd.

There were some straight-edge skinheads in the center, spiraling their fists as the singer caterwauled an *OH!* sound over and over and over.

I thought: she is wailing.

I thought: it is too hot in here.

The singer threw herself on the mass of bodies and they received her. It was all guys, I realized, men whose hands grabbed and tugged and pinched and pressed.

She moved toward me, this broken body on a sea of grasping hands. She floated above the heat waves.

I could not breathe.

She was almost on top of me as I sank to the ground, and before I closed my eyes, I recognized her.

"Holy shit, Lexi. I mean, really."

Debbi, my former babysitter, had one hand on each of my knees. "I thought I was having some sort of drug-induced flashback, although, like, I don't use at all."

I rubbed my eyes. "It's really me."

We used to listen to Taylor Swift and play tennis rackets as guitars and made Charlie be the drummer in the background.

"Shit, girl, what happened?" Even when she was our babysitter, Debbi swore too much.

"I was hot. I got overheated."

"No, I mean, look at you. You grew up. I must be ancient." She turned over her shoulder to her bandmate. "Are we ancient? I used to babysit this girl."

We were backstage in a tiny room with yellow-green walls

covered in handwritten messages and signatures. Seth sat in a fraying armchair at the far side of the room. His beanie was pushed back on his head so some curls were showing. I smiled, but he didn't smile back.

"How old are you anyway?" Debbi asked.

"Fifteen," I said. I bit my tongue to keep from adding "and a half."

"Shit," she said again.

"Is this your job now?"

She laughed. "Nah, I work at a graphic-design place downtown. And before you say that's cool, let me clarify that I don't get to do any actual design. Mostly I photocopy."

"It's still cool," Seth said from the armchair.

"Yeah, sure," Debbi said. "What about you? What about Charlie? I bet he's cute now, huh?"

"That's nasty, Debbi," one of the other women said. "They're kids."

"If you're fifteen, he's gotta be, what? Nineteen. Not nasty."

"He's not cute, he's—"

"So you're in high school?" She leaned back so she was sitting on the floor, but she still had her hands on my knees.

"Yeah."

"You like it?"

"I guess."

"And this d-bag is your boyfriend?"

I couldn't help but smile. "Yeah."

"Right here," he said. "Not a d-bag."

But Debbi ignored Seth. "Still rocking the tennis-racket guitar?"

"Not lately."

"Ever try a real one?"

I shook my head.

"I play," Seth said.

"So what're you into?"

"I don't know." I looked over at Seth. "Mostly YouTube stuff, I guess."

"YouTube?" She looked confused.

"Yeah. Actually there's one artist I think you would like. Her name is Possum and her songs are really pretty, but also sad and angry and—"

"Vaginas of Steel is not going to be interested in someone like Possum. She's all cutesy and girly-girly. They're much more likely to be interested in someone like Jackson Reeder, who is actively engaging in a feminist critique of modern society."

"Actually, I'm interested in all female discourse," Debbi said to Seth. She turned back to me. "Tay-Tay's latest totally rocks, right? I do a pretty rad cover, but you cut our set a little short."

"I'm sorry."

"Hey, no worries. Maybe next time."

"Sure."

She grinned. "Next time, bring Charlie."

"Gross," I said.

She leaned over and kissed me on the cheek. "Night night, time for star flight," she said, just like when I was a kid. And I kind of wished I was home already, and that little again, and she was tucking me in and I was thinking of what kind of trippy spaceship we could take to the stars.

Seth didn't talk much on the car ride home. As we turned onto my street, he said, "So your old babysitter is kind of a bitch, huh?"

"What?"

"And washed up. Like, she's practically thirty and still playing all-ages clubs."

"I thought you liked Sloppy Sue's."

"And making copies? She's like an intern. Shoot me now if that's my future."

"I think she's pretty cool, actually."

He steered the car down my driveway. "Sure you do, Lexi," he said. He kissed me on the cheek. "You're sweet, right. Probably too sweet. But I'm telling you—washed up and dried out." He kissed me again, for real this time. Long and hard and deep. When we stopped, we didn't say anything and I got out of the car before the good moment changed.

NOW

"We have twenty-four dollars and nineteen cents left," I tell them. "Our best bet is to go to the grocery store for food. It will be cheaper. I think we may need to siphon gas to get home. I've never done it, but I've seen it done in movies. We'll need a tube and one of you will need to suck the gas out of the other car to get it going."

"Why us?" Zack asked.

"Because it was my idea, and I'm bankrolling this whole operation, so that ought to earn me something, don't you think?"

We drive up the road until we see a small grocery store. There are a few cars parked outside, and it's lit up like a fancy house in the real estate ads my dad is always looking at.

Grocery stores should all be set up the same way. I mean, really. You're hungry. You need some Pop-Tarts. You get in, you get out. But each one is different. The entrance to this one deposits us in the flower section. Buckets and buckets of flowers in improbable shades of pink and yellow and blue. The smell is overwhelming, but not like real flowers. Like those air fresheners that hang from rearview mirrors. The door hums shut behind us. I sneeze.

Charlie and Zack go to find a bathroom. I don't know why people talk about girls having to go to the bathroom more than guys, because with those two it's pretty much a constant stream. Whizz, whizz, whizz.

But I digress.

And I am distracted from my Pop-Tarts mission by this guy. Well, really, his curls. Seth has curls, but not like this. I've never seen curls like this on a boy: blondish-brown soft cherub ringlets around his face with pink cheeks and full lips. We're talking serious stepped out of a Botticelli and grew up to be a teenager.

It makes me want to barf.

I walk past the flowers into the produce section.

The boy works here. He has a red apron on and he's unpacking pomegranates into a bin. There's another guy in a brown Carhartt jacket who I guess is trying to look tough, but he's scrawny and antsy, so he's like a jumping live wire. "Just cut out early," he says to Angel Boy.

"That would be nice," Angel Boy replies, resigned.

"So, come on, let's go."

"Like I said, that would be nice, but I actually want to get out of this town someday. So I work."

Well, that at least I can relate to, but this trip seems to be showing me that one shit town is no better or worse than any other shit town along the way. They've got the same crappy chain restaurants, the same crappy stores, even the same crappy street names.

The other boy gives a halfhearted "Seriously, Gabe, your dedication to this job is a little boring."

"Says the guy who takes on every extra shift he can get his hands on," Gabe replies.

I step between them and wrap my hand around a lush, red pomegranate, its skin still cool from the refrigerator it was stored in. "Excuse me," I say as I pull the pomegranate close to me. "Thanks."

The boys both watch me as I back away, then pivot.

"All right then," I hear as I pass the banana display. "I guess I'll just catch up with you at the diner after."

"Sure, man. Maybe. Snow's supposed to come in pretty

hard, though."

I leave the produce and walk through the deli and meat areas. The *Good Feelings* book is pressing into the flesh of my hip, so I pull it out and put it in my hoodie pocket. But then I think that maybe this is a store that could use some good feelings, so I leave a slip—*Art is the artist's way of highlighting our world's small beauties*—in the cheese case. And another one by a display of pretzels.

When I round the corner, I find Charlie and Zack. Charlie's hat is pulled down so low you almost can't see his eyes, only the dark circles underneath them.

"A pomegranate?" he asks.

"Yeah, sure. Why?"

"You're lecturing us about a budget, and you pick out the most expensive fruit, and the most difficult one to eat."

I look at the red fruit in my hand. I don't think it's even ripe yet. "This way," I say. I lead them down the cereal aisle. We find the Pop-Tarts and buy the store brand. Strawberry frosted. I leave the pomegranate in the empty space on the shelf, a *Good Feelings* slip beneath it.

Back in the car Charlie switches on the radio and rolls the tuner back and forth. Country, country, classic rock, religious, country, talk radio, country, talk radio, and then, finally, a pop station where the DJs are talking about, who else, Adrian Wildes. "Still no word," the woman's voice, scratchy from cigarettes, says. "So sad."

"You know what I think," a man says, and you can practically hear the laugh track in his head. "This is all one big publicity stunt. He is, like, holed up somewhere with some nice booze, some ladies—"

"Oh, stop."

"No, really, hear me out. He's a smart guy, right? A clever guy? So he's in some bungalow on the beach with the ladies and the booze, and he's just going to stay there. He's going to hang out and then, just when we've forgotten about him, back he'll come."

"You don't really think that," the woman DJ says. "Come on, Dirk. You think he's that manipulative."

"Here's what I know. I know that he's number one on the iTunes album and singles charts. He's got two albums in the top five on *Billboard*. And this from a guy whose sales were slumping. That's all I'm saying. Just putting the pieces together."

"It's not an awful theory," I say as the DJs stop talking and roll into one of Adrian's lesser-played songs, "Sleepheart."

"It's a terrible theory," Charlie says. He has those circles under his eyes and his hair is all crazy, but something about him looks a little less tired.

"Twenty miles, they said?" Zack asks.

"Yeah, about that. I don't think they measured it or anything."

"Because strippers aren't good at math?" Charlie challenges.

"No"—I sigh—"because strippers don't go to summer camp."

This makes Zack laugh his guffawing laugh. "That would

be a pretty fabulous summer camp, though," he says. "I mean, even I would like to go."

Charlie shakes his head.

"Do you think these are still Penn's Woods?" I ask.

Charlie looks back at me. He has a great big gob of crust in the corner of his eye. Sleep, my mom calls it. Like it seeped out of you in the nighttime.

"Wipe your eye, crust lord," I tell him.

He uses his thumb to wipe the sleep away. "William Penn no longer owns these forests, no."

"No, I mean, do you think they are still the same trees?"

"We could cut one down and count rings," Zack says, still wearing his jolly smile. I wonder if he does this at home when his parents are arguing.

Charlie turns back around and watches the road go by. Maybe I was wrong. Maybe he is just as tired as he always was.

"There!" I say. The street sign is crooked, as if it was hit by a plow, but I can still read it: Winsacondor Way.

Zack slows the car, but not quickly enough, and as he makes the turn onto Winsacondor Way we fishtail around until the side of the car is pressed firmly into the snowbank. It's not rough or violent or even all that dramatic. We are sliding and then there is a soft thud and our bodies rock to the side. Then, still. Out my window is a wall of white. I put my hand up to the glass and the cold burns.

Zack opens his door, and I slide across the back seat to get out the driver's side. Charlie has to crawl over the center console and out the door after me.

There's three fresh inches of snow on the road on top of another six or more that have been packed down since previous storms. "Look," I say. "Tracks. Under the snow."

"What are you, some kind of crime-scene detective now?"

But I bend over and brush away some of the powder and underneath there are, indeed, tracks. "I bet the car would be fine since it's all packed down underneath. We could push it out of the snowbank and drive down the road and see what we can find."

Zack shakes his head. "I don't know. She's a fickle kind of car. This might be asking too much of her."

"Why are cars always girls?"

"Not with this right now," Charlie says.

"You know, this is the type of thing we used to agree on."

Charlie turns, but he looks past me instead of at me. "We're here for a reason."

"Yes, sir! Won't stray from the mission, sir!"

"We could walk," Zack says. "We can just walk down, check it out, then walk back and push this nongendered vehicle right out of the snow. Okay?"

I bet Charlie and I would have actually killed each other by now if it weren't for Zack. Not like the fights we had when we were kids, rolling and pounding each other. I scratched. It was one of the only defenses I had. We'd always reach a point where it was like it was too much, too hard, and we'd fall apart from each other. But now, I'm not so sure we'd stop.

"Fine," I say. I open the car, reach in, grab an old sweat shirt of Zack's, and pull it on top of the clothes I've been wearing for what seems like days and days. It's long enough to cover my hands, which I ball into fists. I step over the snowbank and onto the road, which twists away from the highway and into the woods. I start walking away from the car. "Well, come on then, let's go."

EIGHT

Once upon a time, a princess was born in a kingdom on a cliff. The view of the sea was so magnificent that no man could go to the edge of it without throwing himself from it. Many great men were lost, and so the king issued a proclamation: any man who could go to the edge of the cliff and resist it's pull would have his daughter's hand in marriage. Princes and commoners traveled from near and far to test their will, but not one could pass the test. The princess could not bear the loss of life another day. At the break of dawn, she marched out to the cliff's edge. She had passed the test. When she turned, she saw beside her a bold knight. Filled with envy and rage, he charged at her. She tumbled backward off the cliff and down into the water. She sunk down, down, down into the dark and swirling ocean until she found herself in the home of the sea witch.

NOW

Lake Condor looks deep, like it's the kind of lake that when you swim in it, your feet are swallowed up in murky green water. It's iced over, or so we think, with a layer of snow on top of it. It gleams in the sun like a diamond mirror, reflecting back nothing but itself.

It takes us almost twenty minutes to walk the long driveway from the road to the camp, but it's almost worth it because it's just so pretty. Camp Winsacondor sits like a crown atop the lake, and the central jewel is the big dining hall: a giant log cabin with a huge stone chimney climbing up the side. The roof has a good foot of snow on it. It's hard to tell with all the fresh powder, but the camp doesn't look completely abandoned. There are all sorts of divots in the snow, spaced like footsteps, and what looks like a cross-country ski trail. There is no car, though, and no smoke comes from the chimney.

"Dead end," Charlie says. "There's no one here."

"Come on, let's look around. He could be anywhere."

We walk along the central path of the camp toward the lake. On the far side I can see another shore with big houses. The lake itself on that side is dotted with ice fishing shacks. "I don't really understand ice fishing," I say.

Charlie sighs. "They cut a hole in the ice and drop their line down that way. It's not like fish hibernate or anything."

I stop walking. Charlie's feet crunch a few more steps in the snow. "Do you really think I'm stupid?" I ask. "Like monumentally moronic?"

He turns around. His cheeks are pink and his breath puffs in front of his chapped lips. "It had occurred to me," he replies.

"Well, I'm not. I know how ice fishing works. It's not, like, a rod and reel. It's an actual line. And they check it every once in a while. They sit in their huts and drink beer and check the lines and some of the huts even have satellite TV. What I don't understand is, what's the appeal? Because you can drink beer and watch dumb TV at home."

Charlie tugs his hat down. "It's not up to you to decide. You're not the supreme arbiter of what leisure activities are acceptable."

"I'm not saying they can't do it. Or that they shouldn't do it. I'm saying I don't get it. And you should know that about me."

"I should?"

"Sure. Watching dumb sitcoms for hours on end. Laughing at the shitty, lazy jokes. I went along on this stupid adventure to look for some crappy singer who probably is holed up somewhere doing coke like the guys on the radio said. Do I say anything like, 'Hey, why don't you read a book?' or 'Gee, shouldn't you be back at school?' No, I do not."

"Why don't you?"

I'm about to say that it's because I'm not a judgmental waste of air like him or Penelope (gack), but there is something in his eyes that stops me. It's probably just the cold, but it looks like he is crying. So I say, "Because I'm not the arbiter."

Zack is right behind me. I can hear him shifting from side to side in the snow.

A blue jay lifts off from a tree and flies toward the lake.

"There's still a lot more cabins this way," Zack says. "Let's keep walking."

"Fuck this," Charlie says. Charlie doesn't normally swear. Not the F-word, anyway. That's my domain. "Fuck this," he says again. "Let's just go."

"Go where?" I ask.

"Home."

He walks past me back in the direction we came from. Zack still stands right behind me. "Well, I guess our stupid adventure is over."

I don't answer. I look out over the lake, and then I look at the cabins perched on platforms over the water. It would be nice to go to summer camp, I think. You have your set schedule. You get to do things like macrame and archery, and drink bug juice and sing songs. You can swim in the cold, cold water at dawn. But we aren't summer camp people.

"I guess so," I say.

Zack puts his arm around my shoulder while we clomp back through the snow to the road out of camp. It's an unexpected gesture, but I like it. This is what a brother should do, I think: put his arm around you when you least expect it and just when you need it. So I lean into him and put my arm around his soft waist. It's a little hard to walk this way, like we are in a three-legged race. His feet sink into the snow deeper than mine, with a satisfying crunch. It would be nice to be that sturdy. When you said "No, thank you," people would know you meant it.

"No," I say.

Charlie sighs and turns around. "No, what?"

"We came here for a reason. Your reason. We aren't going to just leave."

"We need to find a phone, anyway," Zack says. "I think we need to call a tow truck."

I shake my head. "No," I say again. I feel something swelling up in me. I am like a fire breathing dragon whose stove had been turned back on. I also feel like I am going to cry. Water works and flames battle inside my chest.

I turn, slipping out from under Zack's arm, and walk back toward the lake. The sun shining off it is so bright that, like an Antarctic explorer, I am blinded by all the white, the vastness of it all.

But I keep walking down to what would be a beach if this were summer, but instead is just more snow, its surface brushed by the wind into wafting hills.

My feet crunch through an inch, but the snow holds me up.

I don't know where the beach ends and the lake begins. I walk out and out. Feet crunch behind me. "Lexi," Charlie calls. "Lexi, he's not out there."

I turn around.

From above, I am a speck of red and blue—or maybe muted grays—on the white, white landscape. Just a fleck. An accidental brush of paint on a canvas. And I feel it. I feel that way.

Zack and Charlie stand on the beach. They are the same height, I realize, which is funny because Zack seems so much bigger, so much more solid and present and alive.

I lean my head back and look up at the blue. "Adrian!" I yell. "Adrian Wildes!"

A flock of sparrows rises up from a nearby tree. That's all. The rest of the world is silent.

"Adrian!" I yell again. "Olly olly in free! Come out, come out wherever you are."

Nothing. If he was ever here, he's gone now, but most likely he was never here. We were chasing a ghost. A deliberate ghost.

I look back up at the sky.

A crack like a bullet rings out. Is someone shooting at us? Do they think we are trespassing?

We are trespassing.

Another shot. And another. But where are they? I don't see anyone else and anyway they sound so close. Like I am the one firing shots.

And then I am gone.

The sky pulls back into a fuzzy haze, like a storm blowing in above me.

The cold is instant and so severe that it comes and vanishes almost in half a moment. My bones freeze. My heart freezes. My eyes freeze open and I watch the world pull away from me through a little hole, barely bigger than me and getting smaller all the time.

The world turns green around me and I feel silky fronds grabbing my ankles.

Fern fronds. Fern fairies.

I am going home.

And then I am nowhere at all.

BEFORE

October

Seth took me back to Gwen's house because that was where we first met. Not really, but that was what we said. Maybe he'd forgotten that day in the hall. Maybe Zack was wrong and he was never drawing me. Whatever the case may have been, five weeks after we got together—before Halloween, before Debbi and Vaginas of Steel, but after Remy stopped me in the bathroom—we went back to Gwen's house.

"She's a bitch," Seth said. "She's a jealous bitch and that's all there is to it."

I didn't know what he had planned. Were we going to toilet paper the trees in her front yard? Write *Gwen Osterlow is a virgin who can't drive* in big chalk letters on the front of her house? Maybe we would just sit outside flashing the headlights of his car in her window.

But no. He parked on the road and we snuck through the woods on the side of her house, back down around by the pool, which was covered up for the season. It looked like a big black gaping mouth—a maw like Grendel's mother down in the bottom of the ocean.

Seth slid the lock open on the pool house door and we slipped inside. There was a high window and clear moonlight streamed in. Enough so that after a minute or two my eyes adjusted and I could see the room and Seth. Maybe we were going to do something to the deck furniture. Gwen's parents were crazy about their deck furniture. But no. We weren't going to do anything to Gwen, not really. Seth said what we were doing was rubbing it in her face, but that wasn't true because she didn't know. She'll never know.

The deck furniture was all pressed against the back wall inside the pool house, the chairs piled on top of the table. A huge chaise longue that Mr. Harper made took up most of the floor space. Everything smelled of chlorine.

"In the summer, when all this furniture isn't in here, Gwen and I used to come out here for sleepovers."

"Kinky," he said.

"Not like that." I swatted at him, and he grabbed my wrist, quick as a lizard's tongue. He tugged me and we fell on the chaise.

There was a cricket trapped in here with us, chirping a steady beat.

"You're pretty," he said.

"So are you," I replied. Because he was. He had delicate features and long eyelashes. He frowned when I said it, but he still kissed me. He leaned in and pressed his heavy lips to mine, his tongue like a doctor's probe.

I kissed him back and maybe that's the same as saying yes.

He leaned onto me on the chaise. I shifted away and said, "Whoa there, cowboy." I knew it was stupid as I said it. I wasn't even sure where the words came from. Whoa there, cowboy? How could Seth Winthrop like a girl who said such stupid things? He smiled, but his eyes were elsewhere. His pupils were so large they nearly eclipsed the color in his irises.

With one hand, he stroked my forehead. With the other, he still held my wrist. "So pretty," he said again.

We'd kissed a hundred thousand times before, but this was different. It wasn't just being in Gwen's pool house with the smell of chlorine all around us. It was the way his voice sounded like he was sucking on pebbles and how his eyes made him seem like he was too much there and not there at all. He looked around me and through me and within me.

He slid his body on top of mine.

"No, thank you," I said, digging up words from my toddlerhood. It was what Mom always said to say to Charlie when he hit me or pulled my hair. It was as ineffectual now as it was then.

Still the smile. Still the blank eyes.

And still the chirping cricket.

I tried to move out from under him. He shook his head. His lips ranged over my neck while his hand moved from my forehead to fumble with the snap of my jeans.

No, thank you, no, thank you, no, thank you.

His hands pressed into me through my underwear, rough and thick. "You're hurting me."

Still the smile: parted lips and round teeth.

He tugged and my pants and underwear were around my thighs. "Seth."

"Lexi," he sighed.

He kept one hand on my wrist. His chest pressed against

mine and I couldn't breathe. "Seth, please."

He chuckled. He struggled against my clothes and got them off, mostly. My underpants hung on my ankle.

I started to squirm. "Shh," he said. Like I was his baby and he was soothing me. "Shh." And then he was inside me. Sharp. I breathed in. The scent of chlorine filled my nose.

The cricket chirped faster and faster.

When he was done, he lay beside me with his arm across my chest. "Thank you," he murmured, like I had given him something. He brushed my hair from my face. It was all so tender I wondered if I was the one who had misunderstood.

I slipped from beneath his arm and put my clothes back on. There was blood, but just a little bit.

He left the condom on the chaise longue. I hadn't even realized he had put one on.

NOW

There is something heavy on my chest. Heavy and itchy. Like hair. Like the couch in our grandparents' basement rec room, the one that smells like mildew and pine air freshener. That same smell fills my nose now. My skin is burning, but inside my body feels like it is packed with snow, the kind that's been on the road for three days and turned thick and brown.

I'm naked and I'm afraid to open my eyes.

"Lexi?" It's Charlie. Charlie whispers my name.

I blink open my eyes. He's sitting beside me wrapped in a

blanket. I think maybe he's naked, too, because I can see his chest and the weird little hairs that sprout there. I can't make sense of this at all. "Charlie?"

His body relaxes.

"You fell into the lake," he tells me.

Zack stands behind him. His arms are wrapped around his chest. His whole face is as pink as prom carnations.

"I know," I say. I remember slipping down, the shock of it, and then the way it felt so easy to just let go and watch those ferns and vines come to me. It felt like slipping into some other plane of existence, an actual magical world.

"Charlie pulled you out," Zack tells me.

"We almost both went under," Charlie tells me. His eyes are wide and wild and confused. Did he see that world, too?

I know I should say thank you. I know. Someone saves your life—they pull you out of a frozen lake—you say thank you. But I can't. Because a part of me wishes I was still slipping back into that other world. That peaceful world. And so I close my eyes again.

"Lexi," Charlie whispers. "Come back." But it feels like he's saying, "Take me with you."

"You're too late," I tell him. "You're always too late."

"What the hell?" The voice comes across the room followed by a cold burst of air. There are two men standing in the door-way.

"She fell through the ice," Zack says.

Then the two men are running toward me and as they come

into focus I realize it's the Angel Boy and his friend from the store. Angel Boy skids to a stop in front of me. His face is inches from my own. Maybe I am dead after all. Maybe this is heaven? His curls fall across his forehead. He has buttercup eyes and rosy cheeks. His breath smells of a baloney sandwich, which seems rather un-angel-like, but so it goes. I do like baloney sandwiches, especially fried baloney with ketchup and American cheese, so maybe there's been some sort of mix-up in the design of my own personal heaven.

Which is another goddamn awful Adrian Wildes song.

My skin burns all over: fire three levels of skin deep.

Maybe this is purgatory.

I've never really paid attention to all those religious things, but it seems I am a good candidate for purgatory.

Angel Boy blinks. I didn't know that angels blinked.

"Are you awake?" he asks.

"I'm dead," I tell him. "Let me sleep."

I close my eyes again, but I can still feel his breath (angels breathe?) and smell the baloney. Then I feel his fingers on my wrist, pressing hard.

The rough weight is still there, like a sweater, and the body inside of it pressing down on me. On my bare skin. I am naked, I remember. I am *naked*. I squirm my body backward but there is nowhere to go, just a wall and anyway the Angel Boy follows me.

My throat closes. *I can't breathe*, I scream in my head. But it's only in my head so no one hears me. I squeeze my eyes shut because this cannot be happening again.

"Her pulse is going back to normal," he says. "Open your eyes. I need to look into your eyes."

I blink open my eyes. "Good line," I tell him. He uses my fingers to spread my eyelids back.

"What are you doing?" the boy behind him asks.

"Checking," he says.

"For what?"

"Hemorrhaging and stuff. I can't remember all the details from the class I took. Let me see your toes? I know I need to check the extremities."

Without meaning to, I tuck myself into a ball.

"I just need to check for frostbite and stuff," he tells me, annoyance creeping into his voice.

I shake my head. "Could you get me some clothes first?"

It isn't Angel Boy who moves. It's his friend who shrugs his heavy brown jacket off and lets it fall to the floor. He pulls his sweatshirt over his head, revealing an angry scar down the side of torso. He tosses the sweatshirt in my direction. "Put this on," he says. "I'm going to see if I can find you guys more clothes."

I hear his feet stomp away as I pull the sweatshirt over my head. Licorice and gasoline smells embrace me. My head pops out into the hood and I wriggle the shirt down over the blanket then slip my arms through. The angel boy is still there, feet or inches or breaths away from me, and he watches the whole thing like I am some strange specimen. I feel like eyes will always be on my body.

Angel Boy picks up my fingers and looks at the tips. His hand is gentle but hot, and it's all I can do not to yank my hand away. "So what happened?" he asks.

"She fell through," Zack says. "Charlie went out after her, but I told him he needed to go on his belly."

"Smart," Angel Boy says.

"I held his ankles and he reached down in the water and pulled her up. We got her back in here." He turns to me. "We pumped the water out of your lungs. You barfed rotten fish," Zack says. "Practically, I mean."

They carried me into the dining hall where they found some blankets and started a fire. "Forgot to open the flue at first. Nearly smoked us out of here," Zack tells me.

But they got it going, and put me in front of it, but not too close. Zack couldn't exactly remember what you were supposed to do about bringing someone up to temperature, whether you should try to do it slowly or not. "All I remembered was the best thing was to have skin-on-skin contact. Like in this series with Ben Affleck like before he was Ben Affleck. We watched it in elementary school."

"*Voyage of the Mimi*," Angel Boy says.

"Yeah—exactly. You watched that, too?"

The boy nods and Zack comes and sits beside me. "So that's, you know, what we did. You were out of your clothes anyway, since they were so cold. And Charlie, too, of course. So I took one for the team."

"I knew you were trying to put the moves on me this whole

trip," I say. I want to sound cool and hip and flippant, like being naked under a blanket around strangers is no big deal. But my voice comes out flat and dusty. I tug my wool blanket up around me. The fire crackles behind Charlie.

"It's true," Zack says. "I actually went out and cracked the ice before you got out there. Last night, I mean. And then I crashed the car in the snowbank. Well, first I made it snow to cover up all my tracks. And while you were sleeping, I whispered, 'Go on the ice. The lake is nice. Go on the ice.' I whispered that in your ear all night long. *Then* I crashed the car. And the rest you know."

Angel Boy watches this conversation. His big eyes with their impossible lashes shift back and forth between us, and his cherub mouth looks like it's not sure what to do with itself. Gabe. That's his name. I remember from the store.

"Everything hurts," I tell them. I turn my head away from the fire. I don't want to move too much. I don't want the blanket to fall off my lap. Across the room, I see a girl. The girl is tiny to start with, and then she's got herself all curled up on top of a bench across the room, which makes her look even smaller. She's like one of those gargoyles up on top of an old building. She even has a gargoyle-y expression, with her lips all twisted and her eyes narrowed into laser slits. Lasers which, I realize, are pointing at me.

"Is there really a small gargoyle girl over there?" I ask.

Gabe starts laughing then. "Arabella, she thinks you're a gargoyle!"

The girl—Arabella—unfolds herself. "Easy for a stupid girl to say. Only a pineapple would be stupid enough to walk out on the lake after it's been warm for three days."

"We're not from around here," Zack tells the girl.

"Clearly," she says.

"Your name is Arabella?" I ask.

"She's Clayton's sister," Gabe says.

"Who's Clayton?"

"Me," the other boy says. He clomps across the floor in his work boots.

"She asked if Arabella was a gargoyle," Gabe says, laughing again.

"She thought you were an angel, too, so clearly her judgments are not to be trusted," the boy says.

I tug the blanket around me. Arabella's face is getting darker and darker. I always thought it was just an expression that people's faces got purple—"figurative language," Dewey DeWitt would say—but she is getting redder and redder like a fat seedless grape. Her stringy, straight blond hair doesn't help matters. "I'm not stupid," I say.

"Sure," the girl says.

"Anyway, I got you some clothes," Clayton tells me. "Storage room was stocked with this camp gear. Guess they just cut and ran."

"They died," Gabe tells him. "Remember? The fire?"

Clayton takes a T-shirt, sweat pants, and a sweat shirt from his stack and hands them to me. The camp's color must have been red, because the sweat shirt is a deep burgundy color, like blood. "There's no, like, undergarments or anything. I got the guy some shorts, but I wasn't sure if a girl would like those." I see red appearing on his cheeks.

The guy.

I crane my head around. Charlie didn't speak through Zack's whole tale of what happened to me. He hasn't even snorted again. Now he stares at a space on the floor between his legs.

"Here you go," Clayton says.

Charlie looks up. "Sure," he says. "Thanks." He drops his blanket, pulls his T-shirt and sweat shirt on, then wiggles into the gym shorts and pants, like we haven't all just been lying naked together.

Zack clears his throat.

"Oh, right," Gabe says. Then the guys all turn their backs on me.

It's hard to move my limbs, like they are still frozen in the ice, even though I can feel every square millimeter of my skin. I shimmy into the pants first, the fleece soft against my skin. I bet this was what it felt like when you were a baby, all wrapped up in a flannel blanket. I don't like to go without a bra, but I don't have much choice, at least for now. The T-shirt is a little tight, though, so that feels good. The sweat shirt, on the other hand, is huge, like Zack's was on me. I pull the hood up over my hair, which is nearly dry but tangled beyond repair. When we get out of here, maybe I'll just cut it all off.

"Here," I say, and hand Clayton back his shirt. "Thanks."

"We saw your car," Clayton says. "In the snowbank at the end of the road. Did Gabe tell you that? He wanted to keep driving."

"I didn't."

"You did. You guys are lucky we found you."

"We should have kept driving," Arabella says.

"Here's the problem," Clayton says. "It's snowing again. A lot."

"Meaning?" Charlie finally speaks.

"Meaning we might just need to tuck in here for a while."

Gabe plays the piano in the corner of the dining hall. He's really good and his fingers dance, like Remy with the clarinet. I lay by the fire and watch him and it's a few minutes in before I realize he's playing an Adrian Wildes song. I look across the room to where Charlie is lying on an old leather couch. His eyes are closed and he's got his arm flopped over his forehead, but I don't think he's sleeping. I think he's listening and wondering where Adrian is now.

Arabella watches Gabe, too. Up close she doesn't look like a gargoyle. She has big eyes with long lashes that make her look more like Gabe than Clayton. Her lips are full, but chapped. She keeps biting on the lower one.

"I'm sorry about the gargoyle thing."

"It's the pimples, right?"

I scan her face. I guess there are a fair amount of pimples. Mostly on her forehead, though, underneath her bangs. "No. It was the way you were sitting. And that you are so tiny. And the awful expression you were looking at me with."

"Dagger bolts," she says.

"He's not worth dagger-bolting anyone over," I say.

"Who?"

I raise my eyebrows. I wish I could crawl into her skin and help her straighten herself out, to not be so angry at herself and everyone else. I guess that's a little bit hypocritical coming from me. But watching her, it's painful. I know what she is going to say and what she is going to do, and she might as well be taking a knife and slashing her skin. That's how this anger will feel for her. That's how it feels for me.

"I had a lot of dagger bolts for this girl Remy Yoo."

"What kind of a name is Remy?"

"You've got a small island to stand on there, Arabella."

She blushes. "It means beautiful lion."

"Really? That is kickass."

She shrugs. "So why the dagger bolts for this Remy girl?"

"I thought she wanted to steal my boyfriend, but really she was just trying to warn me."

"Warn you what?"

"It doesn't matter."

"I don't need to be warned about Gabe," she says, then stands up and walks across the room. She sits next to him on the piano bench and together they start playing "Chopsticks."

I know she doesn't need to be warned about Gabe the way that Remy tried to warn me about Seth. I don't think Clayton would let Gabe within seven miles of his sister if he thought that was even a possibility. But it's clear to anyone that Gabe sees Arabella like she's his own little sister. And so she's setting herself up for heartbreak, but she kind of knows it, so she's building that wall around herself and all that's going to do is stop the people who actually care.

Words itch beneath my skin, but I can't find the right ones to tell her that it doesn't do any good to tear down other girls or herself or anyone or anything. It doesn't do any good to try to protect yourself, because you can be as hard and sharp as a mace, and someone will still find a way to get in. Even if you have a code like Harper, sometimes it seems like the whole world is set up just to hurt you, a pinball machine made of glass shards, and you have to find a way to get through each day. I can feel those words tingling on my lips, but it's not what she wants to hear. Isn't what she is ready to hear. And so what can I tell her? She won't listen. I mean, I didn't either, right?

"I think we're going to need more wood for the fire," I say. I say it like a thought. Just throwing it out into the ether.

Without a word, Clayton picks up an ax and goes outside. He comes back with his arms loaded with firewood. He carries it across the dining hall, his boots clomping in time with Gabe's piano playing. When he gets to the fireplace, I stand up and take the logs from his arms and lay them in a line on the stone hearth. Some of them are still dusted with snow and ice, and I figure this will give them some time to dry out.

"You always like this?" I ask.

"Like what?"

"Getting stuff done."

He kind of smiles, but also looks confused, like he's wondering if we actually speak the same language or something. "I guess. We needed more wood, so I got it."

Seth would not have gone to get more wood. Charlie wouldn't. Zack might think about it, but I'm not sure Zack knows how to use an ax without cutting off his own fingers. "Okay," I say, feeling about as stupid as a stone. "Thanks."

Zack is in the kitchen. Every once in a while he pops up holding some new treasure he has found: a box of rice, a can of mashed sweet potatoes, a bag of flour.

Clayton goes out again and comes back with another stack of wood, which I help him unload. Then I put a log on the fire. It sparks and sizzles.

Gabe stops playing the piano and comes over by the fire. Arabella follows behind him, but not so closely that it's obvious. Clayton sits down in one of the heavy-looking chairs. It has wooden arms that are beaten up and scratched, and the thick upholstery is woven through with shades of brown. He takes off his boots and puts them beside the chair, holds out his feet. His socks are dirty on the bottom.

"How'd you get that scar?" I ask him. He raises his eyebrows. "On your side. I saw it when you gave me your sweatshirt."

"Oh, that," he says, like it's nothing, but a big grin spreads across his face. "Gabe shot me."

"Jesus, I hate it when you say it like that. It makes me sound like a psychopath. We were hunting."

"According to him, I stepped right into his perfect shot." He lifts up his shirt to show the scar. It is wrinkled and pink. "It just grazed me, but there was blood everywhere. I mean, the snow was bright red. Gabe started crying."

"I thought I'd killed you. Sorry for being sad about it."

"What were you hunting?" I ask.

"It was deer season."

I've only ever seen deer as they run across the road, so strong and delicate at the same time. Too beautiful. "Do you eat them?"

"Sure. Venison stew. Deer-cutting sausage."

I grin at the thought of a crowd of deer sitting around a table cutting up the sausage with their little hooves.

"Now what's funny?"

"Deer cutting sausage." I hold out my hands, fingers together, and make cutting and poking motions.

He shakes his head and tugs a skullcap down over his ears. I bet in the summer he wears a camouflaged baseball cap, the brim perfectly curved. He'd be one of the Wentworth boys back home—the ones who tuitioned into Essex from the little farming town next door, too small to have its own high school. I'm not sure if I've ever spoken to one outside of class.

"Do you, like, take it apart yourself?"

"I field dress them, yeah. You know, cut it open, take out the intestines and all that stuff. My dad likes the heart."

"Oh."

"Then I bring it home and my mom butchers it."

"You really know how to woo the ladies," Gabe laughs.

I blush, and I think Clayton does, too.

Outside it continues to snow.

There's a back door to the dining hall, but it's covered up. When I can't stand the stillness anymore, I open it and see a wall of white. I press the door closed so the snow doesn't fall inside. Next to the door there's a pair of L.L.Bean boots, the kind with a rubber bottom (green) and a leather top. They are far too big for me, but might fit Zack or Charlie.

Just inside the door is a tub filled with a shapeless stack of multicolored fabrics turned gray with dust and sun-faded. It's probably the lost and found. I start to pull them out, unearth them. I disentangle the fabric and lay out the lost property. A camp T-shirt I pair with silky pink soccer shorts and a single yellow flip-flop. A sundress needs a cardigan, especially in this weather. Short jean shorts, a hooded pink sweat shirt, and a fishing hat. I make all these faceless, bodyless people, line them up like students in a class.

Clayton and Gabe watch me like I am a rare bird. Like no one in Pennsylvania ever dug through old clothes and spread them about. Like maybe they should have just kept on driving when they saw our car stuck in the snow.

Arabella, though, she comes over and helps me. It's hard to find a match for everything, but we do it. I give the soccer shorts and T-shirt a fishing vest that still has a lure pinned to its pocket and a compass dangling down from a loop. Arabella's combination of the jeans and denim jacket is a questionable sartorial choice, I know, but some people could really rock that look.

There is only one shirt left in the bottom of the bin, blue like a robin's egg, a purple stain at the belly, and written in laundry marking pen on the collar: *Lexi*.

That's how I find myself at the bottom of the lost and found.

Zack makes us dinner out of the various things he has discovered in the kitchen. It's sort of a sweet-potato-and-rice porridge seasoned with cinnamon. "It could use some butter," he says, "but it'll do."

Gabe goes up a set of stairs and comes back down with a six pack that has lost two members and a bottle of something green. "It's Chartreuse," he explains. "Hayley drank so much of it that she barfed all over."

"That sounds fantastic," I say, and pull one of the cans of beer from the six pack.

Charlie raises his eyebrows, but doesn't say anything.

The beer is warm and flat, but I drink it anyway. I put the can between Clayton and me so we can share it. Zack sits down on the bench next to me and I shift over a little, which puts me right next to Clay. I think maybe he will slide down some more, but he doesn't.

"So you really came all this way looking for Adrian Wildes?" he asks.

I glance over at Charlie. He has a mouth full of food, but he swallows and says, "Yeah, I guess we did." He cracks his knuckles like snapping sticks. He knows I hate that sound, but then, he saved my life. I try to smile at him and my lips split. His face is flat and still as a lake at sunrise. Probably the way this lake is in summertime. I can't tell what he's thinking, if he's mad at me or if he's wishing we were back on the road looking for Adrian Wildes.

"I don't think he ever came out here," Gabe says. "He bought the place and everyone got all excited, but as far as we know he's never been out here."

"Who was it? It was Hayley and someone else, maybe Theresa? Anyway, they said they saw him at the Total-Mart once. In the music section. That's how I knew they were lying," Clayton says. He picks up our can of beer and takes a sip.

"We thought maybe he would come here to just, you know, take a break," I explain.

"You thought he was holed up in a hotel with strippers and drugs," Charlie says.

"But then I met the actual strippers and they told me about the camp, and his coming here made sense."

A hunk of snow slips off the roof and falls to the ground with a crash. I shudder.

"Wait, you went to Sherri's?" Arabella asks.

"What do you know about Sherri's?" Clayton asks her.

"Nothing. Just that Hayley told me that you can make a hundred dollars a night working there."

Clayton stares at her across the table. "Don't even joke about it."

"Who says I'm joking?" She's not looking at Clayton,

though, she's looking at Gabe.

No, no, no! I want to yell at her.

Clayton shakes his head and seems to decide it's better to just move on. "You know that river he went to see, it's got a strong current even when it isn't swollen with rain," he says.

I like the way he says that: *swollen with rain.* It's the type of thing Dewey DeWitt would tell us to pay attention to, but coming out of Clayton it sounds like, I don't know, this is kind of hokey, but it sounds like he talks that way because he actually understands the way that nature works.

"What do you mean?" Charlie asks.

"Just that it would be really easy to be swept away. Even if it wasn't on purpose."

"He didn't try to kill himself," Charlie says, putting down his bent spoon.

"I'm not saying he did," Clayton says. "I'm saying it would've been really easy for him to get caught up in it if he stepped too close. The bank could've given way or—"

"He didn't get swept away," Charlie says firmly.

"Okay, sure," Clayton says.

"He didn't," Charlie says, his voice rising.

"He said 'okay,' Charlie. Ease up," I tell him.

"Anyway," Zack says. "We've had quite the adventure. We got to be interviewed for TV and these junkies tried to steal our car and we went to an old abandoned amusement park and Lexi nearly died of drowning and hypothermia."

"Yeah, it's been a real hoot," I say.

"Shots all around!" Gabe announces.

"Vomit shots?" I ask.

"Hayley is a lightweight."

We don't have shot glasses, of course, so we use the little plastic cups from one of the cabinets, the kind meant for the littlest campers. "It kind of looks like bug juice," I say, holding up my cup. "Or how I imagine bug juice. I never went to camp."

"What about me?" Arabella asks.

"No way," Clayton tells her. "You're thirteen years old. I've already told you that when you are sixteen, I will give you a shot of something—something that actually tastes good. But you are still too young now."

"How old are you?" she asks me.

"Fifteen," I admit. "But, you know, practically sixteen."

"It doesn't matter. Lexi's not my sister. You are."

I glance over at Charlie. We lock eyes for a second, but I can't tell what he's thinking. We certainly never talked about doing shots on my sixteenth birthday, and he's never once stopped me from taking a drink.

"Bottoms up," Gabe says. We all tilt our heads back and gulp the Chartreuse. I try not to taste it, but can't stop from feeling the sour burn.

"I went to fat camp," Zack tells us.

"What?"

"When I was nine."

"When you were nine your parents sent you to fat camp? Isn't that, like, child abuse?" I ask.

"They didn't send me. I asked to go."

"You sent yourself to fat camp?" I ask. "And do they really call it fat camp?"

"No, it was, like, Dr. Dinkleschwitz's Healthful Child Sleep-away Camp or something. It was pretty awful, actually."

"Did you lose weight?" Gabe asks.

Zack pats his belly. "Nah, I held on to it. I figured I would need it later. I'm still growing, man. I need these extra stores."

"So I'm guessing there wasn't bug juice there."

"Nope. Water, water, water."

We clack our cups together and take a second shot. I figure the way Gabe is pouring, it's more like our third or fourth shot, so I turn my cup over.

"You out already, Lexi?" Gabe asks.

"Oh, I could drink you under the table for sure, but I don't like the thought of what that stuff is doing to my insides."

Gabe rubs his eyes and I watch one of his long lashes detach itself and land on his cheek. "You have an eyelash," I say.

"I have many," he replies.

"Girls love 'em," Clayton remarks, looking at his hands.

"No," I say. "A wish lash. On your cheek."

He reaches up and brushes it so it flies to the ground or the table or his clothes, but somewhere it cannot be seen. Lost forever.

I feel my eyes widen. "You can't do that. You can't just brush away a wish lash."

Gabe looks at me with those buttercup eyes, golden green

and perfect. I know what he's going to tell me. That I am too old for wishes. That all of it is superstition. Easy to say when you're an angel. He says, "I lose them all the time. Like a dog shedding. It seems a bit unfair to have so many wishes."

"Maybe you could share them," I say. "A wish charity."

Charlie cracks his knuckles again. The first time maybe it was just getting the stiffness out, but this one is a message, loud and clear as gunfire: *Shut it.*

But then Zack asks, "What would you use the wish for?"

I could tell them, I suppose. I could say how often I wished for Seth to just love me, to not want more of me than I could give. The wishes I was never really able to formulate. Instead I say, "I wasn't thinking of me. I was thinking of, like, starving children in Africa. Political prisoners in Russia. That girl that was kidnapped. The one on the news."

"That's very generous of you with something that doesn't exist," Ari says. She's holding a book. It's an old paperback novel with yellowed pages.

"Wishes exist," I tell her.

"But not magic. Not luck."

And that is true, I guess, for her and for me and for Charlie, pining for Gabe, winding up with Penelope and Seth. There was no magic there, no luck. No love.

NINE

Once upon a time, a princess was born in a kingdom on a cliff. The sea was so magnificent that no man could go to the edge of the cliff without throwing himself from it. The king issued a proclamation: any man who could resist the pull would have his daughter's hand in marriage. Men traveled from near and far, but not one could pass the test. The princess could not bear the loss of life, so one morning she marched to the cliff's edge. When she turned, she saw beside her a bold knight. Filled with envy and rage, he charged at her. She tumbled backward off the cliff and down into the water. She sunk into the dark and swirling ocean until she found herself in the home of the sea witch. "Must I stay below the ocean forever?" she asked the sea witch. The sea witch shook her head. "What you need to do, my fair princess, is fly." The princess said that she did not know how to fly. "Your wings are not broken, dear. Use them."

NOW

"Why'd you go out on that ice, Lexi?" Charlie asks. I thought he was sleeping. His breath has been even and steady, with just a hint of a rasp.

"I didn't realize I was out over the lake."

"Really?" he asks.

We are in a room up above the dining hall. It must have been a lounge for the administrators or something. There's a couch, a small table, and a bookshelf mostly empty except for a few old paperbacks and an outdated phone book. All the boys told me to sleep on the couch like I am more frail than they are, ready to break at any moment, but I said Charlie should have it. That's where he is now, a blanket heaped over him.

"Really. What, you think I went out there on purpose? Like I wanted to go for a polar swim?"

"You nearly died," he says.

"And you saved my life," I reply. "You're my hero, and I think that means I'm going to have to be indebted to you forever and ever. Like Morgan Freeman to Kevin Costner in that Robin Hood movie that Mom likes so much but pretends she doesn't."

"I'm not joking," Charlie says. He's fuzzy under his blanket, like someone has tried to erase him.

"Neither am I. I'll follow you to your classes. Don't worry, I'll sit in the back row, and—" I'm about to tell him that I'll text him the answers, but then I remember that he isn't going to school and stop myself. The sudden break is a hundred times worse, of course, like drawing a big, fat X over it. "Danger, Will ·

Robinson," I mutter.

"Why didn't you ever ask me why I wasn't back at school?" he asks.

"Because Mom and Dad never talked about it. And anyway I just figured it was because of Penelope." I stop myself from adding a "gack." But really: gack.

"It's not because of Penelope." He rolls onto his side. I can see his eyes now, but they are devoid of color, like someone has come along and switched him into black and white.

"What was it then?"

I watch the blanket move. It's like there's a dog under there, snuggling up against him, trying to get closer and closer. But it's just him, his body not sure what to do with itself. Like me. My body feels like it's somebody else's sometimes. Not in these clothes, though, so soft against my skin.

On the other side of me Clayton snores a little.

It's a little too easy to think about what if I had met Clayton first. Like what if I lived in this tiny town, and instead of meeting Seth at that party, I sat down in a pool chair next to Clayton. Clay. What's his last name? I try to imagine. Clayton Banks. Clayton Migillicutty. Clayton Stone. Each one a different version of him.

"I just couldn't anymore," Charlie says. His voice sounds like it did when we were younger and we would play and he would tell me I had lost all the games, the rules always changing. "I would go to class, and realize that the whole thing had passed by and I hadn't heard a word. But I hadn't been thinking about anything either. It was just gone. The time was gone."

"Like you blacked out?"

"No. Like it was too much for it to even stick to me. And then getting out of bed felt that way. It was too much."

"Were you eating? That sounds like how you get when you are hungry, Sloth-Man."

He sighs. A big, fat, heavy, disappointed sigh. Like he is blowing out all the years we spent together. "I'm depressed, Lexi. I went to Health Services finally and they sent me to a counselor and they want me to take Prozac or Xanax or whatever, but I don't want to and—"

"But nothing happened?"

"You mean like an incident to set me off?"

"I guess so."

He shakes his head.

The red of rage is not crimson or fire engine. It is not golden at all. It is deep and dark. More burgundy than the sweat shirt I am wearing. Heavier than blood.

He is sad because of nothing. *Nothing*.

"You know," I say, "you're kind of a dick. I would have been less disappointed if you'd told me this *was* all about Penelope."

He is silent. And then he says in a flat, even voice: "You say you aren't an idiot, but your worldview is so limited you can't see an inch beyond yourself. Just because you are all out of sorts because Seth Winthrop broke your little teenaged heart doesn't mean the rest of us can't make it through a breakup. We can't be upset about bigger things."

"You just told me it wasn't anything."

"It wasn't a douchebag like Seth Winthrop."

And I say, in a voice as flat and even as his: "Seth Winthrop raped me."

I've never said the word before. Not out loud, and not in my own wormy little head. But that's what it is, isn't it? When you say "No, thank you," and he does it anyway, that's what it is.

Clay's snore gets louder. An old man kind of a snore. Then he mumbles, "Sorry," and rolls over.

And after. After.

BEFORE

November

Seth weighed twenty-seven pounds more than me. It wasn't that much. A small dog could weigh twenty-seven pounds. A big cat. And yet, when his body was on top of mine, it felt like a pickup truck stacked with dumbbells parked on me. All my breath went out. He sucked it up like a vampire.

And I thought: this is what happened to Remy Yoo.

And I thought: this is what happens to me.

"No," I said. I put my hands on his shoulders. They were bare and cold and smooth as bowling balls.

He kissed me.

Did I like these kisses once? I used to think I could kiss him for hours, till my lips were raw. Now the rest of me felt raw as an open sore. These kisses were a threat.

"No," I said again.

"What?" he asked, breathy in my ear.

"I said, no. I don't want to do this today."

He sighed and rolled over. "Are you trying to make me woo you or something? Beg you? I didn't think you were so manipulative."

"I'm not—"

"So needy."

"I'm not needy."

Red rage. Where were you all this time?

"So what do I need to do to get past this?" His hand was around my wrist and he rubbed his thumb against my skin, right over my thick, blue vein. His eyes. Those eyes. They were kind.

I frowned. "I just— I think we should take a step back. Like, back before sex."

"You can't rewind like that."

"I'm not talking about rewinding. More like starting again."

"We've barely been together three months. What's to start over?"

"Us. Physically, I mean."

He sighed. "I didn't think you were like this."

"What did you think I was like?"

I wanted to hear this. I wanted to hear how he saw me.

"I thought the crying was just the way you were. Some girls are like that. Emotional."

"I'm not emotional." But as I said it, my voice rose in pitch, and he smirked. I pulled my wrist free.

"I was crying because I didn't want to—not really."

"You either do or you don't. And you never said no."

"I did. I said, 'No, thank you.'"

He chuckled. "That's what girls say. Like you offer them some cake or pie or whatever, and they say, 'No, thank you,' because girls aren't supposed to show an appetite. But you offer it to them again, and they take it. They take it because they want it, but they had to put up a show of not wanting it."

"Well, I didn't really want this. Not yet."

"Shit, Lexi, I knew you were young, but . . ." He couldn't even finish. He shook his head. "We did it more than once."

"I never wanted it, though. I just held still."

"And I'm supposed to know what that means?"

"I should have said it more clearly." But I didn't feel the words as I said them. I said them as a way to move the conversation along. To move away.

"Yes, you should have." He sat up and tugged his shirt and sweater back on. His hair was mussed around his eyes and I wanted to reach up and brush it away. "So I guess this is it."

"What?" I asked.

"We're done."

"No, that's not what I wanted. We could still—"

"I'll see you around, Lexi," he said as he pulled his jeans back on, tight against his skin.

And then he left me alone in his bedroom. I had to pull my clothes back on and walk down the stairs. His mom was in the kitchen working on a laptop. She didn't even look up as I walked by.

I let myself out of the house. I was 4.7 miles away from home, 24,816 feet. I knew this because I had looked it up. I had wanted to know if I could count that high and bring him to me like an incantation. Now I just knew it meant that I was too many steps away from home and I couldn't call my parents because I didn't know how to explain this to them. The only person I had to call was Charlie.

He didn't pick up the first time. It went to his voice mail. So I called again. That was the universal sign for *this is urgent*. But he didn't pick up again. I texted him: I am going to call one more time and you'd better pick up. Or else. Then I dialed one more time.

"What?" he answered.

"I need a ride."

"Not a taxi service."

Really? I thought. *Because it's not like you're doing anything else.*

"I'm at Seth's and I need a ride home."

"Why can't he drive you?"

"He just can't."

There was silence on the line. The kind of silence where you wondered if the call had been dropped.

"I can't," he said.

"Why not? It's Saturday. You don't have class. What are you doing that's so pressing?"

"I just can't, okay, Lexi?"

"Well fuck you very much."

I hung up and started walking.

whI stomp my feet. My sneakers are stiff and still a little wet. It feels like they are freezing around my feet. Maybe they will freeze *to* my feet and I'll be the frozen-sneakered girl for the rest of my days.

Snow crunches behind me. I look over my shoulder and there is Zack picking over the snow in tiny steps, his hands held out to the side like he's a tightrope walker. He slides a little, but catches himself. "Kind of treacherous out here," he says.

"Kind of treacherous everywhere," I reply.

He slides his feet over the snow until he's right up beside me. "So," he says. And then he coughs and claps his hands together. He coughs again. It's like he expects me to say something, but I came out here to be alone, to get out of that stuffy cabin with all those boys and their boy smells and boy noises.

"So," he says again. "Um."

There is a big black hole in the lake where I crashed through, but the rest of it is white and smooth.

"I heard you guys talking in there—"

I keep looking out at the snow. The moon hits it and makes it glitter. It's like a scene in a painting. So still and perfect. Except for that big black hole.

"It's just that—" he tries again.

"Yeah?" I sigh.

"I heard you guys."

"You said that already."

"Come on, Lexi. I'm having a hard time finding an appropriate entry point here."

"So did he," I say. I mime hitting a rim shot and say, "Bah dum dum."

"Don't do that," he tells me.

"Don't do what?"

"Make a joke about it." He kicks the snow.

"No, don't you do that. Don't tell me how to feel and what I can joke about. Don't tell me how to deal with what happened to me. If I want to make a joke about it, then I'll make a fucking joke about it."

"Okay, okay." He holds up both his hands, but it doesn't look like surrender. It looks like appeasement. And I hate him for that. I start to march away. Right toward the water.

"Lexi!"

"Stop following me."

"Stop going toward the water."

"I'm not going back in." But maybe I will. Because it was nice down there. Slipping below had been like going into some other world. The old vines swirled and I could almost believe in little lake sprites living down there. A peaceful world under the surface with fern fairies and maybe even a nice little home for me.

"Lexi!" he says again. His boots stop. So I stop, too.

We don't move. Nothing moves. Not the trees or the moon or the snow on the lake.

"I never said it out loud before," I tell him. "Or in my head.

I never called it what it was. But that is what it was, right?"

"Yes, I think so." He moves slowly toward me. "It's a hard word to say, isn't it?"

"Yes," I agree. But then I yell it out over the lake. "Rape, rape, rape, rape, rape," over and over and louder and louder. Out over the gaping black hole and the smooth ice. Out past the trees that are bent down with snow and look like little gnome houses. I half expect angry gnomes to come crawling out, to raise their fists at me. That's what this place feels like. Like a gingerbread village. Not real. Not permanent.

"I bet you think I'm stupid for staying with him," I say.

"No," he tells me. I want to believe him. He scratches his head through a wool cap he found somewhere.

"I am stupid. He did it over and over and I just stayed with him. Like maybe he would stop or maybe I would actually start to like it or want it or something."

He scratches his head again. "Lexi, I am so out of my depth here. I have no idea what the right thing to say is. But this is what I know. He's an asshole and you're not stupid and I'm just sorry."

"What are you sorry for?"

"That it happened. I'm sure you don't want people to feel sorry for you, but—"

"Maybe you should be sorry."

"What?" He blinks at me. His stubby little lashes hit his bright pink cheeks.

"I sometimes think if one little thing had been different,

everything else would be different, too. Like if you had driven me to school, maybe I would've met one of your dorky friends and wound up with him instead of Seth."

"You wanted me to drive you to school?"

"Of course I wanted you to drive me to school, dumbass. Who wants to ride the bus? Gwen said it would've raised my stock. I don't know about that, but it would've been different."

"You really think none of this would've happened if I drove you to school?" His voice cracks.

"No, of course not. It happened because of me."

"It happened because of Seth."

I shrug. I know he's right, but I can't feel that. I mean, I ache like nothing I have ever ached for before to be filled with righteous anger at Seth. To not blame myself. To not feel small and ugly, but to let that anger fill me up so I rise up like some kind of comic book superhero in thigh-high boots and a bustier and just rain down vengeance on Seth. But I can't muster that. All I can manage is self-loathing and sarcasm. Which makes me hate myself even more. It's this bitter circle, and all I want is to break it but it gets tighter and tighter and tighter until I can't breathe.

"Listen," he says. I hate when people start a sentence with "Listen." They do it because they know you don't want to hear what comes next. "You have every right to be angry at everyone and everything."

"Thank you for that permission."

He grimaces. "But Charlie—I mean some people are depressed because of a thing that happens to them. But some people, it's chemical—the thing that happens is inside them."

"Are you really trying to get me to feel bad for Charlie right now?"

"You must feel a little bad or something or else you wouldn't have come on this trip."

He's right, I guess. "I thought something had happened to him, too. Something with Penelope. Something so awful I couldn't even imagine it."

"It's not always so cause and effect. Like my mom, she's been dealing with this for years. Probably her whole life, I guess. Different diets and like weird exercise programs that are supposed to help her and crystals. She goes on meds, but she says they are calcifying her insides—"

"That's not true."

"Well, sure, but it's not exactly logic at work. And anyway, my dad has had enough of it. Of watching her not do what she needs to do. And so they argue all the time. But it's not about her or anything like that. It's about where to keep the trash bags or whether they should get a new snowblower or where I should go to college. And they never talk about the real problem. But here's the weird thing: my mom is doing better. Like, it seems the more they fight, the better she does. It should be sending her into a spiral."

"That's a good thing, right?"

"Well, no, it's not good because it's not sustainable. But that's not the point I'm trying to make. I'm just saying that it's not like there's always a clear line between something happening and

259

someone being depressed."

"What do you mean it's not sustainable?"

"They can't keep fighting forever. My dad is going to file for divorce any day now. I can see it even if he can't."

"That's messed up. She needs him."

"To fight with her? That's even more messed up." He pulls the cap down over his ears. "I'll be thankful when it's all done, to be honest. But what I'm trying to say to you is to maybe cut Charlie some slack."

"No," I tell him. Because if there is someone I can feel righteous anger toward, it's Charlie. He should have come when I called him. That's what brothers are supposed to do. I bet Clay would come no questions asked from half a world away to help Ari. If he was stuck on a deserted island and he somehow sensed that Ari was in trouble he would build a boat out of banana leaves and the trunk of a coconut tree and he would sail over weeks and months and miles to get back to her to save her. Plus make sure she didn't drink or become a stripper. That's what brothers are supposed to do for you. I could've stepped out on stage at Sherri's, and Charlie wouldn't have batted an eyelash.

Zack nods and stomps his feet on the ground. I look out at the big, black hole in the lake. So does Zack. He doesn't remind me that Charlie dove in to get me. That he showed up when it mattered. But here's the thing: I'm still not sure if Charlie went in to get me out, or to go down with me.

* * *

In the morning Clay sits up and the first thing he does is pull on his boots. The space on the other side of me is empty. "Where's Charlie?"

"Downstairs," Clay replies without looking at me. "He's trying to figure out something for breakfast. You know, you'd think if your best friend works at a grocery store you'd never be hungry, but he's a stingy bastard."

"I'm not," Gabe says. He stretches his arms above his head. Muscles ripple. I'm not even joking. Like something out of a men's health magazine. The curls on the back of his head stand up like a cloud.

"Seriously," I say. "Angel."

Clay scowls. "If you only knew."

But Ari nods.

"Well, sure, no one is really an angel," I say. "Not all the way through."

"So maybe the more on top, the less deep it goes," Clay says.

"And screw you, too," Gabe says as he tugs a shirt on.

Clay stands up. He holds a hand down to me and helps me to my feet. It's weird, though, because even as he's reaching out his hand to me, he's still not looking me in the eye.

We walk down the stairs to the main part of the dining hall. Charlie is banging plastic bowls down on a pine table. I head toward him, then see my dingy beige bra hanging on the back of a chair by the fireplace. I snag it and tuck it under my shirt, then retreat past the guys. I tuck into a nook and slip it on under my shirt.

Gabe and Ari are sitting at the table when I get back. Through the open window to the kitchen I see Clay and Charlie working over the stove. Charlie's back is hunched, his shoulders tight together.

"They're making oatmeal," Gabe says. "I told them to look for mealy moths."

"Eh, it's a little protein."

Gabe looks up through sleepy eyelashes. "Aren't you all glass half-full."

"About as much as you're an angel, it would seem."

Arabella watches our conversation.

He rubs the heel of his hand against his forehead. "So you're a fan of Adrian Wildes?"

"No."

"Not at all?" Arabella asks. "Why are you here, then?"

"It was Charlie's idea. I don't even know what it's all about. I mean, I didn't even realize he liked Adrian Wildes that much. But whatever."

"And you just got in the car with him."

"Everyone is expecting me to jump in the lake, but he's the one that needs watching, not that he has any good reason for it."

"There's a good reason to kill yourself?"

"No one's killing themselves," Clay says as he set a pot of oatmeal down on the table.

"It's going to leave a mark," Gabe says.

"Whoop dee do. Charlie's trying to find coffee so we can all be personable."

"Good."

"Should I wake Zack up?" I ask.

"Let him sleep," Clay says. "All he has to wake up to is snow and pushing cars out of it."

"So you're saying let him stay in dreamland a little longer."

"I guess that's what we'd all want, isn't it?"

Clayton shows me the storage room with all the clothes in it and I layer another pair of sweat pants and two sweat shirts on top of what I'm already wearing. I find some socks, too, white tube socks with red stripes at the top. My shoes have dried, but are stiff and crusty.

"You look like the Michelin tire man," Clay says.

I have both hoods pulled up, the bottom one pulled tight so that it covers the outer ring of my face. "I was going for more of a futuristic Little Red Riding Hood."

He says, "Sure, okay," as he shoves his hands into the pocket of his coat. He turns away from me.

"How big is the scar?" I ask.

"A good three inches."

"Better than a bad three inches."

He smiles and his face relaxes for the first time. It's a funny sort of a face. His nose is flat, his eyes deep set and piercing blue with stubby lashes. He has a crooked scar on his cheek and another one above his eye. That makes three scars, at least.

But then his face goes right back to looking like a snowman melting drop by drop. And I know. He heard.

"You were listening last night. To me and my brother."

He turns toward the floor.

"You didn't say anything. You just eavesdropped and fake snored."

"I was trying to remind you that I was there without making you think I was listening."

"But you were listening, and how could I forget you were there?"

He shakes his head. "Lexi, I—"

"I wish you wouldn't look at me like that."

"Like what?"

"Like you feel guilty for standing next to me."

"I'm not sure how else to look at you?"

"Why?"

"Because—" And then he stops. He can't say the words. *Because he raped you.* Clay's face is pale except for two slashes of red on his cheeks, his scars standing out like chalk marks. *Because he raped you. Because you are broken. Because you are fragile. Because no one will ever want to touch you again, so sure they are that you will shatter into a thousand fragments too small to ever be put back together.*

"Exactly," I say.

"Lexi, I didn't mean that."

"You didn't say anything."

He rubs his flat nose, jams his hands back into his pocket. Then he takes them out and rearranges his hat on his head. I watch him. Just watch him. He closes his eyes longer than a blink but not so long I think he's trying to avoid staring at me. He shifts his weight from side to side.

So I let him off the hook. "Come on," I say. "Everyone's waiting for us."

I push open the closet door and let him follow me out.

"Do you remember Killer Hill?" Charlie asks me. We are walking side by side, our feet crunching into the snow while in front of us Gabe, Clay, and Zack argue about the relative merits of southern rock and modern hip-hop. Arabella trots behind them, trying to keep up.

"It's all party on top," Gabe is saying, "but underneath it's about the protest."

Zack puts both hands on his head. "I can't even believe I'm hearing this."

I think of Seth because I always think of Seth and how he was always so sure about the relative merits of everything.

"So do you?" Charlie asks. He is wearing the L.L.Bean boots from the dining hall and I'm more than a little jealous of how toasty warm his feet must be.

"Killer Hill? Sure." I keep my voice flat. I'm not about to give Charlie an inch. You know what they say about that. And Charlie wouldn't just take a mile. He'd wiggle right in inside me and the next thing you knew I'd be agreeing with everything he said. But of course I remember Killer Hill. My parents took us sledding there. Sometimes kids give a place a name like Killer Hill and really it's just a bump. Like imagination and exaggeration take over and make it bigger in the collective mind's eye. Killer Hill isn't like that.

"Remember that time you were at the top and Scott Mac-Farlane pushed you onto your snow tube and jumped on top of you and rode down?"

"What is this, like, the greatest hits of Lexi's life? Next are you going to talk about the time I got smacked in the head with the baseball at the Fisher Cats game?"

Clay turns over his shoulder and looks back at us. He has his hat pulled down so low I can't see his eyebrows. "If you ask me," he says. "You should forget about southern rock and hip-hop and go for some good old-fashioned country. A little Johnny Cash. A little Dolly Parton."

Zack holds up a hand. "You'll never get me to say a word against the man in black. Or Dolly Parton."

"So when we got to school that Monday," Charlie says as if we weren't interrupted, "I picked up the top layer of snow. You know, the frozen, hard, icy sheet of snow on top?"

"Surrounded by it," I say.

"We're surrounded by fresh snow. I'm talking about a few days after, when it melts a little then hardens up overnight and it's an inch thick and hard and jagged."

"Write a little poem about it, why don't you?"

He reaches up and bats a branch so the snow tumbles down into the woods beside the road. "You make it really hard to apologize."

"You're apologizing? I thought you were reminiscing."

"I'm apologizing. Do you want to hear it?"

"Yeah, go ahead."

"So you know the snow I'm talking about."

"Yeah, sure, what about it?"

"I picked up a big slab of it and I smashed it on Scott Mac-Farlane's face. He got a big scrape down the front of his nose and had to wear a Band-Aid over it for a week. When he talked, he sounded like Bert from *Sesame Street.*"

I don't mean to, but I crack a smile. Then I turn away so he won't see it. Like I said, you can't give Charlie even a millimeter.

"It was a real heroic moment, Lexi. He was holding on to his face and the blood was gushing out and I said, 'Don't mess with my sister.' And then Mrs. Robbins came over and I was suspended."

I turn back to face him, eyes wide. "That's why you were suspended? No one would ever tell me why."

"Mom and Dad didn't want to give you the idea that violence was the way to solve interpersonal dilemmas."

I grin.

"But then they bought me three packs of Pokémon cards, so, you know, I guess they thought I was doing something right."

"What? They never told me that!" And I realize there's probably a lot they haven't told me about Charlie.

We walk on under a heavy bough that crosses over the road like a canopy.

"Anyway, that doesn't sound like much of an apology," I say. "I mean, a very belated thanks and all. No one ever used me as a sled again."

"What I'm trying to say is that if I had known, I would have done something. If I had known, I would have—"

"Smashed snow in his face?"

"Smashed something, Lexi. I would have. Honest."

The cold is starting to seep into my feet, tickling around the edges, testing the waters. "I didn't need you to smash something in his face. I needed you to come get me when I called you."

"Is that when it happened?" His voice cracks. "That time you called and I wouldn't come to get you? That's why you called?"

In front of us, Clay bends over and with a smooth motion scoops up a handful of snow, balls it up, and hurls it at Gabe. "That's for your hip-hop," he says. Another snowball, this one for Zack: "And that's for your southern rock."

Gabe responds in kind: a big, fat one that smashes on Clay's chest.

"Lexi?" Charlie says.

"It was the one time he didn't," I say. I try to storm ahead into the snowball fight, but the snow is too deep.

Charlie grabs my arm. "Lexi," he says. "I'm sorry. I'm so, so sorry. You don't—I can't. I'm so mad at myself. And I just—" His eyes are red and (oh, God, I don't want to see this) tears stream out of them and his nose is snotty and his cheeks are pink.

"Charlie," I say.

"Lexi, no. You called me and you said you needed me and I couldn't. I just couldn't. I remember that day. I was in bed. I hadn't gotten out of bed all day and I didn't even care. I didn't want to get out of bed."

"Well, of course you didn't or you would have."

"Maybe. There are some days I want to—I don't know. That day I didn't. I didn't even want to be the kind of person who wants to get out of bed. But I should have gotten you."

"It doesn't matter," I tell him. It's like having him admit that he was wrong and I was right is making me furious all over again. Like when we were little: *I told you so!* Or maybe I've held this anger so long that I don't want to let it go.

"It *does* matter."

"It was over then."

"Lexi." His voice is so full—full of sorrow and anger and weakness and guilt—that it makes my heart want to break.

"It was all over," I tell him, my voice soft.

Gabe turns then and arches a huge snowball. We watch it falling down toward us. It smashes right in the middle of Charlie's chest, exploding out like a firework. But he doesn't move.

Clay puts a hand on Gabe's shoulder and turns him around, his eyes on me the whole time.

"Anyway, you were there when it counted. You pulled me out of the water."

"I did save your life."

"I'm your Morgan Freeman." Maybe we can joke about this. Maybe we can just joke and move on.

"But still—"

"It's all over, Charlie. It's okay. I'm okay. I'm going to be okay." I say the words even though they are not true. Not yet. Maybe not ever. "That story—when he pushes the princess off, I used to tell myself that she didn't fall. She flew. She flew someplace better. I'm tired of falling, Charlie."

My toes freeze and then I don't feel them, which is fine. Clay tries to give me his hat, but I say "No, thank you," and he tugs it farther down over his ears.

"Colder than a witch's teat," Gabe says.

"A witch's tit," Zack says back.

"It's the same thing," I say. "And either way it's horribly sexist. The frigid woman unable to suckle her child. Mother Nature isn't out to get you all."

"Isn't the whole idea of Mother Nature sexist?" Gabe asks.

"No," I say. "You're just jealous."

"It's true," Gabe replies. "I am jealous of fictional deities."

"And a waster of wishes," Ari says. She grins at me.

"Also, falsely angelic," I say.

"Anyone else?" he asks.

"You fart in your sleep," Clay tells him. "It's nasty."

"Is that who that was?" Zack asks. "I was afraid it had been me. Sweet potatoes don't always agree with me."

Clay has a shovel in his truck (of course) and he starts digging out Zack's little car while I use my arms to sweep the snow off the windshield. When we finally uncover it, the poor thing looks small and neglected. I give it a little pat.

"I thought we could tow it out with my truck, but I'm not

sure what we can connect to without risking breaking something," Clay says. He squats down and looks under the car.

Things Seth Winthrop would never know how to do: use a pickup truck to tow a car.

"Gentlemen, we are going to have to push," Gabe says. I watch his chest puff up with air, his muscles pop.

"Great!" I say. My own muscles tingle a bit.

"Lexi and Arabella, you get in," Charlie instructs.

"In what?"

"The car," Charlie says. "We'll push you and when the car gets going you just need to back it out, okay? You don't even need to turn."

"I can push, too," I say.

"Someone needs to drive the car," Gabe says.

"Why not Charlie?" I ask. "He's practically smaller than me, and I bet you I can lift more. Or Ari. You can steer, right, Ari?"

"Just get in the car, Lexi," Charlie says.

"So you want both of us in the car weighing it down?"

Clay says, "Ari is too small to reach the pedals and I want her in the car where she will be safe."

"Then I'm driving back to town."

"You can't drive yet," Charlie says.

"I'm fifteen and a half. I *can* drive, just no one will let me."

"Do you have a permit?" Clay asks.

"We don't do permits in New Hampshire," I say.

Charlie says, "Stop being such a pain in the ass and get in the car and I will take you driving when we get home."

"You're not old enough to take me driving."

"What are we even arguing about then?"

We stare at each other across the trunk of the car. I think we both know the answer to that question: we are arguing because that's what we've grown accustomed to. "Please, Lexi."

"Fine." I give in. Because in the woods we made a tiny little bit of peace between us, and I don't know how I feel about everything yet, but I know I don't want to break that peace. If it falls apart, I don't want it to be because of me.

I have to hitch the seat way up. Clay stands in the open doorway. "So you just leave it in neutral and as soon as we start you rolling, drop it into reverse and ease it back. Don't hit my truck if you can manage it." He grins.

"What if I put it into drive and roll over you all and then just keep on driving."

His grin falters for a moment. "I guess we just have to trust that you won't do that. Not today anyway."

I shut the door and then look over my shoulder at Ari. "We could keep driving, you know. Where do you want to go? Someplace warm? I have a friend who's working at a restaurant down in Florida."

"I've never been to Florida."

"Florida it is, then!"

The boys all stand at the front of the car. It's so narrow and they are so broad—well, with the exception of Charlie, of course—that they barely fit. They crouch down, their feet in the snowbank. They look like runners ready to explode from starting blocks, dogs ready to chase the rabbit with their squinting eyes and open lips.

They push.

I try to watch Clay, sure that he will nod when it's time for me to put the car into reverse, but it's Charlie who I stare at. He nearly disappears between Zack and Gabe. Not that they are pushing him away, but like he is fading. I can see him erasing himself right before my eyes.

"Now!" Clay yells. "Now, Lexi, now!"

So I do what he said. I drop the clutch down into reverse, feel the wheels grip, then I slide the car back right next to Clay's truck. The engine hiccoughs and farts and the rest of the range of unseemly noises, and a black cloud of smoke belches out behind it, but it is free from the snowbank.

I *could* just drive. I could just put it into gear and pull back out onto the country road. Ari and I could escape. I guess that's one way I could keep her safe. She'd be safe and I could be new. We could keep driving back to the strippers maybe, or in an entirely different direction. We could go to New York and pick up Harper so she wouldn't have to hitch to Florida. We could go to Connecticut to get Annie from the college, too, and help her on her quest for the worthy man. Hell, we could get that reporter and bring her to a more exciting city. We could even go get Caroline and get her away from that guy and whatever drugs she's taking. We'd all go down to Florida together and walk across the warm sand to put our toes in the ocean. Florida could be our Oz and all our wishes would be granted there. And all those boys with their huffy-puffy breathing, their boy smells, their dirty thoughts, their soft lips. We could just leave them.

But we don't.

Because there is no wizard in Oz, and there is no protection and no starting new. You just have to find your code, your costume, your mask, your armor: the way to try to keep yourself safe even in a dangerous world. You have to keep going because there is no way around or over or under. So I put the car in park and open up the door and I step out into the snow-white world.

Clay's truck is clean. Like gleaming surfaces and smooth leather clean. No fast-food wrappers on the floor. No pebbles at the bottom of the cup holders. I let out my breath.

I ride with him while Gabe and Ari ride with Zack and Charlie, so no one gets lost, they say, but I wonder—hope like a little balloon with fading helium—that maybe Clay arranged it this way on purpose. Maybe he does not see me as permanently breakable.

Riding in the truck is like being in a parade float, stacked up on pillows, like being on top of a mountain looking down at the whole tiny world. "I want to move into this truck and live here," I tell him.

He glances over at me, but only for a second. He's a careful driver. "I think you might find it a little small after a while."

I shake my head and run my fingers against the smooth, black dash. "This is your favorite thing, isn't it?"

"What's yours?" he asks.

I have so many favorite things. Small tiny things like shells and ceramic lions and a single black pearl earring. And bigger things like my perfectly soft pillow back home and my zip-up boots and the wig that is all pink and makes me look like a totally different person. But what I think of is my booklet. "It's called a *Good Feelings* book. You write little messages—or they have ones printed in it—and you put them down and it's supposed to bring a little joy to people's life. Which was probably not what you were expecting, right? I mean, what were you expecting?"

"*Make your tomorrow today. You deserve it.*" As he speaks, He keeps his eyes on the road. His nose looks straighter from this direction, almost regal.

"You found it?" I ask. "But it was under the pomegranate."

"Yeah." He rubs his cheek. "I'm not saying I followed you through the store or anything."

"Because that would be weird."

"That would be weird," he agrees.

It changes everything and nothing.

"The truck isn't my favorite thing," he says. "It's maybe my third favorite thing. Or second. But it's not my favorite."

"What is your favorite then?"

"When I was little we went to a carnival and my dad won me this stuffed dog. It has a big black circle around one eye, which is blue, and its other eye is brown. I think it was reject dog."

"Did your dad die or something?"

"What? No. I've just had it forever." Another quick glance.

"It knows all my secrets."

Those lips whispered secrets into the dog at night, filling it up like a piggy bank until there was no more room. I can't imagine what type of secrets a boy like Clay might have.

"They really don't do permits in New Hampshire?" he asks.

"Live free or die, I guess," I reply.

He pulls the truck off to the side of the road. Not quick, abrupt, impulsive, but slow and easy. Miss Ruka drives away. He is going to kiss me, I think. And I also think that I might like it.

"Swap," he says.

"What?"

"You crawl over me and I'll slide that way—and don't try any hanky-panky."

"But why?" I ask.

"Because you're going to drive."

A herd of elephants, a stampede of horses, a pod of dolphins—all under my control. He puts his hand on mine on the clutch. "Foot on the brake?" he asks.

"Yep."

He pulls down and I feel the truck drop into gear.

"All right, foot off the brake and ease onto the gas. You're clear. Pull on out." He sits right next to me, our thighs touching like we are a four-legged, two-headed monster. "Easy. Easy." I know what he means is "Slower, slower." But my foot presses down until the world is spilling by us, the trees blurring into a streak of green, until we take off and head for the moon.

"Well, shit," Gabe says. "That is something I never, ever thought I would see."

"This truck is my new best friend," I say as I climb down out of the truck that I parked across two spots outside the diner.

"Well, shit," Gabe says again.

"I am going to eat through two of the Lumberjacks," Clay declares.

"Our funds are dwindling," I tell him.

He gives me a look. A shared look. A "come on, really, please" look. "We're going to buy you guys breakfast and fill up your tank and pool whatever cash we have left for you to take with you on your drive home."

Inside, there is a group of teenagers in a round booth at the back, piled up on top of one another like piglets in their pen. Next to me, Charlie stiffens. Gabe seems to notice because, after giving the group in the back a wave, he leads us over to a booth closer to the counter and to the door. Clay hands me a menu as thick as a magazine and I begin flipping through it. "Their eggs are really good," he says. "The pancakes are only so-so, but don't tell them I said that. My aunt works here and if it gets back to her I'll never hear the end of it."

I smile. "Lips sealed."

What I want to get is the yogurt with fruit because it feels like I haven't eaten a healthy-ish thing for years. But I don't want them to think I'm one of those girls who won't eat in front of boys. But if I order an omelet or whatever, that will make me seem like a glutton. And I realize that there is nothing on this menu that I can order that is right. Every single thing could be used against me. Like when I went to Ruby's with Seth and got everything chocolatey—how young I must have shown myself to be.

I let the menu fall to the table.

"Everything okay?" Clay asks.

"There are a lot of choices," I reply.

I think of Harper, how she disguised herself—how she had no safe choices either, really. And all of the sudden it's kind of freeing. If everything I can choose is wrong, I might as well choose what makes me happy. Maybe that's why Debbi wore that ridiculous outfit onstage, maybe that leather bra made her happy and she figured she was either going to be called a sexed-up hussy or a joyless feminist or something else, so she might as well wear it, right?

So when the waitress comes I order the yogurt and a coffee and side of home fries which I plan to cover in ketchup.

Gabe says, "Nice combo, Lexi."

And I say, "Yes, it is." After we all order, I realize how I am dressed and how long it's been since I've bathed. "Be right back."

In the bathroom, I take off two of my sweat shirts like I'm a snake shedding skin. I run cold water over my hands and splash it onto my face. There are circles under my eyes, and my hair is snarled and static-y, like Medusa's snakes. I scrub my skin harder and turn it pink.

On the way back to the table I glance at the counter, and

there he is.

Adrian Wildes.

Adrian Wildes with two days' worth of beard hunched over a cup of coffee, a wool cap pulled down over his ears. Adrian Wildes with a plate of eggs and sausages and beans half-eaten and pushed away. Adrian Wildes tipping a salt shaker back and forth.

He looks up, sees me looking at him, and panic shatters his face.

I go back to the table and slip in next to Clay. He has his phone out. "According to this, it'll take you nine hours to get home if you don't stop at all."

"These guys have to pee every hour on the hour," I say.

I can see Adrian Wildes from where I sit. He has terrible posture and the big, heavy cardigan that he wears looks like it would stink of yaks.

Charlie isn't talking. He's staring into his cup of black coffee (Penelope's influence yet again), counting the bubbles, maybe, or watching them pop. He has horrible posture, too. He didn't used to.

"You should probably leave right after breakfast," Clay says. "But you'd be getting home pretty late."

"It's fine," Charlie says. "We can take turns driving."

"Me, too," I say. "I'm pretty amazing, right?"

"Pretty amazing." Clay laughs.

"You're lucky," Gabe says. "Get to drive right on out of here."

"Here we go again," Clay says.

Adrian Wildes swings his foot next to his stool. He's wearing canvas sneakers, like me, and I wonder if his feet are cold. He doesn't have the old tube socks to keep them warm. This is the person that Charlie has been looking for. Adrian Wildes doesn't look too promising to me, but this is the person that Charlie believes can save him.

"Mr. Temple wants me to do a PG year. Do you know what PG years are for? Stupid jocks who can't get into college their first try. I'm not stupid."

"You're not," Ari agrees. "But boarding school sounds kind of fun."

Adrian scratches at the back of his neck. His hair has grown and is curling up underneath the bottom of his hat. Which makes me wonder if he has been planning this escape for a while. Did he start building his disguise while he waited for just the right moment to disappear?

Charlie finally lifts up his coffee and takes a sip.

Can a destined-to-be-faded pop star save your life? Probably not. Maybe it's like wishes and believing enough gives them power. Charlie believes. He believes that finding Adrian Wildes will somehow set him back on the steady road. Charlie saved me from drowning. The least I can do is try to pull him from whatever imaginary-turned-real weeds are pulling him down. The least I can do is try to pull him back.

I slip my *Good Feelings* book from my pocket. I choose one marked *Optimism is hope given wings*. On the back I write, *Watch me. Don't tell anyone.*

Then I tear out another one. This one says *Home is the place they always take you back.* I write: *Your secret is safe with me. Please do me a favor, though, and keep this paper indefinitely on your person at all times. From Lexi, who is trying to believe.*

"Sorry," I say as I slide the paper to Charlie, my hand on top of his under the table. "I need to go to the restroom again."

"And you say we pee all the time," Zack says. "She's the one who had to go to the strip club."

They are talking about the strip club and the strippers and how they are the ones who told us to go to the camp. I go into the bathroom and just stand there. I count to one hundred in my head. I stop at the counter on the way back, right next to Adrian Wildes. He doesn't smell like yak. He smells like maple syrup.

"Excuse me," I say to the waitress behind the counter. "I forgot to order an orange juice."

"Sure, sweetie."

My hand is on the counter, the paper under my hand.

The waitress hands me my juice, and I take it in both hands, the note now right next to Adrian. He looks at it, I think, but doesn't touch it, not at first.

Back at the table, I slip in next to Charlie, across from Clay, who slides his leg forward so his calf touches mine. It's distracting, electricity jumping the line, and I spill some of my juice on the table.

Clay wipes it up for me.

I lift my gaze then and look back toward Adrian. He's gone. So is the note.

TEN

Once upon a time, in a great and beautiful kingdom, a princess was born. The kingdom was built upon a cliff that looked out over the blue, churning sea. The view was so magnificent that no man could go to the edge of it without throwing himself from it. The king was losing his finest knights and soldiers to the ocean. The only way to break the spell of the cliff was for a man to resist its pull. The only beauty more powerful than that of the sea was that of his daughter, the princess. And so the king issued a proclamation: any man who could go to the edge of the cliff and resist it's pull would have his daughter's hand in marriage. Princes and commoners, old men and young, wise and foolish men, they all traveled from near and far to test their will, but not one could pass the test. Each man who ventured to the edge of the cliff threw himself into the sea. The princess could not bear the loss of life another day. At the break of dawn, she marched out to the cliff's edge. There she stood, the sun rising over the ocean which had momentarily stilled. She had passed the test. When she turned, she saw beside her a bold knight, his armor glinting in the early sunlight. He was filled with envy and

rage, and he charged at her. She tumbled backward off
the cliff and down into the water. She sunk down, down,
down into the dark and swirling ocean until she found
herself in the home of the sea witch. "Must I stay below
the ocean forever?" she asked the sea witch. The sea witch
shook her head. "What you need to do, my fair princess,
is fly." The princess said that she did not know how to
fly. "Your wings are not broken, dear. Use them." So the
princess tried. It took her days and days of swimming, but
eventually she burst through the surface of the water and
then she flew right up into the golden light of the sun.

SPRING, OR, WHAT HAPPENED AFTER

When we get home, Mom and Dad hug us like we've been on a journey around the world in a hot air balloon. They hug us like we've been kidnapped by wolves and finally returned. They hug Zack, too.

On the first day of school after February vacation, Zack waits for me in his car at the end of his driveway. He rolls down his window and says, "Hop in."

"You couldn't come down and get me?" I ask.

"That's the opposite direction from school."

"It's not even a quarter mile."

"So you shouldn't mind walking. Do you want a ride or not?"

I open the passenger's side door. I can't say I'm excited to get back into the stink mobile, but if it has one thing going for it, it's that it's better than the school bus. I slide into the front seat. "So this is what it's like when you get out of the cheap seats," I tell him. It actually is a little bit more comfortable up front. The seat is squishy and kind of gives me a little hug. "You wanna let me drive?" I ask.

He doesn't even bother to answer. When we get to school, we pull in right after Seth. I don't think Zack notices until we get out of the car. I sit in the front seat and don't move. "Do you think you could—" I begin. Zack nods. He walks around the car and opens my door. He extends his hand. "My lady," he says. I take his hand, warm and soft, and he pulls me to my feet. "Too bad Clay isn't here with that big red truck. That would show Seth."

"No," I say. "No, this is good, too."

Seth watches us. I can feel his eyes on me. But Zack steers us right toward the door of the school. It isn't until we get to the walkway and I turn and look over my shoulder that I see Hannah standing in Seth's shadow.

In homeroom I think about following Hannah into the bathroom and saying to her just what Remy said to me. But of course that won't work.

Ms. Blythe makes an announcement about a sophomore class community service activity, collecting books and toys for kids in a homeless shelter. "Who wants to sign up?" she asks. I raise my hand. Gwen does, too. I think about the kind of girl

Gwen wants to be—the joiner and the star, but also the girl on the edge. I'm still not sure what kind of girl I want to be, but now I know I want more than the spaces in between. That's why I raise my hand.

Instead of following Hannah into the bathroom, I watch for Remy. She's in the band room a lot of the time, and I wait outside the door during my study hall one day. When she comes out, I call her name. She hesitates, and I think maybe she isn't going to stop. But then she turns to me. "Yeah?" she asks, cautious. I guess I deserve that.

"You were right," I tell her.

Her face crumples and she looks away from me. When she doesn't say anything else, I say, "Thanks for trying."

"I guess I knew it wouldn't change anything, but I had to try, right?"

Maybe Seth is right. Maybe we could've been good friends in some alternate world. But we are in this world, the one with Seth in it, and there is too much debris between us for us to be friends.

I go back to study hall in the library. Zack is there reading *Rolling Stone*, and I sit next to him on the weird little couch. I curl my body against his, and Ms. Blythe doesn't say anything to stop us. I press my eyes against his shirt sleeve and let the tears come down. When the period is over he says, "Lexi Green, you're going to go and make people think I'm straight."

"I'm just that magnetic," I say. And then sniffle like Dewey DeWitt during allergy season.

Charlie sleeps for three days, and I think maybe the whole trip has been a stupid waste.

But on the fourth day he wakes up. He's in the bathroom when I need to get ready for school. Half of me is relieved, but half of me is annoyed. I bang on the door. He opens it and he's dressed and his hair is combed back from his head. "I need to get ready for school," I tell him.

He doesn't move. "There's something I've been meaning to ask you."

"Okay?"

"Why'd you come on that trip?"

"Well, I just knew you would do something stupid like fall through the ice on a lake, and you'd need me to rescue you."

"For real, Lexi. Why'd you come?"

"For real," I said.

"I didn't ever expect he'd save us. I just felt like if we could find him—I felt like then I would know that there was a way through."

"I know," I said. "That's why I came."

We were both looking for that way through. We still are. Not a shortcut. We just want to know there will be something there when we get to the other side. That there *is* another side.

He puts on real clothes and he comes downstairs and eats Cheerios and says, "I have some appointments at school today."

Mom says, "Hmmm," and buzzes in her seat.

Dad says, "That's great," and punches Charlie lightly

on the arm.

I say, "It's about fucking time."

And Charlie agrees: "It's about fucking time."

And so I do what I should have done ages ago, too. I text **Hannah:** If you ever want to talk, I'm still here.

She doesn't reply, which I guess is to be expected. I couldn't ever hear what Remy had to say. And anyway maybe someday she'll come to me and we'll be able to talk and I'll actually be able to help her. Maybe.

Three weeks after we return home a video is posted on YouTube. The user name is Schlockster, and he only has one video. It's shot in silhouette, like when they interview people on TV and don't want to reveal their identities. But if you know someone, you know their shape, even without all the details. And people know this shape. And even if we didn't know the shape, or doubted because of the apparent beard and longer hair, we know the voice. He sings his "Lexi" song, but he changes the last verse:

At the diner on the edge of town,
The boys kept you for their crown.
And I must go, I must go, I must go.
Lexi, won't you follow me home?

He's wrong about the boys and the crown. I never said he was the most astute observer. And of course he doesn't want me to follow him anywhere. Not the me of me, but the idea of me, maybe. Everyone has their own idea of me. And so he can build up that version of me, the one that melds with whoever the original Lexi was. It's become a lot easier to be generous with myself when no one is trying to steal me.

"That's pretty cool, Lex," Gwen says after we watch it for the third time. "Lexi Green, star of an Adrian Wildes song." I know that she will tell people my story whenever the name Adrian Wildes comes up. She'll say, "My friend Lexi saw him. He isn't dead at all."

"What do you think he meant about the boys and the crown?" she asks.

My instinct is to say that she's the lyric analyzer, not me, but I'm trying to be careful. This bridge we're building to each other is fragile, and the two ends don't quite meet yet. I'm not sure they ever will again. I've told her all about our trip and showed her all the pieces of proof I've brought home—the Polaroid of me and Harper, the toothbrush from Annie, the clothes from the camp, the picture of Alana Greengrass, and the *Good Feelings* book with the torn edge that will someday match up with a slip of paper held by Adrian Wildes. I show these things to her as offerings, a way of apologizing for how I acted but also as a test to see if this friendship is worth mending.

"We were sitting at a round table in the diner. Four boys and Ari and me."

"Maybe Ari is the jewel," Gwen said.

"She probably is," I agree. Ari, who added me on Instragram

and posts pictures of gargoyles and the ice on the lake and pictures of Gabe's eyes and Clay's face—she really is more of a jewel than I am. I'm more like sea glass, I think, still wearing off those edges.

Charlie doesn't go back to school right away. He has to wait until the fall. And he still lives at home. His doctors want him to go on medication, but he's not sure he wants to. It takes him a while to agree, and then it takes a while to get the dose right. Some days he'll be moody and mean. Other days he'll be so amped up he can't sleep and so he stays up watching television and posting inspiring messages on Facebook. And sometimes he sleeps for days. When he sleeps like that, I go into his room and do my homework there, or send text messages to Zack or his dorky friends who I guess are becoming my dorky friends. One of them is in my grade. She's almost six feet tall and she's in my math class, so I ask her what the homework is even when I already know it. And in the background I play Adrian Wildes music, which really, when you get right down to it, is not the worst music in the world. Sometimes it's not so much the song as who you listen to it with. That's not one of my *Good Feelings* sayings, but it should be. And so I write it down on one of the blank pages, and one day, when Charlie is out of his room, I tape it to the bottom of his bed. I crawl under between the unmatched socks, the tissues (gack), and the dust bunnies. It looks so lonely there that I start ripping out all the rest of them—except for the two on either side of the one I gave to Adrian Wildes. I rip the rest out and tape them all to the bottom of Charlie's bed, weaving them together into a safety net. If he slips off the edge of this world, they will catch him. We are all of us falling, all of us dancing on the edge of a cliff above a churning sea or a rolling river. Any one of us can slip at any time. Any one of us can crash through the ice—or be pushed down deep to places we never wanted to see. He pulled me out from under that ice. He will pull me out again, and I will be there to pull him back, too. Neither of us is going anywhere.

ACKNOWLEDGMENTS

Thank you to the women who have helped me along the way:

Tamra Wight, who organizes an amazing writing retreat with Anna Jordan, Jeanne Bracken, Laura Hamor, Nancy Cooper, Val Giogas, Denise Ortakales, Cynthia Lord, and Mona Pease. Deep gratitude to Joyce Shor Johnson for reading through a whole early draft.

The aunties: Larissa Crockett, Jessie Forbes, Sarah Newkirk, and Lindsay Oakes.

All the amazing teachers and administrators I've had a chance to work with. All of my students, too.

My mother, Eileen Frazer.

Susan Tananbaum and Audrey Blakemore.

Sara Crowe, who always stands by me and my writing.

And to Alexandra Cooper, whose careful reading and conversations made this book stronger with each pass.